Living Two Lives

by Erin Wade

Edited by Susan Hughes

Living Two Lives
by Erin Wade
© 2018 Erin Wade

ISBN-13: 978-1987764390
ISBN-10: 1987764390
**
www.erinwade.us

DEDICATION:

To the one who has always supported me in everything I have ever undertaken. You have encouraged me and have always been my biggest fan. Life is sweeter with you.

Always yours,
Erin

Acknowledgements

A Special Thank You to my wonderful and witty "Beta Master," **Julie Versoi**. She makes me a better storyteller.

A heartfelt "Thank You" to **Laure Dherbécourt** for agreeing to beta read for me. She has added insight and an incredible knack for catching incorrect homophones.

Erin Wade
LIVING TWO LIVES

Chapter 1

The attractive woman pulled the collar of her raincoat tighter around her neck. The drizzling Texas rain was cold for May. She squinted, trying to bring into focus the gorgeous brunette who was accepting condolences from everyone. She sincerely regretted that Jules Divine was suffering from the loss of someone she deeply loved.

Hidden in the shadow of the lone oak, the woman watched the pomp and circumstance going on below her as mourners paid their respects to the woman she had murdered.

Julie Adair Divine walked to the massive front door of her grandmother's house in Kingston, Texas. She pushed the oversized key into the lock and turned it. She could hear the deadbolt slide back to allow her admittance into the home where she had grown from a gangly teenager to a responsible adult.

Her mind flashed back to the day she had arrived on her grandmother's doorstep looking for a place to live. On her fourteenth birthday, she had announced that she was a lesbian and her parents had thrown her out of the house. Her grandmother, Nana, was the only one she could turn to.

Nana had taken her in and christened her "Jules," exclaiming that Julie was too severe a name for her lighthearted granddaughter.

Nana had provided her a home filled with love, mutual respect, and laughter. Nana had taken her everywhere she traveled and introduced Jules to so many wonders of the world that Jules had lost track of the locations of the splendors Nana had shown her.

Although Nana would never admit it, Jules suspected that she took great joy in showing up for church on Sunday morning with her granddaughter proudly sitting beside her. She took even greater joy in explaining why Jules's Baptist minister father—Nana's son—had turned his back on his only daughter.

Community leaders and staunch examples for Christians, Warren and Martha Divine refused to acknowledge their daughter, saying that "Jules was dead to God and to them."

Nana's response to their ridiculous declaration was less Godlike. "As if God would ever let those two hypocrites know what he thought," Nana had huffed.

Nana—Daphne Adair Divine—made certain that her granddaughter and namesake had all the benefits and opportunities money could buy. Jules worked hard to justify the faith and pride Nana had in her. She had graduated valedictorian from high school and college and earned her master's degree in English from Texas Christian University in Fort Worth, Texas. At the age of thirty-four, she was head of the English department at a high school in Waco, Texas.

Jules's heels clicked on the highly polished wooden floors of Nana's house as she walked through the foyer into the great room. She slipped off her heels, dropped her purse and jacket onto the sofa, and then collapsed onto the overstuffed furniture. She buried her face in her hands and cried.

Nana's funeral had been simple, with almost everyone in their rural town in attendance. Nana was their most famous local celebrity. A well-known mystery writer, she had been writing for over thirty years and had many best sellers to her credit. Thanks to a good investment banker and over a hundred books under her name, Nana was a wealthy woman.

Suddenly, Nana's doorbell jerked Jules from her reverie. "Money, money, money. It's a rich man's world," echoed through the house. She had to chuckle at her eccentric grandmother's choice of chime tones. She wondered who would be ringing the doorbell.

Through the opaque glass of the massive door, Jules could make out the figure of a medium-height person. She pushed the intercom button. "May I help you?"

The figure held up something to the door and said, "Yes, I am police detective Tanner West. I would like to speak with you, ma'am."

Jules unlocked the door and pulled it open. Although Tanner West was five-eight, she was dwarfed by the massive wrought iron door. She pretended to take a moment to scrutinize the high ceilings and dazzling chandelier hanging in the foyer, but truthfully, she was trying to stop herself from drooling over the gorgeous woman standing in the doorway.

"What can I do for you, Detective?" Jules tilted her head slightly and entered into the conversation halfheartedly. She did not move to allow Tanner to enter.

Tanner could tell the woman was weary from the emotional day she had endured and hated to add to it, but the sooner she compiled evidence, the sooner the police would solve their case.

"Are you Jules Divine?" Tanner asked, still holding her badge so Jules could read it.

"Yes."

"If I may," Tanner said, "I need to ask you a few questions about your grandmother's death."

Jules stepped back and motioned for Tanner to enter. "Nana died in her sleep," Jules mumbled. "I don't understand why the police need to question me about her death."

As Tanner followed her into the great room, Jules stumbled. Tanner caught her elbow, steadying her. "Are you okay?"

"I had a slight dizzy spell." Jules shook her head as if trying to clear the cobwebs. "I haven't eaten all day."

"We have several excellent restaurants," Tanner said. "Perhaps we could dine while we visit. Kill two birds with one stone, so to speak."

"That isn't necessary," Jules said, scowling. "I'm sure you won't take long."

"I would consider it a favor." Tanner did her best to look pitiful. "I haven't eaten all day either. It would give me an opportunity to sit down and relax."

Jules looked down at her severe black dress and stockinged feet. "Give me a few minutes to change."

Tanner nodded and tried to keep from staring at the brunette's perfect derrière as she left the room. It had been a long time since she'd encountered a woman as beautiful as Jules Divine.

Tanner walked around the room as she waited. A beautiful portrait of Jules hung over the fireplace, and a grand piano was nestled inconspicuously into a niche to the left of the mantel. The back wall of the great room was glass and overlooked a crystal-clear swimming pool. A waterfall splashed down a ten-foot retaining wall into the pool, providing soothing sounds and a delightful ambience.

Tanner jumped when Jules cleared her throat. "I didn't mean to startle you."

"Oh, um, I was just lost in your backyard paradise," Tanner said, her cheeks flushing. Try as she might, she couldn't keep her eyes from scanning Jules Divine from the tips of her polished toenails to the top of her gorgeous head.

"Did I pass?" A smile flitted across Jules's lips.

Tanner raised a questioning eyebrow. "Pass?"

"Your intense inspection," Jules said.

Chapter 2

Tanner placed a comforting hand on the small of Jules's back as she guided her to a booth in the family-owned Italian bistro.

"Nana said this was an excellent place to dine," Jules said, making small talk as they were seated, "but I haven't eaten here."

"If you like Italian food, you'll love Sabello's," Tanner said.

They placed their orders then silently waited as the waitress placed bread and their drinks on the table. When it was clear they could talk without interruption, Tanner cleared her throat. "What do you know about your grandmother's death?"

"Just that the housekeeper found her in her bed Friday morning. Everyone assumes she had a heart attack." A scowl wrinkled Jules's forehead. "Is there something about Nana's death I should know?"

"I don't know any easy way to say this." Tanner bowed her head then raised her eyes to watch Jules's reaction. "Your grandmother was murdered."

Shock registered on the brunette's face. She seemed to have a problem grasping Tanner's information.

"She was poisoned," Tanner added.

"Poisoned? Nana? Someone poisoned Nana?" Jules found the thought incomprehensible. "Why would anyone want to kill Nana?"

Tears rolled down Jules's cheeks as she fought to maintain control of her emotions. "I . . . I must go," she mumbled.

"No." Tanner placed a firm hand on top of Jules's. "You need to eat something. You'll feel better."

"I need to visit the ladies' room," Jules said as she slid from the booth and walked to the back of the restaurant.

Just then, a voluptuous Italian woman appeared and placed plates and more bread on the table. "It's good to see you, Tanner. We've been missing you."

"It gets busier every day, Max," Tanner said to Maxine Sabello, the restaurant owner. "This used to be a sleepy little town, but it's growing too fast."

"Who's the looker?" Maxine nodded in the direction Jules had disappeared.

"Jules Divine."

Maxine raised a brow. "Daphne Divine's granddaughter?"

"Yeah." Tanner exhaled as Jules walked toward them. "Jules, I'd like to introduce you to Maxine Sabello, the owner of this fine establishment."

"You were at Nana's funeral," Jules said, extending her hand to Max.

"Most of the town was there." Max shrugged. "We all loved her. She was our claim to fame. Daphne Divine was a celebrity."

"Yes, I suppose she was," Jules said. "I never think of her that way. She is . . . *was* just Nana to me."

"Eat your dinner before it gets cold," Max chided. "And watch out for Sherry Martin. She's trying to run down Daphne's heirs to see if the house is for sale."

Jules frowned and turned to Tanner for clarification. "Our local real estate agent," Tanner explained.

"Oh," Jules said, sliding into the booth beside Tanner.

"Is it for sale?" Tanner asked, eager to learn if the beauty beside her would make her home in their town.

"I . . . I don't know. I don't know who Nana left her estate to. I suppose her attorney will contact me sooner or later. I do know Nana had a will."

"Eat," Max commanded. "I'll get you some fresh bread. You've let this get cold."

"How was Nana poisoned?" Jules asked when they were alone.

"Rattlesnake venom," Tanner said.

"Could she have been bitten by a snake?"

"No, she had too much venom in her system for a snake bite. There was enough to kill twenty women her size.

"Our pathologist found a needle mark in her arm. She was injected. There was venom around the puncture wound."

They ate in silence for several minutes before Tanner continued her questioning.

"Did she live with anyone?" Tanner asked.

"No. She lived alone. I usually traveled with her when she had to make book tours or public appearances. She had several scheduled for this summer.

"She had a lot of acquaintances but no close friends. Nana loved writing and that left little time for anything else."

Tanner kept pushing for information. "She had no romantic involvements—no lovers?"

"Romantic?" Jules looked as if the thought of her grandmother being involved with a lover was the most preposterous idea imaginable.

"She was young," Tanner said, trying to suppress her mirth at Jules's prudish reaction. "And extremely attractive—an older version of you. I've seen her around town, even talked with her on occasion. I found her to be delightful."

"I noticed her obituary stated she was only sixty-seven," Tanner continued. "Most of the sixty-seven-year-old people I know are still sexually active."

"I . . . she . . . I must go." Jules blushed a deep red. She reached for the check, but Tanner beat her to it.

"My treat," the detective said.
"Thank you. It was delicious."

Jules watched as Detective West's taillights disappeared at the bottom of the hill. She looked over at the lights in the distance. Nana's house had a view of the town. It was a quaint town, small enough that one could hear the wail of sirens when a firetruck rushed to a burning building anywhere in town.

She wandered into the study and laughed when she spied the high-powered telescope her grandmother had sitting in front of the window that overlooked the town. She fought the urge to look through the instrument and lost.

"Oh, what the hell," Jules mumbled as she pulled a chair up to the telescope and sat down to look through the eyepiece. She wondered what Nana's neighbors would think if they knew she spied on them. Jules focused in on Roy and Ashley Craft, who lived just down the road. Roy was smiling and helping his wife clean up the kitchen.

Jules examined the telescope and discovered there was a device that allowed her to connect her cell phone to the instrument and take pictures and video through the lens. She gave it a try, recording Roy and Ashley as they settled in front of the television in their den. *This is like being in the room with them*, she thought. She soon tired of her voyeurism and walked through the rest of the house.

Jules was still stunned. She couldn't wrap her mind around the fact that Nana had been murdered. She began to plan. She had four weeks left of school. Her principal had allowed her to use ten personal days to handle Nana's funeral and private affairs. She would return to Waco for the last two weeks of school and then be out for the summer.

Chapter 3

Jules couldn't sleep. Detective West's revelation that Nana had been murdered deeply disturbed her. She checked her Kindle to see if it had charged while she showered and was relieved to see the hundred percent sign in the corner.

She downloaded the latest book by her favorite lesbian fiction writer, Darcy Lake. She secretly harbored a crush on Lake and had even stood in line for several hours to get Darcy's autograph on her book.

Lake was as gorgeous in person as she was in the photos on her book covers and website. She was genuinely nice. Of course, she was also very married. Sometimes Jules's stomach would lurch when Darcy posted on Facebook about how wonderful her gorgeous wife was.

Jules was soon immersed in the action of the latest Darcy Lake novel. Lake was a spellbinding storyteller. One felt like they were living the action and romance in her novels. Jules could understand why Lake had been the number one lesbian writer for the past ten years. She was incredible. Lake's novels had even crossed over from lesbian fiction to mainstream fiction and helped open the door for acceptance of lesbian fiction writers. Lake wrote murder mysteries, thrillers, and suspenseful action with lesbian heroines.

Why can't I find a woman like Darcy Lake? Jules thought.

Sometime after midnight, her Kindle slipped from her hands as Jules succumbed to exhaustion.

##

The sound of a lawn mower outside her window pulled Jules from her dreamless sleep. She lay on her back, reliving the last love scene in Darcy's book. She sighed and threw back the covers, ready to face the day. Even if her love life sucked, at least she could read arousing stories in Darcy's novels.

Jules put a coffee pod into the Keurig, pushed brew, and returned to her room to unpack. It had always been her room. Jules's freshman year of high school, Nana had built the house after signing a multimillion-dollar contract for three books in one year. One side of the house was dedicated to Nana's master bedroom and office. The other side of the house was Jules's master bedroom and office, mirroring Nana's.

She pulled on a pair of jeans and a soft Henley. She had a lot to do today and wanted to be comfortable while she worked.

By the time she had poured her coffee and walked onto the patio, the lawn mower had moved to the back of the house. For the first time, she realized whoever was mowing was doing it in her yard. She watched as a sinewy young woman carefully maneuvered the lawn mower around the corner.

Jules relaxed on a cushioned lounge chair and admired the easy grace of the lawn girl. She wondered where Nana had found her. She was tall and attractive in a butch sort of way. Collar-length blonde hair curled naturally around her stunning face.

The lawn mower sputtered, warning its operator it was running out of gas. The young woman turned off the mower and softly cursed under her breath. "Damn! Fifteen more minutes and I would have finished."

She turned on her heel and noticed Jules watching her. For several seconds, the two checked each other out, and then Jules realized she was smiling. "I'm Jules Divine," she said, standing as she introduced herself.

"Chance Howard." The woman flashed a brilliant smile and extended her hand toward Jules but pulled it back just before their hands met. She removed tight-fitting black leather gloves. "Sorry, my hands are all sweaty," she said, wiping her hand down the front of her jeans before again offering it to Jules.

Chance's hand was surprisingly soft for one who made a living mowing yards.

"I recognize you from your picture," Chance added.

"My picture?"

"Over the fireplace." Chance gestured toward the great room.

"Oh, I see," Jules said. She wondered if the young woman was a frequent visitor to Nana's home.

"I keep Daphne's yard for her," Chance said. "I own my own landscaping business. I service most of the single women in this neighborhood and the Crafts."

Service most of the single women? Jules thought. *What a strange way of putting it.*

"I think they're more at ease with me than with the male lawn care teams." Chance displayed her beautiful smile again.

"How many women do you *service*?" Jules asked.

"In this neighborhood, about twenty," Chance said, flashing a grin then turning somber. "I'm sorry that Daphne passed. She was an incredible woman. I saw you at her funeral, but I didn't want to talk business there. I want to make certain you need me to continue taking care of the grounds."

"What does your service include?" Jules asked.

"I mow, weed eat, and pull any weeds that dare raise their ugly heads in my yards. I also do all the landscaping, flower bed maintenance, fertilizing, and insect eradication."

Chance Howard was relaxed and easy to be around. Jules chastised herself for thinking the young woman was anything more than she appeared.

14

"Would you like some ice water?" Jules offered. "It's very warm today."

"No, I'm good." Chance's blue eyes seemed to stop short of laughing. "I need to finish here. I have three more yards to do before it gets too hot. It was nice to meet you."

"I want you to," Jules blurted out.

"To what?" Chance slowly raised an eyebrow.

Jules laughed. "To continue to take care of the grounds. How do I pay you?"

"Oh, Daphne's accountant takes care of all her bills." Chance seemed to know more about Nana's business than Jules. "Unless you make changes, I assume I'll continue to invoice her, and she will mail me a check."

Jules watched Chance walk away to get gasoline. *I would bet a month's pay you're a lesbian,* she thought.

##

"How did you meet my grandmother?" Jules asked as Chance filled the mower with gas.

"The police arrested me on a DUI. I used to stay drunk most of the time. I had real anger issues. I didn't figure my life was worth much, being a lesbian and all. That's what my folks said.

"Before they could book me and fingerprint me, Daphne showed up at the jail and talked the arresting officer into releasing me to her. She paid for counseling to help me manage my anger issues.

"She helped me start this business and taught me how to run a small company so I would succeed. She saved my life."

Jules watched Chance crank the mower. *Nana really was a remarkable woman,* she thought.

Jules finished her coffee then forced herself to enter Nana's world. Nana's office was a spacious room with floor-to-ceiling bookcases lining two walls. Another wall was home to Nana's built-in desk and computer with the largest monitor imaginable. Nana's eyesight had started to deteriorate, so she had purchased a huge monitor. "I work and tan at the same time," she used to tease.

An entire section of one bookshelf was devoted to Daphne Divine's books. Jules inhaled slowly as she recalled proofing every book Nana had ever written. She hadn't exactly proofed Nana's early books, but Nana had read them out loud to her, and Jules had loved Nana's stories.

Sometime during college, Jules had become Nana's official proofreader. She often felt that her desire to be a great proofreader for Nana had led her to major in English. Of course, Nana had beta readers, an editor, and an agent who advised her, but she depended on Jules for the final read before releasing a book to print.

Jules pulled the handle on Nana's private bookcase and found it locked. Nana had always kept it locked. "That is where I keep my ideas, so no one can steal them," she used to say with a chuckle.

Jules jumped when Nana's cell phone rang. She followed the sound and found the phone on the desk beside Nana's computer. The word *Agent* flashed on the phone screen. Jules disconnected the cell phone from its charger and sat down in Nana's desk chair.

The phone dinged in her hand as the caller left a message. Jules played back the recording. "I'm getting nervous. Where's the final manuscript? The printer is screaming for it. Just sign off on the damn thing and email it today. I'm serious. Today!"

Jules was surprised no one had notified the agent of Nana's death. She wondered if she could find the manuscript on Nana's computer but was distracted by the sound of footsteps in the kitchen before she could search for it.

"Hello, is anyone here?" A pleasant voice echoed through the empty house.

"Hello," Jules called back as she walked toward the center of the house. She was surprised to find an attractive, middle-aged woman in the kitchen.

"You must be Jules," the woman said.

"I am. And you are . . .?"

"Daphne's chief cook and bottle washer, Renee Baxter." She extended her hand to Jules.

"I thought you might be here," Renee continued. "I saw you at the funeral. You were her favorite, you know."

Jules nodded and tried to swallow around the knot in her throat. The shock of Nana's death was wearing off, and in its place was a gaping hole of indescribable sadness.

"Why don't I fix you some breakfast?" Renee said.

"That sounds lovely." Jules refilled her cup before sitting down at the kitchen island. She watched Renee as she moved about the kitchen, easily locating what she needed. It was obvious the housekeeper knew her way around Nana's home.

Jules committed to memory the features of the woman. Renee was short, about five-three, and slender. Her shoulder-length brown hair was streaked with red highlights. Her sparkling hazel eyes fit perfectly in a face that laughed more than it frowned. Jules guessed Renee to be in her late thirties.

The doorbell rang as Renee pulled bacon and eggs from the refrigerator. "I'll get it," Jules said as she slid from the stool and walked to the front door. Even through the opaque glass, Jules knew the figure on the other side was Detective Tanner West. She licked her lips and opened the door.

"Detective West, what a pleasant surprise." Jules managed to keep her joy from blooming into a huge grin.

"Good morning, Miss Divine," Tanner said, stopping short of bowing before the beautiful brunette. "I hope you feel better today and we can continue our talk."

"Oh, yes," Jules said, "of course. I'm sorry for abruptly ending the evening."

"It was inconsiderate of me to question you so soon after the funeral. I apologize, but I must move quickly, or any evidence may disappear."

"Detective Tanner West, I'd like you to meet Renee Baxter." Jules swept her hand toward the housekeeper. "Renee is . . . was Nana's housekeeper."

Renee placed a cup of coffee in front of Tanner. "Have you eaten breakfast?"

"No, but I—"

"Then you'll join us," Renee declared as the bacon began to sizzle in the large skillet. "Jules, if you'll set the table and pour the orange juice, breakfast will be ready in two shakes of a lamb's tail."

Chapter 4

Tanner enjoyed the conversation with the two attractive women. She had seen Renee around town and was familiar with her struggle as a single mom raising teenage boys. More than once Tanner had kept her twins from being booked for a DUI.

"Did you find Miss Divine's body?" Tanner asked Renee.

Renee looked down as if overcome by emotion. "Yes," she whispered, tears filling her eyes.

"Would you mind showing me where you found her?" Tanner turned to Jules, "If that's okay with you."

Both women agreed.

Jules stood back as Tanner and Renee entered her grandmother's suite. Nana's latest best seller was stacked on the nightstand along with two other novels by authors unknown to Jules.

"I was told you found her in bed." Tanner frowned.

"That's right."

"But her bed is made and—"

"I'm so sorry," Renee mumbled. "I thought Daphne died of natural causes. I gave the house a thorough cleaning to get it ready for Jules.

"I laundered all the bed linens, towels, and Daphne's clothes. I also polished all the furniture and waxed the floors."

"That pretty much destroyed any evidence that might have been here." Tanner couldn't hide her disappointment. "Are you always this efficient?"

"I . . . I was just trying—"

"Detective West, Renee said she was trying to have the house cleaned for my arrival. None of us knew Nana had been murdered."

Tanner nodded but it still perturbed her that any evidence that would help her catch a killer had been eradicated by the housekeeper. She couldn't even be certain if Daphne's bedroom was the crime scene or if the mystery writer had been murdered somewhere else and then placed in her bed.

Renee had called an ambulance, and Daphne had been rushed to the nearest hospital where she was pronounced dead on arrival. Two days later, the medical examiner had declared her death a homicide. Tanner was two days behind the killer and losing ground fast.

"Did she have company the night she died?" Tanner asked. "Was there any evidence of two wine glasses or two dinner plates? Anything like that?"

"There were two glasses of wine," Renee said. "But I—"

"Ran them through the dishwasher," Tanner said, her frustration growing. "Did the glasses have lipstick on them?"

"Yes," Renee confirmed. "Daphne didn't wear lipstick, so it had to belong to her visitor. It was bright red."

"The wine bottle . . . what happened to the wine bottle?" Excitement colored Tanner's voice. "Maybe we can pull prints from it."

Renee's eyes brightened. "I put it in recycling. It should still be in the utility room."

The three hurried to the small room off the kitchen. "That's it." Renee pointed to an empty Siduri Pinot Noir bottle.

"Dessert wine." Tanner narrowed her eyes as she carefully used her pen to pick up the bottle. "Was there evidence that someone dined with Miss Divine?"

"There were two dinner plates in the sink," Renee said as she pulled a gallon ziplock baggie from the shelf and handed it to Tanner.

"Thank you," the detective mumbled as she placed the bottle into the bag. She was certain the case could have easily been solved if all the evidence hadn't been destroyed.

"Well, I must get to work," Renee said before heading back to the kitchen.

"Jules, do you have my number in your phone?" Tanner asked.

"No, I haven't entered it yet."

Tanner pulled her phone from her pocket and pressed the buttons to send her contact information to Jules. Then she sent a photo of herself leaning in a doorway. She held out her hand for Jules's phone and synced the photo with her phone number.

"Now you have me at the top of your friends' list," Tanner said with a chuckle. "Please don't hesitate to call me if you need anything. I do mean anything—a friend to talk with or a dinner partner. Anything."

Jules led Tanner to the front door. "Thank you for stopping by, Detective," she said as she opened the door.

"Please, call me Tanner."

"Thank you, Tanner."

Only after the door closed behind her did Tanner West realize that she'd been dismissed. *Jules Divine is very smooth*, the detective thought.

##

Jules located Renee in the dining room, where she was polishing the magnificent table that filled the room. Jules sighed as she recalled her relatives gathered around the table on holidays.

Nana had always hosted family gatherings in her home. The huge table seated twelve people, just enough room for Jules, her parents and older brother, Lucas, Uncle Buddy—Nana's other son—and his family of seven, including Aunt Page, two boys, and three girls.

After Jules's parents disowned her, they refused to dine at Nana's because Jules was at the table. Jules recalled being surprised and pleased when her parents didn't show up for Thanksgiving that year but everyone else did. Even Lucas opted to dine with her and Nana instead of their parents.

"Renee, do you mind telling me your arrangement with Nana?" Jules asked.

"Every morning I cooked her breakfast. Then I straightened anything that was out of place in the house. I did all the grocery shopping and cooked any other meals Daphne needed."

"Did you cook her last meal?" Jules asked.

"I think I did. She often had me prepare dinner for two and leave it in the refrigerator. That's what I did that day."

"You should've told that to Detective West."

"I'll call her and give her that information. Do you want me to continue as your housekeeper?" Renee asked.

"I'm not certain what I'll do. I don't know what will happen to the house. I know nothing about Nana's will."

"Why don't you call her lawyer and find out?" Renee suggested.

"Do you know her lawyer's name?" Jules asked.

"No."

"Neither do I." Jules knew she had a lot to learn about Nana.

"I'm sure you can find it on her computer," Renee said. "She kept her life on that thing."

"Until everything is settled, let's maintain your regular routine."

"Thank you." Renee bowed her head. "This job makes it possible for me to care for my boys."

Jules left Renee to her chores and wandered into her grandmother's suite. She turned on Nana's computer and watched as the screen requested a password. She uttered a quick prayer that the password hadn't changed and typed in *Jules1410*. The computer opened to Nana's emails.

The first email was a complimentary ticket to the awards ceremony for Rainbow Award Winners (RAW). The International Rainbow Literary Society was holding its annual convention and awards banquet in Dallas, Texas. The guest speaker at the banquet was Darcy Lake. Dallas was only an hour's drive from Kingston.

Jules inhaled sharply as she realized that she could use the ticket to see her favorite author. She quickly checked the date and location of the annual meeting. It was three days away. The convention started Friday morning and ran through Sunday afternoon. It would be held at Dallas's most elite hotel, Rosewood Mansion on Turtle Creek, and attendance was limited to 400 people.

Jules printed the ticket and itinerary for the convention. Two of the pages pointed out how popular Darcy Lake was and that she had won every literary award offered to a lesbian writer and several mainstream awards. It touted the fact that Mrs. Lake would be unveiling her latest novel at the convention and would be on hand to autograph her new book for the duration of the convention. Jules was certain that Darcy Lake's appearance was responsible for the sellout of the convention.

An email from Agent dinged into Nana's computer. It had two attachments. The subject line of one read manuscript; the other was titled approval.

The agent's email said, "Sign the damn approval so I can send this to the printer. We're in real danger here. I must have this today, or you can kiss the book release goodbye until next month. We have too much riding on this to wait. You've proofed it a dozen times. Just sign it."

Jules considered proofing the attached manuscript but knew it would take her at least a day to read one of her grandmother's books. The email sounded frantic. Jules opened the approval form, attached Nana's electronic signature to it, and returned it to agent@sbcglobal.us.

I can't believe I have a ticket to attend the awards ceremony where Darcy Lake will be the guest of honor, Jules thought. She turned off Nana's computer as she thought about buying a new dress to wear to the banquet. *I'll need shoes and a matching purse.*

Jules returned to her suite, and picked up Darcy's last novel from her bedside table. *I'll take it and get her to autograph both her newest release and this one too,* Jules thought.

She moved to her bookshelf and surveyed the many Darcy Lake novels she owned. She left them at Nana's for safekeeping. She had every novel Lake had written.

Nana often teased her about reading "that lesbian trash." She would laugh as she hugged Jules's slender shoulders. "How can you jump from Shakespeare to Darcy Lake?" Nana would ask.

Jules would argue that Darcy Lake was one of the finest mystery writers of their time. The fact that her heroines were lesbians didn't keep mystery fans from buying her books.

Nana would simply nod and walk away laughing. "Lake certainly outsells me," she would admit.

Jules could almost hear her grandmother's laughter.

"Room reservations," Jules said out loud. "I wonder if Nana made room reservations." She found the hotel's number in the convention information and called the reservation desk. A quick check confirmed Nana didn't have a room reserved.

"The only thing we have available is the executive suite," the reservationist said. "We had a cancellation; otherwise, we would have nothing."

Jules pulled her credit card from her purse and provided the necessary information to reserve the suite. It was pricy, but how often does one get to spend the weekend with Darcy Lake?

"I have cleaned everything," Renee said as she tapped on Jules's open door. "Do you want me to make you lunch?"

"No. I'm going shopping. I'll grab something at the mall if I get hungry. Thank you, Renee. I appreciate you taking care of Nana's house."

Jules gathered her purse and key fob then followed Renee from the house.

"See you in the morning," Renee said with a wave.

Chapter 5

The porter removed Jules's luggage from the trunk of her Lexus as she turned the car over to the valet. She followed her bags to the registration counter and handed her confirmation to the cashier. The young woman typed information into her computer and looked at Jules.

"I'm sorry, Miss Divine," she said, frowning at her monitor, "but your room isn't quite ready. It'll be another hour before you can get into it.

"I'm going to give you the keycard and have the porter hold your luggage until he can deliver it to your room. In the meantime, please accept this chit for free wine and hors d'oeuvres in our private club until your room is ready. The club is through that door." She motioned to a gold-trimmed mahogany door across from the registration desk.

Jules accepted the items. Hors d'oeuvres sounded good. She had skipped lunch in her eagerness to check into the hotel and possibly catch a glimpse of Darcy Lake.

The private club was spectacularly decorated with plush carpet and secluded circular booths along the walls. A young bartender beamed as Jules entered the club and motioned for her to sit at the bar. She gracefully slid onto the barstool, cognizant of the bartender's admiring glances.

"What may I offer you, M adam?"

"A glass of merlot," Jules said.

"May I recommend my personal favorite? It's Island Mist Black Raspberry Merlot."

Jules laughed. "Sure. Why not?" His enthusiasm was contagious.

The young man watched Jules as she took her first sip of the wine. Her pink tongue lightly licked her lips. "This is delicious."

"Everyone has the same reaction," he said, obviously pleased by her compliment. "It's good, isn't it?"

"It is different."

"Young man? Young man!" a woman's voice called from one of the booths. "Can we get some service over here?"

The bartender winked. "Duty calls. Don't go away. I'll be right back."

Jules sipped the wine as she thought about her day. Agent had sent a text message to Nana's phone. "We will make this by the hair on our chinny-chin-chin. We must talk when this is over," the message had read. Jules wondered if Agent had a real name.

Jules had packed her suitcase, loaded her car, and driven to Dallas, anxious to get a look at Darcy Lake. The convention brochure had also promised that Lake's camera-shy wife would attend the convention with her.

"Excuse me, is this seat taken?" A dark, silky voice spoke softly beside Jules. It sent heat down her spine.

Jules looked at the mirror over the bar and watched in stunned silence as Darcy Lake sat down beside her. She didn't answer the question. She couldn't find her voice.

"Are you okay?" Darcy asked.

"I . . . I . . ." Jules licked her lips. Everything was desert-dry. *Dammit, I'm a thirty-four-year-old adult, and this woman has turned me into a stammering idiot,* Jules thought.

"Mrs. Lake!" The happy bartender was back. "It's good to have you with us. What would you like?"

"Any wine will be fine," Darcy said.

Jules managed to find her voice as she held up her wine glass. "This is delightful."

"Then I'll have some of that." A beautiful smile slowly spread across Darcy's face.

"There you are!" A boisterous voice filled the sedate club as a tall, redheaded, raw-boned woman strode toward them. "And you've finally produced your gorgeous wife. What is your name, dear?"

Darcy smiled and nodded to Jules to answer.

"Jules," Jules squeaked. She cleared her throat and said her name louder.

"You really must join us for dinner," the woman insisted. "Everyone will be so thrilled to meet Jules. You know we were beginning to believe that she was a figment of your imagination. You've kept her hidden from us all these years. You're right; she is gorgeous." The woman trailed her fingertips down Jules's arm and licked her lips before flashing a toothy grin.

Darcy grabbed the woman's wrist and pulled her hand away from Jules's arm. "That's why I never bring her with me." Her voice was a low growl. "I don't like people touching my wife."

The woman stepped back as Darcy stood. "I'm sorry."

"We've just arrived," Darcy said. "We'll pass on the dinner invitation. I'm certain we'll see you tomorrow."

Darcy's hand cupped Jules's elbow and gently urged her to stand. Jules picked up both wine glasses and allowed Darcy to propel her to one of the secluded booths at the far end of the room.

"I'm so sorry," Darcy said as they settled into the booth. "I didn't want to leave you to the vultures, and I didn't want them to know I'm alone. Thanks for being a good sport."

Jules nodded. The closeness of the other woman was overwhelming. The touch of her soft hand, her beauty, and the soft fragrance of her perfume combined to send shockwaves through Jules.

"What happens when your wife shows up?" Jules asked.

"She won't," Darcy said.

"The brochure said she would be here," Jules mumbled.

"It's problematic." Darcy shrugged. "The least I can do is buy your dinner." She motioned for the waiter.

"So, you're here for the awards?" Darcy said after they placed their order. "Are you a writer?"

Jules giggled like a school girl. "Oh, no. I . . . uh . . . came to . . . get your autograph." She rushed out the last three words, hoping she didn't sound too starstruck.

"So, no one here knows who you are?" Darcy raised a perfectly arched eyebrow.

"No, this is my first time to attend a lesbian literary awards banquet," Jules replied.

"Listen, Jules. I have a proposition for you. I'll pay you a thousand dollars a night to be my wife this weekend."

Jules sat in shocked silence. She finally summoned the ability to respond. "Mrs. Lake, I may seem like a groupie, but I can assure you I am not a hooker."

"A hooker?" The look of astonishment on Darcy's face was comical. "Oh! No, you think I'm offering to buy your services. I didn't mean that. I—"

Jules tried to scoot out of the booth, but the blonde caught her by the wrist. "Please, I'm in trouble. I need your help. I didn't mean to insult you. I don't want to sleep with you."

Jules stared at Darcy's hand on her arm and then slowly raised her gaze to meet the author's sparkling blue eyes. The truth was, she'd dreamed of sleeping with Darcy Lake.

"Please let me explain," Darcy pleaded.

Jules nodded and settled back into the booth.

"As you know, I'm the featured speaker this weekend. I'm supposed to unveil my latest novel at the convention and let them meet my wife of ten years."

Jules motioned for Darcy to continue.

Darcy took a deep breath. "As of right now, my books haven't arrived, and I have no idea where they are. My wife isn't here and won't be. I'm just generally screwed."

Jules laughed at Darcy's last statement. She was surprised to hear such everyday slang coming from the gorgeous woman sitting beside her.

"Don't they know your wife?" Jules asked

"No, I've been careful to keep my wife away from these functions, and no one has ever seen a photo of her."

Jules frowned. "If I agree to help you, what do you want me to do?"

"Pretend to be my wife," Darcy said with a sigh. "Stay by my side so no one hits on either of us, and pray that my books arrive before the convention is over. These women can be vicious when things don't go as planned. Several of my rivals would love to see me with egg on my face.

"Of course, you'll have to dance with me and maybe even steal a kiss for the cameras, but I'll make certain the angle is such that your face won't be visible.

"You can sleep in your own room. Just don't let anyone see you coming or going."

Jules thought about the repercussions of the arrangement Darcy was suggesting. If her plan fell apart, the only one who would suffer would be the author. If it worked, it could provide an exciting weekend. The thought of being on Darcy Lake's arm all weekend definitely appealed to her.

"Would you autograph my book?" Jules said, regretting the pitiful-sounding request the minute it came out of her mouth.

"Of course." Darcy laughed. "I'll sign all the books you want."

The waiter served their dinner as six women from the convention entered the room. Jules recognized four of them as well-known lesbian writers. She didn't know the other two. The women looked around the room and then zeroed in on the couple.

"Here we go," Darcy mumbled as she laced her fingers through Jules's.

"Darcy!" a woman with green-and-red-streaked hair gushed as she closed in on the two women. "Connie said you were in here . . . and this must be your lovely wife. Oh my! She's a looker. No wonder you've kept her hidden from us."

"Honey, this is Rita Lafame. Rita, this is my wife, Jules," Darcy said. "Why don't the rest of you introduce yourselves?"

The women rattled off their names, and Jules graciously acknowledged them.

"We've just gotten our food," Darcy said. "We're going to eat before it gets cold and then get some rest before the festivities start in the morning."

"We could drag some tables together and eat as a group," Rita suggested.

"No, not tonight." Darcy's response was firm and final. "I haven't seen Jules all week. I'd like some alone time with her before the convention starts."

I wouldn't mind spending the night in your bed, Jules thought before she could stop herself.

Jules stopped listening as Darcy encouraged the other women to leave. She watched Darcy's lips as she spoke. They were full and beautifully shaped, covering perfect white teeth. Without a doubt, Darcy Lake was the most desirable woman Jules had ever met.

"Don't you think so, honey?" Darcy squeezed Jules's hand, pulling her from her reverie.

"Whatever you say, baby," Jules mumbled.

Darcy looked down at her and neither of them spoke as Jules held the blonde's gaze. "I was just saying we were tired and wanted to go to bed early tonight," Darcy said without moving her eyes from Jules's.

"Yes," Jules whispered.

"Registration starts at nine," Rita informed them. "You need to make an appearance sometime before noon. Call me and I'll meet you for brunch."

Darcy nodded as the women moved away, filling the club with noise as they pulled enough tables together to accommodate all of them.

"Umm, you're right," Darcy said, resting her free hand on Jules's. "This wine is excellent."

Jules couldn't explain the feeling that flooded her body at the other woman's touch. "I'm glad you like it."

Jules and Darcy talked as they dined. Darcy pointed out the good, the bad, and the crazies as the lesbian authors congregated in the club. Jules laughed as the writer used humorous adjectives to describe her peers.

You have no peers. You are in a class all by yourself, Jules thought as she gazed into the face of the woman she had nursed a crush on for the past ten years.

Darcy ordered one crème brûlée and two cups of coffee. "You must taste their crème brûlée," she insisted. "It's the best in the world. If we share it, we won't eat too many calories."

Jules flinched when the waiter ignited the dessert with a small blowtorch. The sight of Darcy's lovely face in the glow of the dancing flames took her breath away.

"Thank you," Jules said as she finished her half of the dessert. "That was wonderful." She was acutely aware of the glances and nods they were getting from the other diners. "I think they're talking about us."

"We should give them something to talk about." Darcy grinned mischievously. She slowly leaned down and placed her lips against Jules's.

Darcy's lips were soft and smooth like . . . like rose petals. Of its own accord, Jules's tongue lightly traced Darcy's bottom lip. Darcy tasted sweet and dangerous at the same time, like crème brûlée and intoxicating wine. The room fell away. The entire world disappeared as Darcy increased the pressure on Jules's lips and touched the tip of her tongue with her own.

Jules had no idea how long the kiss lasted. It could have been seconds or a lifetime. The only thing she knew for certain was that no one had ever kissed her the way Darcy had kissed her.

"Now *that* was wonderful," Darcy murmured against Jules's lips.

Jules bowed her head to hide the turmoil raging in her mind and body. For the first time, she was aware of the total silence that had settled over the room.

Darcy signaled the waiter for the check and then led Jules from the club. Shouts and wolf whistles followed their departure.

"What's your room number?" Darcy asked as the elevator door closed.

"Three-ten." Jules pulled the key card from her purse.

"That's perfect." Darcy's smile illuminated the elevator. "My room is three-twelve. Our suites are right next to each other. We can pull this off, Jules."

Jules nodded. She was still reliving Darcy's kiss.

"What time do you want to go to breakfast?" Darcy asked as she unlocked her room. "It would be good if we can go down together."

"Is nine okay?"

"Perfect." Darcy ducked her head into her room "We have adjoining suites. Unlock your door when you get inside."

Jules took a deep breath and unlocked the door between her room and Darcy's. Darcy was waiting on the other side.

33

"This couldn't be any better if we'd planned it."
Darcy's enthusiasm was overwhelming. "Now, if they'll
deliver my books, we'll have an awesome weekend."

"Yes," Jules said. "Right now, I just want to take a
shower and get some rest. *Preferably a very cold shower.*
Good night, Darcy." She walked into the bathroom, leaving
the door between their rooms ajar.

Jules towel-dried her hair as she walked from the
bathroom. She was surprised to see the door between their
rooms had been closed. She left a wake-up call for seven
and slipped between the clean sheets. She hoped sleep
would come soon. Reliving Darcy's kiss was pumping
adrenaline into her body at an alarming rate.

Jules was no novice when it came to women. College
had been a true education for her both academically and
sexually. A beautiful woman by anyone's standards, she'd
had flings with lesbians and straight women just checking
out the "college experience."

After graduation, she had settled down and devoted
herself to becoming the best teacher possible and making
Nana proud of her. It startled her to realize that Nana hadn't
crossed her mind all the time she was with Darcy.

Jules fell asleep wondering if making love with Darcy
would be like the smoking love scenes the author wrote in
her books. If the way she kissed was any indication, it
would be.

Chapter 6

Jules put the finishing touches on her lipstick as a soft knock sounded on the door between their rooms. "Come in," she called out.

Darcy looked beautiful in her tight designer jeans and long-sleeved, open-collared blouse. The sleeves were cuffed above her wrists, and high-heeled boots made her look like a model for women's casual clothes.

Jules was glad she had dressed in similar attire.

"Wow!" Darcy's approval seemed sincere. "You are just as breathtaking as I remembered. I was afraid I had dreamed you."

Jules dipped her head as a light blush crept up her neck. The compliment hadn't embarrassed her, but the desire to wrap her arms around Darcy had.

Darcy pulled a ring from her pocket and slipped it onto Jules's finger. "They'll wonder why my wife has no wedding band," she explained. "Jules, I owe you big-time for this. If I can ever do anything for you—speak to your book club or send you a personally autographed copy of every book I have ever written—please...."

"You don't owe me anything." Jules pulled her hand from Darcy's and walked into the writer's bedroom. "We should both leave through your door."

Darcy opened the door and motioned for Jules to step into the hallway.

Rita Lafame strode toward them as Darcy closed the door. "Good morning. I had the registration desk put me on

35

your floor. Did you get some . . . umm, rest last night, Darcy?" The woman wiggled her eyebrows, reinforcing the salacious look on her face.

"We had a nice night," Jules said. "Thank you for asking."

Darcy smiled as she placed her hand on the small of Jules's back and guided her toward the elevator. Rita stomped after them.

"You'll be happy to know your books arrived after midnight last night," Rita said.

"Then all is right in my world," Darcy said as she laced her fingers through Jules's and pulled her close.

##

The morning passed quickly as Darcy autographed books and Jules kept a steady supply of the paperbacks stacked beside her. During a lull, Jules got a green tea macchiato for Darcy and a strong black coffee for herself.

Darcy stood and stretched then took a sip of her beverage. "How'd you know I drink green tea macchiatos?"

Jules tilted her head in thought. "Your main characters always order that drink. I figured you liked it."

"I do." Darcy smiled and leaned down to brush her lips against Jules's. "Thank you, darling."

A low "aww" went up from the women crowded around Darcy's table. "Time to get back to work." Darcy blushed for the first time.

Jules found herself wondering if the quick kiss had been spontaneous on Darcy's part or another show for the onlookers.

##

Darcy glanced at her watch. It was almost two. "Are you hungry?" She placed a large GONE TO LUNCH sign in the center of the book table and took Jules's hand in hers.

"I am," Jules said. "Your admirers shanghaied us before we could get breakfast."

As they dined, Darcy seemed to be genuinely interested in Jules's life. "Tell me, Jules, what do you do when you aren't chasing autographs?"

"I'm an English teacher," Jules said proudly. "And I don't chase autographs. Yours is the only one I have."

"Really?" Darcy held Jules's gaze for several seconds. "I'm flattered."

Jules cleared her throat and changed the direction of the conversation. "Tell me about your next book."

"I'm not sure."

"I heard writers always have four or five books working at once. What have you cut from the herd and singled out to finish?"

"Right now, nothing," Darcy said. "I also have a day job, you know." Before Jules could ask for details, Darcy changed the subject.

"I know you read my books, but tell me, what other lesbian authors do you read?"

"I don't read just lesbian novels. I read all genres. I adore Daphne Divine," Jules said, giving Nana a plug.

"So do I," Darcy declared. "I have every book she has ever written—a hundred, I think. I have several autographed copies."

Jules wondered if maybe the two had been friends. "Do you know her?"

"I've had the privilege of visiting with her on several occasions. Have you read all of her books too?" Darcy's eyes twinkled as she teased Jules. "She doesn't write lesbian fiction."

"Yes, I've read every book she's written. I've also read everything William Shakespeare ever wrote."

"Did I just get reprimanded, teacher?" Darcy's look of mischief was endearing. "I didn't mean to insinuate that you only read lesbian books. I apologize."

"Are you always so nice?" Jules asked.

"No, not always." Darcy shrugged. "You seem to bring out the best in me."

"I could be your muse," Jules's tone was teasing. "But I'm certain your wife holds that envied position."

Darcy looked across the room for several seconds and then returned her attention to Jules.

"I wonder if Daphne Divine has ever read any of my books. I sent her an autographed copy of my last book. I sent it to her publisher. They probably haven't forwarded it to her yet."

"Is she a fan of yours?"

"I don't think so," Darcy said. "I don't think she's into lesbian books."

Jules started to tell Darcy that Daphne Divine was her grandmother, but the look of distress on Darcy's face stopped her.

Darcy glanced across the room again. "Steel yourself. Here comes the head bitc . . . battle axe."

"Darling!" A brassy blonde leaned down and planted bright red lips on Darcy's cheek. "They told me you were already here. As always, I'm running late. It's difficult when one is in such great demand."

Darcy didn't stand. She looked up at the woman and said, "Honey, this is Lacy Lawrence. Lacy, my wife, Jules."

Jules dutifully used her napkin to remove the lipstick from Darcy's face.

"My ball-and-chain is around here somewhere." Lacy's loud voice went up an octave as she looked around the room. "There she is. Bade! Bade, over here."

A tall, heavyset woman dressed in tan slacks and a tight-fitting sweater swaggered toward them. She perked up when she saw Darcy.

"You must be the gorgeous wife I've been hearing about all morning." Bade held out a hand toward Jules. "Nice catch, Darcy."

"Oh, she didn't catch me," Jules said, deciding to add to Darcy's reputation. "I shamelessly chased her."

Lacy pulled out a chair and sat down at their table. "You must tell me how you managed to convince this gorgeous creature to marry you," she said to Darcy.

"Honestly," Darcy's eyes twinkled as she looked at Jules, "she chased me until I caught her."

Jules laughed and squeezed Darcy's hand. "We should get back to your booth, darling. You can't keep your fans waiting."

She turned to Lacy. "Darcy has been signing autographs nonstop all morning. She likes to stay on top of it or the line gets too long."

"Humph." Lacy gave her a wicked look. "I'm sure that isn't all she likes to stay on top of."

Darcy shot Lacy a disgusted look and stood, pulling Jules up with her. Without another word, they walked away from the lewd woman.

"Who was that?" Jules asked as they headed for the convention hall.

"She fancies herself as my archrival," Darcy said with a chuckle. "She writes smut I can't stomach reading."

"Do her books sell as well as yours?" Jules frowned.

"Not really. She sells her books for less than three dollars. My books sell for six times that price. We may do the same volume, but her income is a lot less."

"Darcy!" a short, dishwater blonde called out as they reached the convention hall door. "Darcy, it is so good to see you." She wrapped her arms around Darcy and hugged her tightly. Darcy hugged back.

"Marta, it's good to see you too. I hoped you would be here." Darcy pulled free from the woman's arms and turned to Jules.

"Jules, this is Marta Wayne, my wonderful beta. Marta, I want you to meet my wife, Jules."

A dark red blush crept up Marta's face as she held out her hand to Jules. Jules instantly knew the woman was hopelessly in love with Darcy Lake.

"It's a pleasure to meet you." *I guess you and I are in the same boat*, Jules thought.

Marta nodded and acknowledged Jules's words before turning to Darcy. "I haven't received your latest manuscript," she said.

"I thought it was sent two weeks ago," Darcy said, frowning. "I'll check on it."

"Quickly," Marta instructed. "I have this week open for your book. After that I have others scheduled."

Darcy looped her arm through Marta's as they entered the hall. "I know how busy you are, Marta. I'll make certain it happens Monday. I promise."

"See that you do." Jules could tell Marta only pretended to be agitated. "Save a dance for me at the party tonight."

"You're the first name on my dance card," Darcy promised as she glanced at Jules, "right after my wife."

Jules wondered if Darcy was as solicitous of her real wife as she was of her.

Chapter 7

Jules looked in the mirror, checking everything one last time. She was pleased by what she saw: perfect makeup; glossy hair curling around her face and cascading onto her shoulders; stunning dress, long and fitted and showing just enough cleavage to make anyone drool. She jumped when Darcy knocked before entering her room.

"Oh! Wow! Just wow!" The look of delight on Darcy's face was worth the effort Jules had made to look good. "You are gorgeous." Darcy shook her head as if trying to remove from her mind pictures that shouldn't be there.

"Tonight I'll have the most beautiful woman at the convention on my arm." Darcy's smile widened. "You are stunning."

"The same could be said for you," Jules replied.

Darcy wasn't just beautiful. She was devastatingly magnificent. She looked the part of an arousing romance writer. Everything about her screamed, "sensuous, exciting and desirable."

Darcy was wearing a black evening dress that accentuated all her assets. The thigh-high slit exposed long, lean legs when she walked. She was flamboyant and sexy as hell.

Darcy moved closer to Jules. An inch more and their lips would meet. Jules stepped back and picked up her purse. "Shall we show them our best moves?"

##

The party was in full swing when the couple entered the ballroom. A soft murmur ran through the room as eyes turned to stare at Darcy Lake and her wife.

"How do you ever get used to this sort of attention?" Jules whispered.

"You don't," Darcy answered as she pressed Jules's arm tighter against her side. "It's a bit overwhelming, but bearable with you by my side."

Darcy spoke to everyone they encountered. She often stopped to chat with a group or another couple and introduce Jules.

Marta beamed as she caught Darcy's arm and pulled her toward a round table of six. "You're seated with us." It was in the front row of the tables circling a dance floor already filled with dancers.

A younger, androgynous-looking woman sat at the table. "Look who I found," Marta said, addressing the epicene female.

The woman scanned the couple, obviously liking what she saw. "Are you two together?" she asked.

Darcy smiled. "Yes. I'm Darcy Lake and this is my wife, Jules."

"I'm Marta's significant other." The woman held out her hand. "My name is Janet Price.

"Are you really married to each other?" Janet asked as everyone took their seats.

"Yes," Darcy said.

Janet snorted "You look like the same side of a coin. Which one of you is—"

"We don't discuss our personal life with others," Darcy snapped. "How we fit together is no one else's business."

Janet held up her hands. "Hey, no need to get all huffy about it. It's just unusual to see two extreme femmes together. I'm just saying."

"Looks can be deceiving," Darcy replied. Then she turned to Jules and smiled. "I believe this dance is mine."

Jules was trying to decide whether to lead or follow when Darcy placed the palm of her hand on the small of Jules's back and pulled her close. There was no doubt about who was leading. Darcy was a strong, smooth dancer and guided Jules around the dance floor. Darcy held her just tight enough to telegraph her every move. Her arm wrapped firmly around Jules made it easy to follow her lead.

Jules relaxed and enjoyed being in Darcy's arms. The scent of her was overwhelming and made her dizzy.

"I hope you're having a good time," Darcy whispered in her ear.

Jules closed her eyes and savored the feel of Darcy's lips and warm breath so close to her ear. She knew she was getting dangerously close to reaching a point that would only result in pain for her. Still, she nestled into the blonde's arms.

The band took a break and Jules reluctantly slipped from Darcy's arms. As they approached their table, a flashing light from Jules's clutch bag announced a phone call.

Jules removed her cell phone from her purse to turn it off, but the sight of Tanner West's face stopped her. "I have to take this call," she informed Darcy as she looked for the closest exit.

"Hold on, Tanner," she said over the chatter in the ballroom.

Jules exhaled as the heavy double doors closed behind her, muting the music and laughter inside the ballroom. "Tanner, hello. Is everything okay?"

"As okay as a murder case can be. I stopped by your home today, and Renee informed me you were in Dallas."

"Yes, I'm at a publishing convention."

"I wish you'd let me know when you're going to be out of pocket," Tanner grumbled.

"Oh, I didn't realize I had to answer to you," Jules said, her tone terse.

"I'm sorry, Jules," Tanner said. "Daphne's case is driving me crazy. I keep hitting dead ends. I was hoping you could answer some questions for me. When will you be back?"

"Late Sunday," Jules replied.

"Maybe we could have dinner together Sunday night," Tanner suggested.

"I'm not sure I'll be home in time for dinner. Why don't we plan on breakfast Monday morning?"

"I guess that'll have to do." Tanner's answer was almost a growl.

"Tanner, I'm sorry." Jules felt a warmth at her elbow and realized that Darcy was standing behind her.

"Jules, I really need your help on this case," Tanner said, using her sweetest voice.

"I know you do. I'll call you Sunday. We can talk while I drive home."

Tanner's mood seemed to improve. "I'd be delighted to keep you company while you drive."

"I'd like that too," Jules said. "Look, I have to go" She disconnected the call, and Darcy slipped her arm around her shoulders.

"Is everything okay?" Darcy asked. "You seem upset."

Jules thought about sharing her distress with Darcy but remembered that Darcy was only a brief acquaintance, someone she had agreed to help for the weekend. Someone she would never see again once Darcy returned to her real wife.

"I'm fine," Jules said.

"You don't look fine. Problem with your girlfriend?" Darcy asked.

"A friend." Jules didn't want to tell Darcy that Tanner was the detective investigating Daphne Divine's murder. "No one that matters to you."

"Would you like to go to your room?" Darcy asked. "I'll tell everyone you have a headache."

Jules sighed. "No, I'd rather stay with you."

"I'd like that." Darcy's arm tightened around Jules's shoulders.

They returned to their table as RAW Chairman Rosalind Reynolds tapped on the microphone. "Welcome, everyone." Reynolds quieted the crowd. "I just wanted to give you a quick rundown on a few changes in tomorrow's schedule. Then you can get back to enjoying yourselves."

Once they were seated, Darcy protectively slipped her arm back around Jules's shoulders.

Jules was drawn to Darcy like a magnet. She leaned into the blonde and thought how wonderful it would be if she really was Darcy's wife.

"I'm going to the ladies' room," Jules whispered in Darcy's ear. The blonde removed her arm from the back of Jules's chair and nodded.

Jules was halfway across the ballroom before Darcy noticed she had left her clutch bag on the table. She picked up the purse and Jules's cell phone fell from it. When Darcy looked up, Jules had disappeared.

Knowing it was wrong, Darcy couldn't stop herself from pulling up the last phone call Jules had received. The photo of a stunning, green-eyed woman filled the screen. Her auburn hair was shoulder-length and feathered around her face. *Pretty*, Darcy thought.

A text message from the woman dinged into the phone. "I have so much to share with you. Can't wait until Sunday."

Darcy quickly slid the phone back into Jules's purse and chastised herself. *You knew a woman as beautiful as Jules would have a girlfriend.*

"Those are the changes for tomorrow," Rosalind said, finishing her announcements, and Darcy realized she hadn't heard a word.

"I do want to recognize our speaker for tomorrow night's banquet," Rosalind continued. "Darcy Lake, please stand."

Darcy stood as Jules arrived at her side. "She's here with her gorgeous wife, Jules."

Darcy looked down at Jules, who squeezed her hand and smiled. *I wish you were my wife*, she thought.

"Darcy, why don't you and your lovely wife lead off the next dance?" Rosalind said as everyone else clapped and murmured in agreement.

Darcy led Jules to the dance floor and slowly pulled the brunette into her arms. She didn't want to dance with Jules. She didn't want to be in a crowd with Jules. She wanted to be alone with Jules. She wanted to make love to Jules.

Darcy closed her eyes as Jules's smooth cheek lightly touched her own. The images that filled her mind as Jules's soft breasts pressed against hers were totally wrong and impure. She tightened her arm around Jules's waist and pressed her tighter against her body. Darcy continued to hold Jules long after the song ended. A tap on her shoulder brought her back to reality.

"I believe you owe me a dance," Marta said, beaming.

"I . . . uh, yes," Darcy mumbled. She suddenly realized she was still clinging to Jules. Neither woman made a move to separate.

Jules looked up at Darcy. "You probably should let me go."

Darcy stepped back, and Marta pushed her way into the writer's arms as the music started.

"Looks like you're stuck with me," Janet said as she caught Jules's hand.

Jules kept the woman at arm's length the entire dance—not only because Janet kept stepping on her toes, but because she had no desire to be close to her.

"Time to switch partners," Darcy said as she pushed Marta into Janet's arms and pulled Jules into her own.

"Thank heavens!" Jules giggled as she snuggled into Darcy. "My poor toes will never be the same. I've danced with adolescents at school dances who were better than Janet."

"I didn't like you out of my arms," Darcy said, her voice deep with emotion.

"Neither did I," Jules replied.

The band broke into a driving beat that set everyone's feet to tapping. "Can you dance to this?" Darcy asked.

"Oh, yeah." Jules laughed as she danced backward away from her partner. Darcy did not disappoint her. Her eyes sparkled as she danced in pursuit of her elusive date, finally pulling Jules into her arms and kissing her soundly. "For my fans," she whispered.

Chapter 8

Jules finished blow-drying her hair and slipped into a pair of designer jeans and a lavender sweater that hugged her curves. She carefully applied her makeup to hide the circles under her eyes.

Her night had been a long and sleepless one. She'd tossed and turned, trying to drive the feel of Darcy from her mind. Her kisses were so real, so honest. She held Jules as if she were the most wonderful woman in the world.

Jules's tumultuous night had been filled with dreams of Darcy's kisses and Darcy's strong arms wrapped around her. She wondered if the writer was thinking about her. *Probably not,* she concluded. *This is just a business arrangement for her.*

"Good morning!" Darcy's happy voice filled Jules's room. Suddenly everything was right in her world.

Jules scanned the other woman. She was dressed in black slacks, low heels, and a pink silk blouse. The top two buttons on the blouse were unfastened. An ancient gold coin encircled by small diamonds dangled from a thick chain that directed one's eyes to the coin's resting place between the slight rise of Darcy's breasts.

Jules licked her lips and raised her eyes to meet Darcy's. The tip of Darcy's pink tongue traced her own bottom lip. The room was thick with desire as the two women fought the fire burning between them.

Jules slipped her purse strap over her shoulder and walked to the door. "I'm starved."

Rita Lafame was waiting for the elevator and grinned broadly as Darcy and Jules approached. Darcy caught Jules's hand in hers and pulled her a little closer.

"Well, if it isn't the lovebirds." Rita gave them a secretive grin as if they shared knowledge no one else had.

"You two certainly raised the bar on dancing last night," she added. "Darcy, I had no idea you could dance like that."

Darcy laughed. "I believe my partner deserves credit for our gambol. She's an excellent dancer."

"Yes, I noticed," Rita said. "Are you ready for your big speech tonight? Speaking in front of all our peers . . . . I'd be as nervous as a nun in a brothel."

"I'm fine," Darcy said, scowling. She hated it when others tried to get into her head.

"Did you streak your hair red and green for this occasion, or do you always wear it like that?" Jules's sweet expression hid her dislike of Rita's attempts to rattle Darcy.

Rita fluffed her hair. "This is special for the convention. One has to stand out at these functions. Unlike Darcy, I must depend on things other than my incredible good looks to sell books. It's good that *I* am a *talented* writer."

Jules started to confront the woman, but Darcy squeezed her hand and whispered in her ear. "She's not worth it."

Oh, but you are, Jules thought.

##

The day passed too quickly as Jules and Darcy sold hundreds of books. Jules had no idea conventions were such a source of revenue for authors. Although she had accompanied Nana to many conventions, mainstream conventions didn't seem as exciting and tumultuous as the lesbian convention.

"How many books did the printer ship you?" she asked Darcy.

"Five thousand. It's a good thing the convention ends tomorrow. I hope we have enough to last the day."

"Your poor hand." Jules frowned as she massaged Darcy's fingers and the back of her hand. "You must be dying."

"Oh, yes. I'm in major pain." Darcy gave her an impish grin. "You may have to massage my hand every time I get a break."

Jules ceased movement as she looked up into Darcy's eyes. A smile slowly spread across her face as she realized that Darcy was playing with her.

"Please don't stop," Darcy whispered. "I like the way you touch me."

"Unfortunately, I like touching you," Jules replied.

"Jules, I—"

Suddenly, Rosalind Reynolds approached their booth. "Darcy, I need to speak with you," she said. She looked around at all the women standing in line to get an autographed copy of Darcy's book. "In private."

"Roz, look at this line," Darcy argued. "We'll have a lot of upset women if I walk away."

Rosalind surveyed the crowd again. It would probably cause a minor uprising if she dragged Darcy away. "Make certain you talk with me before the banquet. This is important."

Darcy nodded as she accepted another book to autograph.

##

The traffic at Darcy's booth had been steady all day. Women were still lined up at her table when the lights dimmed in the convention hall. A low murmur spread throughout the women as the hall doors were locked.

"I'll be happy to continue signing your books," Darcy announced to the line at her table.

They stayed an hour after closing, but Darcy didn't disappoint any of her fans.

"It looks like we may have a hundred books left," Jules informed her as she packed things up for the night.

"Hopefully things will be slower tomorrow," Darcy replied. "It should be quiet until church is out, but then it'll pick up. The convention ends at two."

Darcy looked at her watch. "We have just enough time to shower and change for the banquet." She laced her fingers through Jules's and led her to the door where someone was waiting to let them out of the hall.

"I want to tell you again how much I appreciate all you've done for me this weekend," Darcy said as they rode the elevator to their floor. "You literally saved my reputation."

"Or ruined it," Jules said, laughing. "What'll you do when your real wife shows up at the next convention?"

"She won't," Darcy said.

The elevator stopped on their floor and Darcy held the door for Jules.

"What are you wearing tonight?" she asked as she followed Jules from the elevator.

"It's a surprise," Jules said.

A glow radiated across Darcy's face. "I can't wait to see."

##

As Jules fastened her bra and pulled her slip over her head, a commotion in the hallway caught her attention. The door between their rooms flew open and Darcy whispered, "Please come with me."

Without thinking, Jules followed the blonde into her room as someone hammered hard on Darcy's door.

"Just a minute," Darcy called as she closed the door between their rooms, ruffled the bedcovers, and motioned for Jules to sit down on her bed. For the first time, Jules realized that Darcy was only wearing a dressing gown.

The knocking started again.

"Okay, okay," Darcy said as she opened the door. "What is so important—"

"I told you to see me before the banquet," Rosalind said as she pushed her way into the room.

"As you can see,"—Darcy gestured toward Jules—"I had much more enjoyable things to do."

Rosalind gaped at Jules. For a few seconds, she was speechless. "Well, yes, I can understand your hesitancy to abandon your wife, but I have news you need before you give your speech tonight."

"What?" Darcy demanded.

"Your latest book just hit number one on the New York Times Best Sellers list."

Darcy gasped. "How? It was just released this week. I was concerned the printer wouldn't get copies here in time for the convention. It just came off the press."

"Preorders," Rosalind explained. "The minute your book was off the press and posted on Amazon, all the preorders were filled. It was unbelievable.

"The Rainbow Literary Society's switchboard locked down yesterday due to the volume of calls from people trying to book you for events. My God, Darcy, you've put lesbian writers on the map!"

"That's nice," Darcy said. "Thank you for the information."

"You need to include it in your speech tonight," Rosalind said.

"I don't want to toot my own horn." The look of humility on Darcy's face was real. "I probably won't do that."

Could she do anything else to make me love her more? Jules thought as she watched the gorgeous author usher Rosalind out the door.

Darcy turned toward Jules and stood still, as if committing to memory the scene before her. Jules sat on the bed in a black slip and bra. Her glorious hair cascaded around her neck and shoulders like a dark cloud. Her brown eyes were almost black. Darcy recognized that look. She was certain her blue eyes were darker than the ocean right now. Desire did that to eyes—the windows to one's emotions.

Jules stood. In two quick steps, Darcy was in front of her, pulling her into her arms. Without a word, their lips touched—slowly at first, and then eagerly as their passion fanned the flames of desire and need. A chorus of moans rose from the depths of each woman's core.

Without breaking their kiss, Darcy eased Jules back onto the bed. "I want you," she whispered.

"What about your wife?" Jules murmured as warm lips captured hers again.

Darcy's hand gently caressed breasts she had dreamed about. Jules caught her wrist, stopping her from going any further.

"Please, Jules? Please, let me make love to you," Darcy pleaded. "Please say yes."

"It's not right." Jules sobbed as she pushed Darcy off her. "It will never be right."

Jules was out of the room before Darcy could pull her thoughts from the desire-induced confusion raging in her mind.

"God, what am I going to do?" Darcy whispered.

##

Half an hour later Jules stuck her head into Darcy's room. "Are you ready? Your public awaits."

Darcy turned from the mirror, where she'd been trying to figure out how to zip the back of her dress without asking for help.

Jules closed the distance between them to lend a hand. "You are breathtaking," Jules said.

Darcy turned to face her, careful to keep her hands at her sides. "You steal my breath, my mind, and my heart."

"We should go." Jules walked to the door and opened it just as Lacy and Bade Lawrence walked past.

"Have you heard the good news?" Lacy crowed. "I'm ranked number two in Amazon's lesbian book sales. What do you think of that, Darcy?"

"That's nice," Darcy said.

"Who's number one?" Jules asked.

"I haven't the slightest." Lacy waved her hand as if dismissing a tiresome gnat.

"Where are you on the New York Times Best Sellers list?" Jules needled the arrogant woman.

Lacy snorted. "Lesbian writers never make the Times Best Sellers list."

Darcy caught Jules's hand and squeezed it tightly. She smiled when the brunette didn't pull away from her.

##

The ballroom had been converted into an exquisite banquet room. Low lighting, pink tablecloths, and rose-bouquet centerpieces created a lovely ambience for women attending the festivities.

Jules sat beside Darcy at the head table and made small talk with those around them. Darcy was strangely quiet during dinner.

Jules was captivated by Darcy's speech. The woman's voice held the audience spellbound. She was as eloquent on the podium as she was at spinning her stories. She told humorous anecdotes about her experiences as a writer and then settled into sharing the difficulties lesbian writers had to face. She discussed the need to write good murder mysteries, love stories, and action/adventure stories, regardless of the gender of the characters.

"We must create a following that reads our books because they are spellbinding stories, not because they are about lesbians," Darcy said, concluding her speech.

Darcy received a standing ovation.

Rosalind moved to the microphone and waited for the applause to quiet. "Thank you, Darcy. Your speech has rekindled my enthusiasm for what we do, and so have your accomplishments. Darcy is too modest to tell you this, so I'm going to share something amazing with you."

A hush fell over the banquet hall as attendees waited for Rosalind to continue.

"Darcy Lake's latest novel is number one on Amazon and the New York Times Best Sellers list. Not just in lesbian fiction, but in all books."

A rumble ran through the crowd as they jumped to their feet and applauded their fellow writer. Darcy Lake was a trailblazer for all of them. Tomorrow she would be their biggest competition. Tonight, they loved her.

Jules could not suppress the tremendous feeling of pride she felt for Darcy. She was glad she had met the incredible woman, even if her heart was already breaking.

The band started playing, and couples moved to the end of the room where a large dance floor provided adequate space for the attendees to dance.

"Let's get some fresh air." Darcy took Jules's elbow and steered her to large double doors that opened into a hallway leading to a private garden in the center of the hotel.

Darcy inhaled deeply, holding Jules's hand as they strolled along the path winding through the garden. "It's nice here," the author said.

"It is," Jules said. She was unsure why Darcy had brought her to the garden.

"I wanted to apologize to you," Darcy said. "I acted like an animal. I don't know what came over me. You didn't deserve that kind of treatment."

"Unfortunately," Jules said, her voice low in the quiet garden, "I'm afraid we both wanted the same thing."

Darcy turned to face the woman who haunted her dreams. "May I kiss you?" she asked.

"Yes."

It was a kiss both women would carry in their hearts for a lifetime. It was sweet and passionate and promised things Jules knew would never come to fruition. For the first time in her life, Jules knew what it felt like to be loved above all others.

"Darcy, I—"

Darcy's lips silenced her. "I had to kiss you one more time," she declared as she released Jules from her arms. "I will never forget you, Jules. When you read my books, know they are dedicated to you."

"You will always hold a special place in my heart, Darcy Lake."

Chapter 9

Darcy opened the door between their rooms. Jules was gone. *She probably checked out early to beat the rush,* Darcy thought.

She packed her things and pulled her luggage to the elevator.

"Are you checking out already?" Lacy said as she followed Darcy into the elevator.

"I'll have the bellman hold my luggage so I can grab it and go when the convention ends," Darcy said.

"Where's your wife?" Lacy inquired.

"She went down ahead of me," Darcy explained. "She probably opened our booth and put out books for me to sign. She's sweet like that." *So sweet.*

Darcy handed her luggage to the bellman and headed to the convention hall. Jules was nowhere in sight. Darcy's books were neatly stacked beside two pens. Darcy relaxed as she saw everything was ready to start the day. She looked around for Jules. Her day couldn't start until she found the beautiful brunette. Happiness engulfed her as she anticipated watching Jules walk toward her.

Darcy pulled out her chair and sat down. She straightened her books and then offset them the way Jules had placed them originally. She spied a white envelope under a lone book on the corner of her table. Darcy's hands trembled as she opened the flap and removed the single piece of hotel stationary. She read Jules's note.

Dear Darcy,

Thank you for a memorable weekend. I will never forget being your wife for a few days. It was exciting and wonderful to get to know you. You will always be my favorite author.

I had to leave. I was getting weak. I knew I wouldn't be strong enough to tell you goodbye in person.

I'm afraid I have fallen in love with Darcy Lake the woman, not Darcy Lake the author.

Always yours,

Jules

Darcy fought back the tears that threatened to run down her cheeks. She ran to the front desk to see if Jules had checked out.

"What's the last name?" the cashier asked. "I don't have anyone by the name of Jules."

"I . . . I don't know." Darcy scanned the lobby looking for a sign of Jules.

"She was in room 310. Can you look up 310 and see who was staying in that room?"

"No, Mrs. Lake," the cashier said, a look of genuine sorrow on her face. "We're not allowed to give out that information, but the room has been released."

"May I speak to the manager?" Darcy asked.

"You may, but she won't give you any more information than I have. It's illegal for us to give out someone's name."

Darcy bowed her head and walked away from the counter.

I can't get her out of my mind. I think I'm falling in love with her, and I don't even know her name. The thought made Darcy's stomach churn. *How will I find her?*

##

Jules was halfway home when her brother called her. She pushed the phone button on her steering wheel to answer the call. "Hi, Lucas."

"Hello, baby sister." Lucas's crisp baritone voice sent a warm feeling over her. "Where are you?"

"On my way home from Dallas," she replied. "What's up?"

"Do you know a Detective Tanner West?" Lucas asked.

Jules took a deep breath. "Yes. Why?"

"She's looking for you." Lucas's voice took on a worried tone. "Are you in trouble or something?"

"What did she say?"

"She said she needed to talk to you," Lucas answered. "What's going on, Jules?"

Jules debated telling her brother that their grandmother had been murdered but decided it was best to tell him in person. Lucas had loved Nana too.

"I've spoken with Detective West," Jules said. "Can you come to Nana's house for breakfast in the morning? We need to talk, but not over the phone."

"I've got to meet the framers at the construction site early in the morning," Lucas said. "Is nine okay for breakfast?"

"Perfect. And just to put your mind at ease, Bro, I am not in trouble. As soon as we hang up, I'll call Detective West."

Lucas chuckled. "You know I worry about you. Everyone knows how wild you single teachers are."

"Ha-ha," Jules pretended to laugh. "Keep that to yourself. See you tomorrow."

If he only knew how much self-control I exercised this weekend, Jules thought, *he would be amazed.* She wondered how long it would take her to get over Darcy Lake.

"Call Tanner," Jules directed her car's hands-free system. The detective answered after the second ring.

"Detective West."

"Tanner, this is Jules."

"Thank you for calling. I appreciate it."

"I was able to get away sooner than expected," Jules explained. "It seems I'm free for dinner tonight, if your offer is still open."

"Of course it is," Tanner said, beaming. "I'll pick you up at seven, if that's okay. Sabello's is serving their specialty tonight."

"That's perfect," Jules said.

##

While she waited for Tanner to arrive, Jules wandered through Nana's expansive home. She smiled as she recalled how the family had teased Nana when she built the house. Everyone called it The Mansion, which embarrassed Nana because she was not a pretentious woman. Over the years the home had become simply the Manse.

Jules had loved growing up there. She loved when she and Nana would curl up in front of the fire on a winter's day, and Jules would read Nana's latest manuscript aloud.

"You must read a manuscript aloud to get a feel for the flow of it," Nana said.

Jules also loved snuggling under her downy comforter at night and reading Darcy Lake's novels. A pang akin to a stab in her heart struck Jules as Darcy's name flitted through her mind. She hoped Tanner West would take her mind off Darcy Lake.

##

"Tell me about your weekend," Tanner said as they settled beside each other in the circular booth at Sabello's.

"I, um, attended a teacher's convention in Dallas," Jules said. She did not intend to tell Tanner West that she'd been at a lesbian literary convention all weekend.

"I'm not trying to get into your business," Tanner said, "but until we arrest whoever murdered your grandmother, please let me know when you leave town. I worry about you."

Jules nodded. "Do you have any leads?"

"Nothing that has panned out." Tanner frowned. "I need to start looking at Daphne's business connections, people she was close to in the publishing industry."

"I haven't had the heart to get into her computer," Jules admitted. "I haven't been able to bring myself to go through things I know were very personal for her. I'll try to do that tomorrow."

"At the risk of upsetting you, I have to ask the question again. Did Daphne have a lover?"

"I don't think so," Jules replied. "After my grandfather died when I was ten, she never dated. She did have friends but no boyfriends. I can't think of any reason someone would kill Nana."

"We pulled a woman's fingerprints from the wine bottle I took from the house." Tanner searched for the right words to move forward. "Your grandmother may have had someone special in her life that you were not aware of."

"A woman?" Jules said incredulously. "Nana?"

"Are you up to giving me a quick synopsis of your family and their history?" Tanner asked.

"Nana had two sons—my father, Warren, and Uncle Buddy. My parents had me and my brother, Lucas. Uncle Buddy and Aunt Page have two sons and three daughters.

"I'm certain you know my parents, Warren and Martha Divine. He has been the pastor at the First Baptist Church for the past twenty years. My brother owns Divine Construction Company, and I'm an English teacher."

"I've interviewed your brother, but I haven't been able to contact your father." Tanner stared pensively at her half-empty drink. "This may be a touchy matter, but I have to ask why you moved into your grandmother's home when you were in the eighth grade."

"I needed a place to live." Jules recalled how scared she had been. "Nana took me in and introduced me to the most wonderful life imaginable. She was my savior."

Tanner pressed on. "Why didn't you live with your parents?"

"My parents threw me out of the house."

A shadow passed over Tanner's face. "Why?"

Jules turned in her seat to face the detective "Because I'm a lesbian," she said, her voice cold and filled with pain.

Tanner sat silently as the waitress placed their order on the table, refilled their tea glasses, and walked away.

"How did your parents find out?"

"I announced it at my fourteenth birthday party." Jules snickered. "My father, who had always taught me to tell the truth, was mortified and tried to convince me I should never tell anyone my deep, dark secret." She looked away for a minute and then continued.

"Only, I didn't want it to be a secret. I was tired of hiding who I was. Nana took me in and taught me to be proud of who I am and my accomplishments. She taught me that my sexuality didn't define me as a good or bad person. Only my actions and how I treated others could do that."

Tears rolled down Jules's cheeks. "I miss her so much."

Tanner slipped her arms around the sobbing woman and held her as she cried against the detective's shoulder. Jules regained her composure after a few minutes and her sobs gradually ceased. She continued to lean against Tanner. Tanner West felt warm and safe . . . and comforting.

Chapter 10

Tanner rang the doorbell for the third time. She knew eight in the morning was a little early to be calling, but she hadn't been able to catch Warren Divine at any other hour. Maybe the only way to get to the man was to catch him before he started his day. Tanner leaned on the doorbell and listened as it continuously chimed.

"Okay! Okay!" A disgruntled male approached the door. "Who is it?"

Tanner held her badge in front of the peephole. "Detective Tanner West."

"Can't you come back at a decent hour?" the man yelled.

"No, sir. I must talk to you now. I can speak with you in your home, or I can drag you down to the police station. Either way, I'm not leaving here without talking to you."

Tanner could hear a woman's voice on the other side of the door as the two discussed the officer's presence. The door opened a crack.

"How can we help you, officer?" Martha Divine's slow southern drawl oozed through the opening.

"Ma'am, I need to come in and speak to you," Tanner replied. "Or I can take both of you to the police station for questioning."

"Oh, officer, that won't be necessary." Martha opened the door, introduced herself, and motioned for Tanner to enter. "Please, join us for coffee."

Tanner followed Martha into a breakfast room where a coffee pot and various sweetbreads were sitting on the table. Martha pulled another cup from the cabinet and filled it with coffee. "Do you use cream or sugar?" she inquired.

"Black is fine." Tanner looked around the room as she placed her file folder on the table. "Where is Reverend Divine?"

"He's getting dressed." Martha placed two of the pastries on a plate and handed it to Tanner. "He does have to maintain a certain appearance, you know."

Tanner almost rolled her eyes. "Yes. Appearance is everything."

"Exactly." Martha beamed, missing the sarcasm in Tanner's voice.

"Officer West!" Warren Divine strode into the breakfast room as if he were delighted to see an old friend. "How kind of you to call on us."

"I've been trying to speak with you for two weeks." Tanner glared at the man. "I need to talk to you about your mother's death."

Warren nodded. "Oh, yes. Nasty business. My son said she was murdered. I don't know how we can help you. We traveled in different social circles from my mother."

"Wasn't she one of your parishioners?" Tanner said between sips of her coffee. "According to your church accountant, Mrs. Divine made huge contributions to your ministry."

"To the Lord," Warren corrected Tanner. "She was very generous in supporting the Lord's work."

"Everyone in town speaks highly of her. You must have been very proud of her."

"My mother was . . . special," Warren said in a noncommittal tone.

"Does anyone in your church have anything to do with rattlesnakes?" Tanner queried. "Raise them, catch them or sell them?"

Warren puffed up. "Look here, detective. We're not some kind of snake-worshipping cult. What kind of question is that?"

"Did your son tell you how your mother died?"

"He said she was poisoned." Warren narrowed his eyes and glared at Tanner.

"Yes, with rattlesnake venom. Do you know of anyone who might want your mother dead?"

"No," Warren said. Weariness settled over his features. "Other than her competitors in the book world. My mother was harmless."

"Mother often commented on how cutthroat the publishing business is," Martha chimed in.

"Did she ever mention any names or anyone she was having problems with in the publishing industry?"

"No," both Divines chorused.

"Did your mother have a will?" Tanner asked.

"Yes, but her attorney has been out of town," Warren said, his brow furrowed. "I spoke to the law firm yesterday. They're supposed to call us this week to set an appointment to read the will."

"Do you believe she left you anything?" Tanner watched the minister's eyes as they darted about the room.

"I honestly don't know." Warren sighed. "Mother and I didn't see eye to eye on many things."

"Was there contention between you and your mother over your treatment of Jules?" Tanner had found that bluntness always caught people off guard.

"I . . . I suppose one could say that," Warren mumbled.

"I understand you stopped being involved in family functions when Mrs. Divine took in Jules. Would she leave you out of her will?"

"I would contest it if she did," Warren growled. "She knew we wanted the Manse."

"We have as much right to her money as anyone," Martha declared vehemently. "Certainly more than Jules. Warren is her son. Jules is only her granddaughter."

"Are you aware that Daphne legally adopted Jules on your daughter's sixteenth birthday?" Tanner stifled a laugh at the bewildered expression that covered Warren and Martha's faces.

"What does that mean?" Martha asked.

"I'm no lawyer"—Tanner hesitated just to make them suffer—"but I'm fairly certain that gives Jules the same legal standing as you and Buddy."

"That's preposterous!" Warren blustered. "There's no way Jules is now Mother's daughter."

Tanner slowly opened her folder and pretended to search for something. After several minutes, she pulled stapled sheets from her files. "Oh, here it is," she said. "This is a copy of the adoption papers."

Warren snatched the papers from Tanner's hand as Martha moved to stand behind her husband. "The old bitch," Warren mumbled under his breath.

"I'm sorry." Tanner leaned toward the minister. "What did you say?"

"I said, I can't believe this," Warren replied. "Can I keep this?"

"No, but you can get a copy from the county clerk, just like I did." Tanner shoved the papers back into her files. "You evaded my question when I asked it, so let me ask again. Does anyone in your church have anything to do with rattlesnakes? Raise them, catch them, or sell them?"

Tanner didn't miss the quick glance between the husband and wife.

"No!" Warren grumbled.

"If you have no other questions," Martha said, "Warren has Bible study in an hour. He must prepare the lesson."

LIVING TWO LIVES

The Divines walked Tanner to the door. After the door closed behind her, the detective leaned close to it, listening to the raised voices.

"You promised me that house," Martha screeched. "I've waited years for the Manse."

"Don't worry, dear," Tanner heard Warren say. "We'll get it one way or the other."

Chapter 11

Jules studied her face in the mirror as she removed her makeup. She looked like hell. She hadn't slept more than four hours a night in the last two weeks. Thoughts of Darcy Lake haunted her sleeping and waking hours. She alternated between hating and loving the beautiful author. She dreaded the impending sleepless night.

I can't believe she hasn't tried to contact me, Jules thought. *I guess I'm easier to forget than she is. I was the one who left without saying goodbye. What a fool I am.*

The wail of a siren abruptly ended Jules' pity party. She walked to the front of the house and opened the door as an ambulance pulled into the driveway next door. The siren stopped but red and blue lights continued to light up the night, casting eerie shadows on the houses in the neighborhood.

The Manse was situated at the top of a hill and overlooked surrounding neighbors. From her viewpoint, Jules could see that someone was being rolled from the house on a gurney and lifted into the ambulance. She knew that Roy and Ashley Craft lived in the house where all the activity was taking place. She wondered what was happening.

Roy and Ashley had moved next door to Nana the summer before Jules's senior year of high school. She recalled how enthusiastic and bubbly thirty-year-old Ashley had been and how much in love she was with Roy. They were a beautiful couple. Roy's dark good looks perfectly complemented his wife's fair, Norwegian features.

They had married right after Ashley graduated from high school and Roy had graduated from college. A hard worker, Roy had taken over his father's failing automotive parts business and had doubled the size of the company. He was considered one of the town's success stories.

Now in their early forties, their only sadness seemed to be their failure to have children. Roy often bemoaned the fact that he had no sons to take over his business one day.

The ambulance pulled from the drive with lights flashing and siren blaring. Roy walked back into his house, and Jules surmised that Ashley had been taken to the hospital. *I'll check on her tomorrow*, Jules thought. Nana and Ashley had always been good friends.

She walked through the house, making certain all the doors were locked. She armed the security system and headed to the kitchen. *Maybe a glass of wine and a good book will help me sleep.*

As she stood in the middle of Nana's office, a text notification dinged on Nana's cell phone. It was from the mysterious person known only as Agent.

"Your sales are off the charts. I need to hear from you. Check your email."

Jules carried her wine to Nana's desk. Although Tanner had hounded her for information on Nana's publishing contacts, she hadn't found the courage to dig through her grandmother's computer. *Now's as good a time as any to start*, she thought.

Jules sipped her wine as the computer whirred into action. She typed in the password and watched as files filled the monitor's desktop. She studied her hands on the keyboard. She still wore Darcy's wedding ring. She couldn't bring herself to remove it. The computer announced it had opened all programs.

Nana's last two novels were on the desktop along with a file folder marked *Jules.* She clicked on the folder with her name on it.

A single letter was in the folder. Jules read it with a heavy heart.

My Darling Jules,

If you are reading this it means I am no longer with you. Hopefully, by now you have met with my attorney and the will has been settled. I won't dwell on that. I know the attorney handling my last will and testament will see that my wishes are carried out to my specifications.

Everything you need to know is in an envelope in the locked section of my bookcase. The key is taped to the bottom of my external storage drive.

My precious Jules, please know that I have always loved you and always worked hard to set a good example for you. When you go through the items in the envelope, please do not judge me too harshly. Just know I loved you above all others.

Nana

Jules sat in stunned silence as she reread the letter. In a stupor, she tilted Nana's largest storage drive and located the key taped to the bottom of it.

She reverently approached Nana's bookcase and slipped the key into the lock. She took a deep breath and unlocked the cabinet.

The case was filled from top to bottom with books written by one author—Darcy Lake. Nana had every book Darcy had ever written.

It took Jules a moment to fully grasp the significance of her discovery. Was Nana a closet lesbian? Had she hidden her true nature from Jules and others all her life? Did Nana have a lesbian lover as Tanner suspected? Did Darcy know Nana better than she had let on?

"Oh God!" Jules struggled to breathe. She fell into the closest chair and put her head between her knees until the dizziness passed. Nana was a lesbian. Warren Divine would have a field day with this discovery.

Jules suddenly had an overpowering desire to see Darcy. *I can't see her,* she thought. *Hell, I can't even call her. I have no idea how to get in touch with her.* She picked up one of Darcy's novels and looked at the back of the book jacket. A breathtaking photo of the writer smiled at her. *Website. Of course she has a website. I've been to it a thousand times.*

Jules rolled the desk chair in front of Nana's computer and logged onto the internet. She typed in www.darcylake.com and hugged herself when the site opened. She realized that Darcy's webmaster had updated the website with photos from the convention.

There was a new video of Darcy holding her latest book and a photo of Darcy accepting the RAW award from the Rainbow Literary Society. The photo that caught and held Jules's attention was one of her and Darcy gazing into each other's eyes as if nothing else existed in the world.

She closed her eyes as the feeling of Darcy's kiss swept over her body and made her catch her breath. Jules took several deep breaths and then opened her eyes and scanned the website for an email address. She quickly opened Nana's Outlook and sent an email to darcy@darcylake.com.

Jules leaned back in the chair and closed her eyes. She had written a simple message—*Please call me*—and added her cell phone number.

The swish of a new email arriving made her smile. Darcy had answered her instantly. Maybe she was missing her too.

To Jules's dismay, the email wasn't from Darcy. The email she had sent had been returned to her. "Damn," she muttered. Why did Nana's email have to go crazy tonight, of all nights?

A splitting headache took up residence behind Jules's eyes. "I can't do this right now," she sobbed. "I just can't do this right now."

Jules rested her head on Nana's desk and cried until exhaustion overtook her and she slipped into a restless sleep.

The ringing of her cell phone woke her. She shook the haze from her swollen eyes and answered her phone.

"Hey, little Sis, how's it going?" Lucas's cheerful voice made her smile.

"I'm doing fine."

"Are you catching a cold?" her brother asked. "You sound funny."

"No, I fell asleep in front of my computer. That's exhaustion you hear."

"I just wanted to remind you that we have an appointment with Nana's attorney at ten in the morning."

"Oh my gosh! I had forgotten," Jules mumbled. "Do you have their address? I don't even know the name of the firm."

"Reed, Crane and Weidman," Lucas informed her. "I'm shooting over their information now."

Jules checked the information when it dinged into her cell phone. "Got it," she said. "Thanks for reminding me, Bro. It had slipped my mind."

"Forgotten?" Lucas feigned shock. "According to Father tomorrow will be the most important day in our life."

"Right." Jules snorted.

"Jules,"—Lucas's tone became serious—"you know Father is planning to throw you out of Nana's house as soon as the attorneys announce that she left it to him, right?"

"It won't be the first house our father has tossed me out of." Jules tried to hide the pain she felt. "Will Uncle Buddy and his family be there?"

"Yes, they're driving in early in the morning and will meet us at the law office."

"At least we'll get to spend some time with them," Jules said. "It will be good to see them."

"Jules, you knew Nana better than anyone. Do you have any idea what's in the will?"

Jules thought of her recent discovery of Nana's stash of lesbian novels. "I'm not sure any of us knew Nana very well. She was a fun-loving old bird. I have no idea what's in her will. She'll probably require us all to participate in a winner-take-all survival-of-the-fittest contest."

Lucas laughed out loud. "That would be just like her. Get some rest, Sis. We'll need our wits about us tomorrow.

"Let's hope the attorney doesn't cancel again," Lucas added. "You know this is the third appointment we've had for the reading of the will. And tomorrow is Friday. If we don't see the attorney tomorrow, it'll be next week before we can reschedule."

"I have to be back at school Tuesday," Jules said. "If we don't do this tomorrow, it'll be two more weeks before I return."

Chapter 12

It had taken Jules half an hour longer than usual to make herself presentable. The dark circles beneath her eyes had required careful makeup to cover them. A little extra blush and a bright red lipstick had helped too. She checked her reflection in the elevator doors just before they opened, spilling her into the reception area of Reed, Crane and Weidman. *The point of no return*, she thought.

"I'm here for the reading of Daphne Divine's will," Jules informed the receptionist.

"Right this way." The young woman led Jules down the hall to a large conference room. "I believe you are the last to arrive. Everyone else is here. I'll let her attorney know you're ready to begin."

"Jules!" Uncle Buddy and her cousins engulfed her in hugs and sincere greetings. "It is so good to see you again."

Aunt Page held her at arm's length. "You look lovely, dear." Then she hugged Jules and whispered in her ear. "I know this is difficult for you. You were so close to Nana." She gave Jules an extra squeeze.

Jules hugged all her cousins and her brother. She leaned heavily against Lucas's strong chest and cherished the comfort she found there.

"The attorney will be here shortly," the receptionist said as she placed a tray of cold drinks beside the carafe of coffee and cups. "Please, help yourself to refreshments while you wait. If you need anything, just let me know."

Everyone seemed to talk at once, and Jules laughed at how comforting it was to be with her family. Only her mother and father had distanced themselves from everyone else. They sat at the far end of the huge conference table.

Jules walked to the windows that overlooked downtown Dallas and admired the view. The city had changed since her last visit. Although she and Nana had lived in a small town only an hour south of Dallas, she rarely frequented the downtown area.

"I'm sorry for keeping you waiting," a sultry, silky voice said. "I was on a conference call and couldn't convince my clients we had concluded our discussion.

"I am Daphne Divine's personal attorney. My name is Darcy Reed."

The fine hairs on Jules's neck stood up. A wave of joy mingled with pain swept through her body. She willed her hands to stop trembling and moistened her lips before turning around to face the attorney.

Darcy was looking down at her file as she spoke. "Is Julie Adair Divine here?"

"Yes," Jules said, her voice barely a whisper.

"Miss Divine, it is a pleasure—" Darcy halted in midsentence as she raised her eyes from the file folder. ". . . ah, um, to meet you." She took a deep breath and forced herself to tear her eyes away from the woman who had made her life a living hell for the past two weeks.

##

Darcy Reed's mind raced over the many ways she had tried to locate Jules. She had never considered that Jules was a nickname for Julie.

She fought to control her emotions and conduct the business at hand in a professional manner. Every part of her being wanted to run to Jules and kiss her soft, red lips. She placed the file folder on the conference table.

"This may take a long time," Darcy said. "Would any of you like to visit the restrooms before we start?"

"That sounds like a great idea to me," Uncle Buddy said. "We just made a four-hour drive."

Uncle Buddy's family followed him from the room.

"I should probably join them." Lucas wrinkled his nose at Jules and left the room.

"I have a private powder room in my office," Darcy said to Jules. "If you'd like to . . ."

"Yes." Jules walked to the blonde's side and followed her out of the room.

They walked in silence to Darcy's office. The attorney opened the door and stepped back for Jules to enter. She closed the door and turned to face Jules.

"Oh God, I've missed you!" Darcy gasped as Jules threw herself into her arms.

"I could just scream. I'm about to explode," Jules mumbled between kisses and soft moans. "I can't get you out of my mind."

"I know! I know!" Darcy groaned as Jules crushed her against the door. Her hands traveled up and down Jules's arms, finally resting on both sides of the brunette's face as she slowly lowered her lips to kiss Jules. "I've dreamed of this moment."

Darcy's kisses always left her breathless, but Jules was having trouble thinking or seeing. Her heart was pounding so hard she could hear the blood rushing in her ears. "We've got to get through this," she whispered. "I . . . I can't breathe."

"Oh, yes," Darcy said. "Business first. Oh God, Jules, I've looked everywhere for you, and you've been right under my nose all the time." She caught Jules's left hand. "You're still wearing my ring?"

"I couldn't make myself remove it," Jules whispered against Darcy's lips.

"I'm glad." Darcy held Jules tighter and kissed her with all the desire of a woman who'd found what she'd searched for her entire life.

"Miss Reed?" Lucas said with a knock on the office door. "Everyone is reassembled."

"I'll be right there," Darcy called as she tried to catch her breath.

"We have makeup smeared all over our faces," Jules whispered. "You fix yours then I'll fix mine and arrive in the conference room after you."

Darcy quickly pulled herself together and walked into the hallway. "Your sister is still in the powder room," she informed Lucas. "This is very upsetting for her."

"I'll wait for her," Lucas said. He watched Darcy Reed walk toward the conference room. "Jules has all the luck," he muttered.

"I'm ready," Jules announced as she left the powder room.

"Not quite." Lucas grinned as he pulled his handkerchief from his pocket. "It won't do for you to go into the conference room with the attorney's lipstick smeared all over your cleavage."

A trapped-animal look spread across Jules's face as Lucas carefully wiped the lipstick from the top of her breasts. He checked her to make certain no other telltale signs of passion were apparent and hugged her tightly.

"You always did get the gorgeous women." He chuckled as he pulled his sister's arm through his and they walked into the conference room.

Chapter 13

Darcy took a few seconds to regain her composure. All she could think about was getting Jules back in her arms. She avoided making eye contact with the brunette.

"I want to thank all of you for appearing here today." *Some of you more than others,* Darcy thought as she looked around the conference table. "As I said earlier, I'm Darcy Reed. I'm the personal attorney for Daphne Divine. I have handled Mrs. Divine's affairs for the past five years.

"I'd appreciate it if you would introduce yourselves, so my assistant can get a list of those attending." She nodded at Buddy to begin the introductions.

"I'm Bradford "Buddy" Divine. Daphne was my mother."

"I'm Page Divine, Buddy's wife."

Uncle Buddy's children introduced themselves.

"I'm Lucas Divine, brother to the lovely creature seated next to me and Daphne Divine's grandson." Lucas wiggled his eyebrows and cast a mischievous glance at Jules.

"I'm Julie Adair Divine." Jules suppressed a smile that threatened to spread from ear to ear. "Everyone calls me Jules, and I'm Daphne's granddaughter."

Darcy turned her gaze to Jules's parents. "And you are?"

Warren puffed out his chest and assumed his most pompous demeanor. "I'm Doctor Warren Divine, and this is my wife, Martha. Daphne was my mother. Lucas is my son."

Darcy looked down at her file. "Doctor?" She raised a quizzical eyebrow.

"He has a doctorate in theology," Lucas explained. "He isn't a *real* doctor. He's just being self-important."

"Ah!" Darcy nodded. "You're the minister. Daphne told me about you."

"Just read the will." Warren glared at his son. "Skip all the wherewithals and to-whom-it-may-concern nonsense. How is her estate divided?"

"Mr. Divine, I am certain you are familiar with the rules and decorum of reading the last will and testament of one who has left this earth. I will conduct this reading with the respect befitting one as great as Daphne Adair Divine."

Darcy read from the will.

I bequeath the following to my beloved family:

To each of my grandchildren: Lucas, Robert, Robyn, Randy, Rose and Marla, I leave one million dollars.

To my children I leave the following: two million dollars to my son Buddy and his wife, Page. I leave one thousand dollars to my son Warren and his wife, Martha.

To my adopted daughter and granddaughter, Julie Adair Divine, I leave the remainder of my estate including, but not limited to, all my intellectual properties such as copyrights I hold on books written under various aliases, all royalties from my novels, oil and gas holdings, real property and investment portfolios.

My attorney has a complete description of everything I wish Julie to receive from my estate. And finally, I leave Julie the Manse. I hope you enjoy the home as much as I have, dear Jules. I have enjoyed sharing it with you. It is designed for loving and living.

To my domestic help Renee Baxter and Chance Howard I leave one hundred thousand dollars to each.

Darcy closed the file folder and looked around the table at the relatives of Daphne Divine. "Are there any questions?"

Everyone shook their heads. "I had no idea she was that wealthy," Buddy said. "She has truly blessed each of us." His family muttered their agreement.

"She left me much more than I expected," Lucas said. "I don't need her money, but I'm thankful she thought of me."

"The Manse!" Martha Divine gasped. "She left Jules the Manse."

"This is ludicrous," Warren Divine said, slamming his fist onto the conference table. "There's no way this can hold up in court. I *will* contest it."

Darcy leaned across the table and glowered at Warren. "I promised Mrs. Divine that this will would be administered exactly as she desired and completely intact.

"I will counter any attempt to undermine it with every legal means at my disposal. In short, Reverend Divine, I will personally destroy you if you contest Daphne Divine's will. I will keep you so tied up in lawsuits it will drain every penny you own. I will keep you in court until the day you die."

Darcy handed Warren an envelope as he dragged Martha from the room.

"I have cashier's checks for each of you in the amount designated by Mrs. Divine," Darcy said, distributing envelopes to Uncle Buddy's family and to Lucas.

"I'd like to take a moment to give thanks to our Lord for allowing us to be part of Daphne's life," Uncle Buddy said. Everyone bowed their heads while he prayed.

After the prayer, Buddy and his children shook Darcy's hand and thanked her for her work. Lucas closed the door behind his family and turned to face his sister and the attorney.

"I'm assuming you two know each other," he said with a devilish grin, "or my sister has become much looser than I ever dreamed possible."

"Your sister and I are old friends," Darcy explained. "We reconnected at a book convention in Dallas a couple of weeks ago."

"Book convention?" A light came on in Lucas's eyes. "You're Darcy Lake! I've seen your photo on the back of your book jackets in Jules's room."

Lucas hugged his sister. "I'll just leave you two to enjoy the rest of the day. Darcy, do you know any good investment bankers?" He waved his check in the air.

"I do," Darcy said. "I'll set up an appointment with her on Monday, if that's convenient for you."

Lucas nodded and pulled the door closed behind him.

"I can't believe your brother recognized me. Maybe I'm farther out there than I thought."

Jules laughed. "Don't worry. Lucas only knows of you because we often read your books together."

"Seriously?" The look on Darcy's face was whimsical as she tried to imagine a brother and sister sharing Darcy Lake books.

He's only two years older than me," Jules explained, "and we've always done everything together. He stayed at Nana's house as much as possible. I must admit I think I'm older than him in many ways, but he sees himself as my protector and I treasure that."

"I like your family," Darcy said. "All except the great Reverend Divine. Exactly how does he fit into the family dynamics?"

"He's my father." Jules laughed out loud at the shocked look on Darcy's face.

"I'm certain there's a story there," Darcy said, "but right now I just want to go somewhere, get two glasses of wine and look at you. I have so much to tell you."

Darcy told the receptionist she would be gone for the rest of the day and led Jules to a decorous wine bar around the corner from her law firm.

##

Darcy couldn't keep her eyes off Jules as the waitress placed their wine in front of them and walked away. "You're so beautiful" she whispered

She watched as a telltale flush crept up Jules's neck and across her cheeks.

"I'm sorry. I didn't mean to embarrass you. It's just that . . . well, I haven't been able to get you out of my mind. The past two weeks have been pure hell.

"I searched everywhere for you, but I didn't know your real name. I cancelled our first two meetings on Daphne's will because I thought I had a lead on you. Little did I know you were Daphne Divine's granddaughter."

A glorious smile lit Jules's face as she listened to Darcy prattle on about missing her. It was obvious the blonde had experienced the same sense of loss Jules had.

"I don't know where we go from here." Darcy finished her declaration and gazed into Jules's eyes, hoping to find her feelings were reciprocated.

"Why don't we get to know each other better? And there is the elephant in the room," Jules said, a look of concern on her face.

"Elephant?"

"Your wife," Jules said, wide-eyed, obviously surprised that Darcy could forget that she was married.

"Oh, that." Darcy tilted her head back and laughed. "I'm not married. I made up a wife to keep men and other lesbians from hitting on me. I'm certain you know how difficult it is for a beautiful, successful, single woman."

Jules nodded at the left-handed compliment. Darcy's heart skipped a beat at the look of relief she saw on Jules's face.

"The first time I attended a lesbian book convention I was swamped with women wanting to sleep with me," Darcy explained. "I didn't want to hurt anyone's feelings or anger anyone, so I decided the best thing to do was invent a wife. That had worked well for me until the Dallas convention, when everyone was clamoring for a look at my wife.

"A friend agreed to help me out, but her baby became ill the day before everyone arrived. That's why I was so distraught when I met you. Offering you money to act as my wife wasn't one of my smoothest moves."

They laughed as they recalled Jules's haughty reply to Darcy's offer at the convention.

"I have to attend a book signing along with several other authors at The Farmers Market all day tomorrow," Darcy said. "Would you mind attending as my wife? I would love to take you to dinner tonight so we can continue to get to know each other. I have so many questions to ask you."

"Yes, to both," Jules said, placing her hand on top of Darcy's.

"When I met you at the convention, I thought you were a godsend." Darcy said. "You were gorgeous, educated, and everything I wanted in a wife. You were so sweet to agree to help me with my weekend charade."

Jules turned the ring on her left hand. "May I continue to wear this while we date?"

"You would do that?" Darcy beamed. "You would date me and wear my ring?"

"If you think I'm going to let you go to those lesbian gatherings without me, you're crazy." Jules's eyes sparkled, half teasing and half serious.

Darcy took Jules's hand in hers and gently ran her thumb over the back of her hand and the ring. "I would be lying if I told you I wasn't instantly attracted to you, and I could feel you liked me too. As the weekend progressed, I found myself easily living the lie I was telling. Even worse, I found myself loving it.

"When you refused my attempt to make love to you, I knew you were different from other women I'd met at the conventions. You had high morals and scruples. You refused to sleep with a married woman—something I had never encountered before. I already knew you had a great sense of humor, were intelligent, and gorgeous. Your strong moral character pushed me over the top.

"Thoughts of you kept me awake all night, and I resolved to have a serious discussion with you about our future the next day. When I couldn't find you the next morning I went crazy. I cancelled my law appointments and spent all my time trying to track you down. Little did I know that by canceling the appointments to read Daphne's will I was canceling the opportunity to see you."

##

After dinner Darcy walked Jules to her car. For the first time in a long time, Darcy was content, happy to be Darcy Lake lesbian fiction writer.

"What time do I need to be at the Farmers Market tomorrow?" Jules asked.

"Eleven. That will give us time to set up and prepare for the onslaught." Darcy reached for Jules's hand and laced their fingers together. "Wear something comfortable but breathtaking, okay?"

"Whose breath will I be taking?"

"Mine, always," Darcy mumbled.

"Why don't I wear—"

A firm, soul-searching kiss silenced Jules as Darcy pulled her into arms that ached to hold her. "God, I have missed you so much. Spend the night with me, Jules." Darcy's voice was deep with desire and need. "There's no reason for you to drive home tonight."

"I should go home," Jules whispered, her voice soft but resolute. "I'm not a fan of U-Haul romances."

"You're right." Darcy sighed. "That's not what I want from you either. See you in the morning then." Darcy bent down and kissed her, slowly fanning a flame neither woman wanted to extinguish.

##

Darcy pulled a bottle of water from the fridge and dropped onto her living room sofa. The day had been a roller coaster ride, and she was exhausted by the myriad of emotions she had experienced.

Finding Jules had ended the unbearable loneliness she had lived with for the last two weeks. In its place was now an unfathomable desire to be with the woman. She knew she should take it slow with Jules and give her time to fall in love with Darcy Reed the attorney. She also knew she should share her ultimate secret with Jules if they were to have any chance at happiness.

Make her fall in love with me, and then tell her the truth, Darcy thought as she walked to her bedroom. For now, she was looking forward to the autograph signing tomorrow.

##

Darcy finished putting all her books in place and located her favorite pen—the one that flowed beautifully when she autographed books. Her face broke into a brilliant smile when she spotted Jules at the far end of the aisle.

Darcy shook her head. She had never met anyone as graceful and gorgeous as Jules. As she watched the woman walk toward her, she realized she was holding her breath. *Jules truly is breathtaking.*

"Darcy Lake!" A smooth, viperous voice reached her ears, pulling her eyes away from Jules. "I thought I'd find you here."

"Cat!" Darcy turned to face Cat Webb, her agent. "I didn't know you were hunting for me."

"You aren't returning my phone calls." Cat's frown let Darcy know how unhappy she was. "You haven't answered my emails and you're ignoring my text messages."

"I'm sorry." Darcy hoped the look of alarm that crossed her face was convincing. "I've been so busy that I haven't thought about anything but my next book. I'm on a roll."

"Perhaps I could come to your place when this shindig is over, and you can read some of your new book to me over a glass of wine." Cat slid a polished nail down Darcy's arm and raised her eyebrows.

"Darling!" Jules had heard enough to know Darcy was being propositioned. "I'm sorry I'm late." She moved behind the autograph table, pulled Darcy's head down, and kissed her soundly.

"My wife, Jules," Darcy explained to Cat as soon as she caught her breath. "Honey, this is my agent, Catrina Webb. Everyone calls her Cat."

"Darcy has told me all about you," Jules said.

"She has?" A look of pure disbelief settled on Cat's face as she looked from Jules to Darcy.

"Maybe not everything," Darcy mumbled as she squeezed Jules's hand. "If it wasn't important, I didn't mention it."

Cat glared at Darcy. "Wasn't important!" Cat raked her eyes over Jules and wondered if she was aware that Darcy had warmed her bed on more than one occasion

"Cat, I'm assuming you tracked me down for a reason."

"Yes." Cat hissed the word. "You've been awarded another literary award, and you need to go to New York to accept it."

Darcy scowled as if she had been told to give up breathing. "I'd rather not. Can't you accept it for me?"

"If you don't start attending these affairs, they'll stop giving you awards," Cat warned. "They like to think they're important enough to the writers for them to show up."

"Send me the information. I'll see if I can work it into my schedule," Darcy said. "I don't know how you expect me to write and run all over the world at the same time."

"If it will put a smile on your face," Cat said, attempting to pacify her most successful author, "your new book is already your best seller. You just keep getting better.

"I sent you all the information a week ago," Cat continued. "Please open your damn email and respond. That's the least you can do."

"I will." As Darcy watched Cat walk away she tried to hide the concern that was nagging at the back of her mind.

"Are you okay?" Jules asked.

"I am now that you're here." Darcy's mood lightened as she looked at the brunette. "Thank you for coming."

The rest of the day went without incident. Darcy spent the day signing autographs and amiably deflected advances from her fans and fellow authors.

On more than one occasion she reminded people she was married and that her wife had graciously agreed to accompany her to the book signing.

Jules was happy to run interference for the besieged author as Darcy bantered with her fans and signed autographs until her wrists gave out.

Marta Wayne and her partner, Janet Price, joined them at Darcy's autograph table.

"I didn't realize you would be here," Marta said to Jules.

"She'll probably be with me at all functions from now on," Darcy said as she caught Jules's hand. "She likes traveling with me."

"Humph! I didn't receive your newest manuscript, so I've dropped you to the bottom of my list."

"I'm sorry, Marta." Darcy ducked her head and cast her best little-girl look at her beta reader. "I'm running behind. I'll let you know when I'm close. Okay?"

Marta gave Darcy a sullen look and motioned for Janet to follow her. "I'll be waiting for your book."

"I'm not certain what's going on." A dark scowl settled on Darcy's face. "I don't know why she hasn't received the book."

Jules stood behind Darcy, massaging her shoulders.

"Oh my God, that feels good." Darcy leaned back into the strong fingers of the woman she was falling more in love with every minute. "How did I live without you?"

"From the comments I've heard today," Jules said, "you've never wanted for female companionship."

Darcy threw up her hands in surrender. "I plead the fifth. Just remember that was before I met you."

"You and Cat?" Jules said.

"Nothing." Darcy shrugged. "It meant nothing to me. I would've told you about it. We should probably sit down sometime and pour out our past to one another so neither of us are blindsided like that. You handled it beautifully. I'm not sure a real wife would have reacted so nicely."

"I don't care about the ones before me," Jules half teased. "There can never be anyone after me."

"You have my word." Darcy caught Jules's hand and turned to face her. "So, does this mean you might be considering me a big part of your future?"

"Might be." The look in Jules's eyes told Darcy her chances were good.

##

"I must return to school on Tuesday," Jules informed Darcy over drinks. "I have to take care of some of Nana's business Monday, and then I'll drive to Waco Monday night."

"What do you have planned for tomorrow?" Darcy watched Jules from under dark lashes.

"My hometown, Kingston, is celebrating Founders Day," Jules said "Why don't you join me for lunch? We have some great restaurants."

"I have a better idea," Darcy said. "Why don't I go home with you tonight so we can spend the entire day together tomorrow?"

"I don't think—"

"Don't you have an extra bedroom I can use?" Darcy placed her hand on Jules's arm. "I promise nothing will happen between us until you're ready."

"It's not you I'm worried about." A soft blush covered Jules's face.

Chapter 14

"I'm glad you agreed to let me come home with you," Darcy said as Jules signaled to exit the interstate. "I've never been to a Founders Day celebration."

Jules didn't respond. *What in the world have I done?* she wondered.

A warm tingle ran through Jules as Darcy trailed her fingertips down the brunette's arm. "No fair, torturing the driver." Jules sighed.

"Do you know what I want to do?" Darcy's voice was deep with desire.

"I have a pretty good idea," Jules said, trying to focus on the road ahead. "I bet it's the same thing I want you to do."

"How much longer?" Darcy whispered as she nuzzled Jules's ear and then trailed kisses down her neck.

"Ten minutes." Jules sighed. "You need to sit back in your seat. Half the people in this town know my car."

"I'm sure they do," Darcy said, laughing. "How many gorgeous women drive a metallic red Lexus sedan? You couldn't own anything more conspicuous, and I love it."

Jules realized she had no idea about Darcy's car. "What kind of car do you drive?"

"I'm embarrassed to admit it, but it's almost identical to yours."

"Oh my God!" Darcy whispered as Jules turned into a cul-de-sac and started up the hill. "That is the most magnificent home I've ever seen. Don't tell me that's the Manse?"

"I'm afraid it is," Jules said with a heavy sigh. "I've lived here since I was fourteen."

"Daphne Divine was more successful than I ever dreamed," Darcy said in awe. "Do you live here alone?"

"Yes. And I'm certain your income is comparable to Nana's."

Darcy tilted her head to the side and studied Jules for a long time. "It is . . . but not because of the Darcy Lake books. My law firm is my bread and butter."

Darcy surveyed the resplendent grounds as Jules pushed a button on her steering wheel that opened the iron gates across the driveway. She pulled her car into the garage and lowered the door behind her. She caught Darcy's face between her hands and kissed her sweetly. "I want to know everything about you, Darcy Lake."

"Reed, Darcy Reed," Darcy corrected her.

Darcy followed Jules into a hallway that led past a master bedroom suite and opened into the great room which was the center of the Manse.

"This is beautiful," Darcy gasped. "It's so . . . so pleasant and peaceful."

"I love living here," Jules said. "It's my sanctuary."

"Yes, I can see how it would be one's haven." Darcy walked to the glass wall across the back of the great room and watched the waterfall splash into the pool. "Do you swim?"

"Like a fish." Jules laughed.

Darcy couldn't stop the way her heartbeat accelerated at the rich, throaty sound of Jules's laughter reverberating throughout the Manse.

Jules slipped her arms around Darcy's waist and pressed her soft breasts against the blonde's back. "I'm glad you're here," she whispered into Darcy's ear.

They stood like that for a long time, simply enjoying the feel of their bodies pressed against one another.

"Come." Jules caught Darcy's hand. "I'll show you where I work."

Darcy allowed herself to be pulled down a long hallway into a beautifully appointed two-room suite consisting of an office that flowed through an archway into a bedroom.

"Oh Lord," Darcy chortled as she surveyed Jules's bookshelves. "You do have every Darcy Lake novel ever written."

Jules pressed her lips to Darcy's. "I told you, I'm a *big* Darcy Lake fan."

Darcy pulled away from her. "We need to talk before this goes any further."

"I don't understand. Don't you want me?" The hurt in Jules's eyes was painful to see.

"Oh, more than anything," Darcy said. "The last morning of the conference I went crazy trying to find you. I wanted to tell you I wasn't married and ask you if we could date. I couldn't get you out of my mind. I thought about you every waking minute and dreamed about you each night. I'm fairly certain you're the woman I want to spend the rest of my life making happy."

"I feel the same way about you," Jules assured her.

"You don't really know me," Darcy said, bowing her head. "You're in love with Darcy Lake the novelist. The woman who writes torrid love scenes that leave you aching all over."

"And that is wrong because . . .?" Jules raised a perfectly arched brow.

"Because I'm not that woman." Darcy took Jules's hand and led her back to the great room. "It'll be easier for me to think straight, if we aren't in your bedroom."

Jules sensed she wasn't going to like what Darcy was about to tell her.

Darcy pulled Jules onto the sofa beside her and searched her mind for a starting point. She had been Darcy

Lake for so long that it seemed she had always been the novelist. "Ten years ago, I was a starving student—and I mean that in the most literal way. I waitressed, wrote essays for other students, modeled at auto shows, you name it. If it wasn't immoral or illegal I did it to keep myself in school."

"Didn't your parents help you?" Jules asked.

"My parents died in a car accident my senior year of high school. They had no life insurance and were heavily in debt. I graduated valedictorian, so I had a free ride to college academically, but things like food, housing, and books weren't covered by the scholarship.

"I modeled one summer at an auto show. You know . . . the beautiful, scantily clad girl who smiles and hands out brochures. About two weeks after the auto show I received a letter in the mail, asking me if I would be interested in a job that would pay all my expenses for law school. A phone number and five hundred dollars cash were enclosed.

"I was thrilled but cautious. I called the number and spoke with someone. I couldn't tell if it was a man or a woman. It was obvious a voice-altering device was being used. I assumed I was speaking with a female. She said she was conducting an experiment. She was a well-known author who wanted to write a series of lesbian books. She needed me to be the face of her alias. I couldn't find a downside to the offer, so I accepted.

"A week later, I received a contract detailing my duties and stating that I would be the face of the author as long as she wrote the lesbian books. A cashier's check for twenty thousand dollars was included. Jules, I needed the money so badly. I signed the contract and have never looked back. The name of the author was to be—"

"Darcy Lake," Jules whispered.

Darcy nodded. "My benefactor selected the name using my true first name and a bogus last name. She said it would make it easier for me to function, and it does.

"Darcy Lake novels have taken the best seller lists by storm. Thanks to the author, I could get my law degree as Darcy Reed and travel all over the world as Darcy Lake. She provided ample funds for my travels and to maintain the façade of a successful novelist."

"Do you know her name?" Jules asked.

"No. I've tried to uncover her identity, but I've failed."

"When your grandmother engaged me to handle her estate, I thought she was my benefactor, but I was wrong. She is a great novelist, but she's no Darcy Lake. She said she found my law firm on the internet."

"That's true. She's no Darcy Lake." Jules laughed as she thought of Nana writing some of the smoking lesbian love scenes written by Lake.

"So where does that leave us?" Jules asked.

"You are the woman I have fallen in love with, Jules. I know who you are. I know I want to be with you always. I don't want to enter a relationship with you only to find out a year from now that you're in love with Darcy Lake the novelist, not Darcy Reed the woman.

"Only I could be both the women in the same love triangle." Sarcasm dripped from Darcy's voice as she realized the irony of her situation. "My own competition."

"I'm willing to get to know the real Darcy Reed. In the meantime, I assume you will continue to shill for Darcy Lake?"

Darcy shrugged. "I won't lie. I enjoy playing the part of a wildly popular novelist. It's a huge charge for my ego, but in the back of my mind I keep wondering when the real author will come forward. I'll be exposed as a fraud. That's a fear I live with every day."

"To be completely honest with you," Jules said, "I fell in love with the Darcy Lake novels partly because they're exciting and spellbinding and partly because of the photo of the gorgeous author on the back cover."

"Then I've won half the battle." Darcy's face revealed her delight.

"How do you contact the writer?" Jules asked.

"Her email is darcy@darcylake.com. I also have a cell phone I can text. On occasion, I call her, but she never answers. She only texts me back."

"So you've never heard her real voice?" Jules asked.

"Never!"

Both women jumped as the ringing of Jules's phone interrupted their thoughts. Tanner West's face filled the screen.

"Jules, this is Tanner," West said when Jules answered the phone. "I just wanted to check on you and make certain everything went okay at the attorney's office."

"Oh, yes." Jules's twinkling eyes scanned Darcy's face. "Everything was perfect. Thank you for asking."

"I thought you might like to eat dinner and talk with someone," Tanner said, her words rushed.

"I . . . um, I already have dinner plans," Jules said. "May I have a raincheck?"

"Of course." Jules could hear the disappointment in Tanner's response. "Jules, please be careful. I haven't found one lead on your grandmother's killer. Until I can find a motive, please don't entertain strangers."

"Oh," Jules chuckled, "I'm having dinner with an old friend."

They said their goodbyes and Jules ended the call. "Dinner is not a bad idea. Are you hungry?"

Darcy nodded. "Is it safe for us to be seen together? I mean, with your father and cousins in town. After all, I am Daphne's attorney."

"Uncle Buddy and his family are on their way back to the family farm in Childress, and Lucas is probably out chasing women. I couldn't care less what my parents think. I'm dead to them anyway."

"Dinner it is," Darcy said, laughing. "I would love a good steak and salad."

"I know just the place." Jules tilted her head for a kiss and Darcy did not disappoint her. *Dear Lord, the woman can kiss*, Jules thought.

Chapter 15

"May we have the circular booth in the far back corner?" Jules asked the hostess as she led them deeper into the restaurant.

"Of course," the girl wiggled her eyebrows. "It's very secluded."

Darcy and Jules exchanged glances. "We have business to discuss," Jules explained. "The booth is private and quiet."

A waitress materialized as soon as the women were seated. "What would you like to drink?"

"Iced tea," Jules answered.

"Same here," Darcy said.

"Are you a beer drinker?" Darcy asked after the waitress departed.

"No, wine and an occasional piña colada around the pool," Jules said.

"Same here." Darcy moved so that her thigh touched Jules's under the table. The feel of the brunette was intoxicating. "I love these circular booths, they allow us to sit side by side."

"Have you ever been involved in a serious relationship?" Jules asked, though she was certain she knew the answer.

"No, not really," Darcy said. "Just the usual college experiments. But when the Darcy Lake novels became popular, I was inundated with women wanting to sleep with Darcy Lake. It was insane. After a few one-night stands, I realized that wasn't what I wanted. The sex was meaningless, and I felt dirty. I'm a commitment kind of gal." Her expression told Jules she was telling the truth.

"How about you? Any ex-lovers I should be worried about?"

"A year-long relationship with a fiery redhead named Raylene," Jules admitted, "but we parted on good terms. We just weren't that compatible in . . . well, in bed."

"Oh?" The surprised expression on Darcy's face told Jules she had questions but wasn't certain she should ask them. "Well, I suppose we don't all like the same things," Darcy said.

"There are certain things that I like a lot and some I don't like at all," Jules explained.

Jules's eyes danced as she pulled a notepad and two pens from her purse. She tore a sheet from the pad and handed the pen and paper to Darcy. "We could resolve our issues right now before we cause emotional pain for one another.

"We'll ask each other questions, and we'll write down our answers. When we finish talking, we'll see how compatible we are."

Darcy nodded. "You go first."

"Okay. Simple yes or no," Jules said. "Do you want children? Be honest. Don't write what you think I want to hear."

They wrote their answer on the sheet and exchanged notes.

"You don't want children?" The surprised look on Darcy's face made Jules smile.

"No. I don't want to raise them, and from what I've seen as a teacher, they cause their parents more misery than joy."

Jules looked at what Darcy had written. The "No" in bold letters made her happy. "We're compatible so far."

"Where would you want to live?" Darcy asked.

They scribbled their answers and passed them to the other. Both had written, "wherever you are."

Darcy scooted closer to Jules. "Let's cut to the chase," she said. "What do you like that your former lover didn't like?"

Jules wrote two words on her notepad and shoved it in front of Darcy.

Darcy stared at the words and swallowed hard. "Who would wear it?" A concerned look crossed Darcy's face.

"Only you!" Jules declared.

"Do you have one?"

Jules blushed as she nodded.

"Jules Adair Divine," Darcy said. "You are truly the woman of my dreams. Women like me are drawn to women like you—like a moth to a flame."

The waitress placed their orders on the table. "Do you need anything else?"

"No." Darcy beamed. "We're perfect." *For each other.*

"Do you have any questions for me?" Jules asked as she cut into her grilled chicken.

"Will you marry me?" Darcy's expression was somber and hopeful.

"Yes, Darcy Reed. I'll marry you. I honestly can't imagine my life without you."

Darcy leaned down and kissed Jules. "I love the way you kiss," she said.

The figure sitting at the booth across from them grimaced as the two kissed.

Chapter 16

Jules was slow to rouse as she snuggled into soft warm arms. She stiffened as she realized she was lying naked next to Darcy and then relaxed as she recalled the incredible night they'd spent together.

"Having morning-after regrets?" Darcy murmured in Jules's ear as she pulled her closer.

"My only regret is that I didn't meet you ten years ago," Jules said with a feathery kiss between her lover's breasts.

"Are we going to be compatible in bed?" Darcy's question was a serious one.

"Oh, heavens, yes." Jules sighed as she pushed harder against Darcy. "I do think you've had more experience than you said. You're an incredible lover."

Darcy kissed along Jules's jawline, down her neck and back up to her lips. "I can't believe you let me do that to you."

"I can't believe you're so good." Jules slid under Darcy as she pulled the blonde on top of her. "There is that one thing you did that drove me insane."

"Just one?" Darcy murmured against Jules's lips.

"Maybe more than one," Jules whispered.

##

Jules pushed the button to start the coffee maker. She was thankful that Renee didn't work on the weekends. Darcy was still sleeping, and she didn't want to disturb her. They'd made love and talked all night. A warmth spread through her body as she thought about spending the next two days with the blonde.

Darcy had been everything Jules knew she would be. She may not have written the love scenes in the Darcy Lake novels, but she certainly brought them to life.

The coffee maker gurgled as it spit out the last of the water. Jules poured a cup of the black liquid and headed for the patio. Darcy intercepted her in the great room.

"Hot coffee," Jules warned as Darcy slipped her arms around her from behind.

Darcy took the cup and sipped the coffee. "Mmm. And you make perfect coffee too." She leaned down and kissed Jules. "I'm going to hop into the shower then join you on the patio."

"I'd like that." Jules watched as the blonde—clad in only a T-shirt—walked from the room. *How can anyone look so sexy this early in the morning?*

She was still watching the empty space where Darcy had disappeared when the doorbell rang. As she approached the door, she recognized Tanner's build and stance.

"Good morning, Tanner." Jules couldn't keep the happiness out of her voice. "What can I do for you today?"

"I have a few questions you can answer for me," Tanner said.

"Coffee?" Jules held up her cup and walked toward the kitchen.

"That would be great," Tanner said.

"Good coffee," Tanner said following her to the patio. "You certainly seem happy this morning."

"I am." Jules opened the patio door. "I love it out here." Jules motioned for Tanner to sit in the chair beside her. "Now, how can I help you?"

"I've been trying to find anyone who deals in rattlesnakes or rattlesnake venom," Tanner said. "I visited a snake farm in New Braunfels, and they gave me a list of men who regularly bring them live rattlesnakes. One of them lives in Cleburne, three live in Glen Rose, and four live in the Grandview area." She handed Jules a sheet of paper. "Do you recognize anyone on this list?"

Jules studied the names. "This man goes to my father's church," she said, pointing out the name of Rowdy Rains. "He's a rancher. As far as I know he raises cattle, not rattlesnakes."

The two continued to talk and were laughing when Darcy walked into the great room. She wore a pair of shorts and a long T-shirt that belonged to Jules. She poured a cup of coffee and watched as Jules interacted with Tanner.

From courtrooms to negotiations, Darcy had become an expert at reading body language. What she was reading right now did not make her happy. The look of joy on Tanner's face when Jules laughed and placed her hand on the detective's forearm told Darcy all she needed to know.

It was obvious the woman was enamored with Jules.

"Time for me to stake my claim," Darcy said out loud as she walked to the patio.

Jules and Tanner looked up at her as if surprised by her appearance. Darcy leaned down and kissed Jules on the cheek before the brunette could acknowledge her.

"Good morning, darling. Thank you for letting me sleep late." *That should let the detective know she's pursuing my woman*, Darcy thought.

Jules caught Darcy's hand and pulled her down beside her on the sofa. "Detective Tanner West, I'd like you to meet my"—Jules hesitated, and Darcy wondered what she was to the brunette after last night—"fiancée, Darcy Reed. Honey, Detective West is investigating Nana's death."

"Investigating?" Concern spread across Darcy's beautiful face. "I thought she died of natural causes."

Tanner shifted away from Jules. "We're just tying up some loose ends. Nothing to worry about." Tanner stood and looked at her watch. "I must be going. The Founders

Day parade starts in an hour. The chief has all of us working today.

"Thanks for the coffee, Jules. I'll let myself out."

"Pretty woman," Darcy commented after Tanner left the patio.

"Yes, but not as pretty as you." Jules scooted onto Darcy's lap and wrapped her arms around the blonde's neck. "I think you're the most beautiful woman I have ever seen."

"I don't know." Darcy shook her head. "I know a brunette that would give any woman a run for her money."

Jules nipped at Darcy's bottom lip. "Have I told you how much I love the way you kiss?"

Darcy pulled Jules closer and kissed her as if nothing else in the world mattered. "I love you, Jules."

They sat on the patio, holding each other and planning their day. "Why don't you shower while I cook breakfast? We can eat out here on the patio," Darcy suggested. "Then we can check out the Founders Day celebration. I bet they have a Ferris wheel."

"I love Ferris wheels!" Jules exclaimed, kissing Darcy one more time before standing.

"Somehow, I knew you would." Darcy's delight at the prospect of sharing something Jules loved showed in her expression. "How do you like your eggs cooked?"

Tanner's post for the Founders Day celebration was the department's mobile observation tower. Rising two stories above the crowd, the detective had a wide view of the activities taking place.

The tower, which had been dubbed Sky Guard by the city council, had state-of-the-art technology, including four HD full-color, movable cameras that could zoom in on things as far as the eye could see. Everything was connected to a large screen that allowed Tanner to monitor several locations at once. A loudspeaker was mounted on each corner of the tower.

Main Street had been closed and turned into a virtual fairground. Vendors' tents covered the mile-long stretch designated for those hawking their wares to celebrators. A traveling carnival had set up on the parking lot at one end of Main Street. A sturdy Ferris wheel was cutting a circle through the blue sky as other rides added to the music and mayhem. The Ferris wheel featured metal cars, each with a wire cage across the top and around the upper sides. Riders were visible from their shoulders up.

At the other end of the street, a stage was being readied for the band performing at tonight's street dance. On the camera surveilling the parking lot, Tanner spotted a gang of teenage boys sidling toward a decked-out Chevy pickup. She radioed her ground coordinator.

"Perkins, it looks like a vehicle theft is about to go down on lot three. Four teenage boys are approaching a red Chevy pickup on row J. One of them is carrying a slim jim."

Slim jims were popular tools among car thieves. The thin piece of metal with a hook on the end could easily open most vehicle door locks. The criminal simply slid the device down the window into the car door, caught the car's locking mechanism, and pulled up, unlocking the door.

Tanner recorded close-ups of the boys using the tool to unlock the truck. They were in the process of stealing an iPhone, a camera, CDs and a boombox from the vehicle when three policemen arrested them.

She watched with satisfaction as her team worked tirelessly to keep their citizens safe. She caught her breath when Jules Divine's smiling face suddenly appeared on her monitor. Her joy was short-lived as she watched Darcy Reed appear beside Jules and hold out an ice cream cone.

The eye sex between the two as Jules wrapped her hands around Darcy's hand and licked the ice cream made Tanner want to throw up.

Tanner watched the couple as they strolled through the temporary fair grounds, stopping at vendors and talking to people along the way. They laughed and occasionally leaned their foreheads together and whispered to one another. For the first time, Tanner thought Darcy Reed looked familiar.

The detective was too busy watching the couple to notice the figure stalking them.

Chapter 17

Tanner watched as Jules pulled Darcy into a restaurant named The Brewery Bar and Grill. The low lighting in the air-conditioned dining area made it intimate and inviting. Music was blaring from the restaurant's sky bar but couldn't be heard by diners below. Tanner was surprised that Jules had selected the hideaway. It was a place frequented by young lovers. It made Tanner ill as she admitted that Darcy and Jules were intimate.

A jolt jerked Tanner back to her surroundings as the Sky Guard lowered to the ground. Another officer keyed in the code to the lock and opened the door to the watch tower. "Time for your break," he announced.

Tanner checked her watch. "Times flies when you're having fun," she commented.

"Yeah, I've been dying to get my hands on this baby," the officer said.

Tanner debated between entering The Brewery or getting a hotdog from one of the vendors. She longed for the coolness of the restaurant but didn't want to run into Jules and her fiancée. She scowled at the vendor as she ordered a hotdog.

"I love the dress you're wearing," Darcy said to Jules as they slid into the booth at The Brewery. "I'm having trouble keeping my hands off you," Darcy whispered in Jules's ear as they waited for their order.

"Who says you have to?" Jules grazed Darcy's lips with her own, happy that the dress had accomplished its purpose.

"There is one thing I want to do today." Darcy's smile was wide and playful. "It's at the top of my bucket list."

"You wiped out my bucket list last night," Jules said, her eyes dancing as she teased her lover. "So, let's start scratching things off your list. What's at the top?"

The blonde whispered in Jules's ear.

Jules blushed as Darcy's warm breath sent desire ricocheting through her body. "Here? Today?"

Her incredulous look made Darcy laugh out loud. "If you don't want to . . . ."

"No! No, I'd love that. I've always wanted to do that. I've never met anyone I wanted to do it with."

Their conversation lulled long enough for the waitress to place their orders in front of them.

"I have to return to my job," Jules said. "I've got to leave Dallas tomorrow by three."

A look of anguish crossed Darcy's face. "This is our last night together?"

"For this week." Jules's eyes filled with affection for the woman who was now so important to her. "I have to close out the end of school. I owe it to my students to be there. Then I'll resign. I'll be home in two weeks."

"Home!" Light flickered in Darcy's eyes. "You just called this home. Does that mean you'll move back here?"

"I guess it does," Jules said. "Nana's has always been home to me, even though I haven't lived there in five years."

"Do you want us to make our home here?" Darcy asked.

"I . . . what about your law firm?" Jules wanted to live in Nana's house—now her house—but she didn't want to be unfair to Darcy.

"I can open an office here," Darcy said. "I've already given it a lot of thought. My partners can continue to run the Dallas office, and I can consult there until I build a thriving business here."

"Really?" Jules drawled the word as her perfect lips spread into a brilliant smile.

"Really!" Darcy captured those perfect lips with her own. She didn't care who saw them.

Suddenly, someone nearby cleared their throat, pulling the lovers back to earth.

As the daze of desire cleared, Jules acknowledged her brother and his best friend, Trent. "Hi, guys!" she said as she slid from the booth and hugged them both. "What are you two up to?"

"I was all set to watch a little porn, but your brother had to make our presence known and ruin it," Trent said with a grin as he ran his eyes over Darcy, all but drooling at the sight of her.

"My fiancée, Darcy Reed." Jules made the introductions as she sat down in the booth. "Honey, you already know my brother, Lucas, and this is our best friend, Trent Leymen. We grew up together."

Darcy greeted the two men with a cordial nod. "Please, join us." She scooted closer to Jules as the men slid into the other end of the booth.

"Fiancée?" Lucas raised a brow as he addressed his sister. "When did this happen?"

"Yesterday." Jules placed her hand on top of Darcy's.

"I guess that explains the PDA." The darkness in Lucas's eyes belied his teasing tone.

Darcy's body stiffened as she held back a curt retort. Jules squeezed her hand, reminding her that nothing mattered but the two of them.

"I can explain the PDA, bro." Jules tilted her head and fixed her brother with a stern look. "I adore her, and I can't keep my hands off her."

Both men started laughing. "Calm down, little Sister," Lucas's laughter turned into a grin. "We're just razzing you. We're jealous, plain and simple. You always get the gorgeous women while Trent and I are left trying to figure out what happened.

"But, um, if you plan on teaching in this town," he added, "you really shouldn't be so demonstrative in public. I swear, just watching you two made my toes curl."

"I'm afraid I'm to blame," Darcy started to explain.

"No doubt about that," Lucas said.

"Enough teasing," Jules declared. "What are the two of you doing here?"

"We have dates," Trent said, beaming.

Jules took her best shot. "Real women or the inflatable kind?"

"Touché," Trent said. "We deserved that."

"We met two ladies at the street dance last week," Lucas explained, "and they're meeting us here tonight."

"Do you like them?" Jules asked.

"Well . . . not enough to get engaged on the second date, but enough to ask them out again," Lucas said.

Darcy couldn't stop the half smile that curved her lips. Jules's brother was witty in an offbeat way.

Just then the men spotted their dates across the room and excused themselves. "We can join you two if you like," Lucas said. One look from Jules and the idea was dismissed.

"Message received loud and clear, Sis." He gave her a happy salute as he backed away from the table.

"I like your brother," Darcy said. "He's obviously devoted to you."

"When our parents threw me out of the house, he defended me. They almost threw him out too. I convinced him to bite his tongue and complete high school before he broke with my parents, and he did. He has always been my biggest supporter."

"You both are lucky to have a friend like Trent," Darcy said.

"I'm lucky to have someone like you." Jules leaned in for a quick kiss. "Now, about that Ferris wheel ride you promised me."

Darcy and Jules had almost reached the Ferris wheel when they encountered Jules's neighbors Roy and Ashley Craft. Jules introduced them to Darcy.

Roy was exuberant and intent on riding all the adult rides the carnival offered. Ashley acknowledged Jules's introduction of Darcy with a nod.

"We were so sorry about Daphne," Roy said and his wife gave Jules's arm a sympathetic pat. "We wanted to tell you at the funeral, but you were surrounded by people."

Jules grimaced, finding no words to respond to Roy. Darcy gave her hand a supportive squeeze.

"I saw the ambulance at your house last week," Jules said. "Is everyone okay?"

"We're fine." Roy put his arm around his wife's shoulders. "Twinkle Toes here got her feet tangled up and fell down the basement stairs."

Ashley bowed her head but didn't respond to her husband's teasing.

"I'm glad you're okay," Jules said.

"Come on, ladies," Lucas said, catching his sister's arm. "We're going to ride the Ferris wheel."

"Y'all have fun," Roy called after them as Lucas herded the group toward the carnival ride.

"You have to meet my date," Lucas said. "I think she may be the one."

"Don't you think it's a little early to be declaring that?" Jules hugged her brother's arm, wishing she could protect him.

"Says the woman who has agreed to marry a woman she has only known a few days."

"Point taken," Jules mumbled.

As they approached, Jules smiled at Trent and the two women with him. He introduced his date, a dirty-blonde named Phyllis, and Lucas's date, a brown-haired beauty named Rachel.

"I've purchased tickets for all of us," Trent informed Jules as he handed two tickets to Darcy. "Each car holds four passengers, so you and Darcy can ride with us if you'd like."

Darcy had other ideas. "We're okay alone," she said. "I'm sure your friends want to remain together."

As the three couples visited and shared anecdotes with one another, Darcy approached the ride operator. With her back to the others, she tore a fifty-dollar bill in half and handed it to the operator. "If my car gets stuck at the top for fifteen minutes," she said, "you'll get the other half when the ride is over."

"Yes, ma'am." His eyes opened wide as he slid the half bill into the pocket of his jeans.

As Jules joined her, Darcy handed their tickets to the ride operator and entered the waiting car. She closed the door behind them before anyone else could join them.

"Your brother likes to spend time with you," Darcy declared as she pulled Jules's hand into her lap. "It's easy to see that the two of you are very close."

"Do you have siblings?" Jules asked as the Ferris wheel began to move so the next group could enter the car.

"No." Darcy looked over her shoulder. "Your brother and his friends are in the car next to us."

"I guess we have to behave ourselves." Jules pretended to pout.

"I fall deeper in love with you by the minute," Darcy murmured as the ride operator moved their car higher into the air and loaded more passengers.

111

All the cars filled, and the Ferris wheel began to spin. Jules watched the lights whirl by in a blur as the ride picked up speed. "This is beautiful," she said. After the third rotation, the wheel began to slow.

Darcy pulled Jules closer and leaned down to press her lips against the brunette's. She sensuously moved her full bottom lip against Jules's to illicit a soft moan.

Jules leaned back against the seat and welcomed the woman into her arms. "Did I tell you I love this dress?" Darcy murmured against eager lips as she caressed Jules's thigh.

"Uh-huh." Jules breathed faster.

"It's so—"

"Accessible." Jules groaned as Darcy moved her hand further up her thigh.

"You're not wearing . . . ." Darcy pulled back to gaze into Jules's eyes.

"This Ferris wheel won't stay up here all night," Jules said, her voice husky as she pulled the blonde onto her as much as possible in the carnival ride.

Darcy moaned as she found the pulse spot in Jules's neck and sucked it gently. The world fell away as they hung suspended in the night sky with nothing but the moon and stars to witness their passion.

The Ferris wheel jerked as it started turning again. Darcy held her tightly against her shoulder as Jules cried the blonde's name into the night.

Darcy sat up in her seat and straightened Jules's dress. She removed a tube of lipstick from her jeans pocket and handed it to Jules. "I think I licked all yours off," she said, ducking her head in embarrassment. "Your brother will notice."

Jules applied the lipstick and then returned it to Darcy who did the same.

Jules was thankful the ride made three more rotations before aligning their car with the ground. Her knees were weak. "I'm not sure I can walk." The look on her face told Darcy she wasn't teasing.

"Lean on me, Jules. You can always lean on me." Darcy helped Jules from the car and shook hands with the ride operator as she passed him, palming the other half of the fifty to the young man.

They waited as Lucas and his group poured from their car and walked toward them. Jules stood up straight and moved slightly away from Darcy. "I've never known anyone like you, Darcy Reed."

Jules could tell by the look Lucas gave her that he knew what had happened in her car. "I think you had a better ride than I did," he teased as he hugged her, whispering in her ear. "Be careful, Sis."

"I am," Jules said as she pulled from her brother's embrace and walked to the Ferris wheel operator.

Darcy watched in silence as Jules spoke to the young man.

"Did you just tip him?" Darcy asked as Jules slipped her arm through hers.

"I might have." Jules's face glowed as the lights from the carnival danced in eyes as black as the night.

"I did too." Darcy chuckled as the others crowded around them.

"Great minds . . . !" Jules wrinkled her nose and hugged Darcy's arm between her breasts.

"We're gonna' dance," Lucas said, grabbing Jules's elbow. "Come dance with us. Can you dance, Darcy?"

"A little." Darcy was still enthralled with his sister and only wanted to return to the Manse. She went along good naturedly as the other two couples swept them toward the band.

"Can you do the Carolina Shag?" Lucas's date asked Darcy after the band completed their second set.

"Not really," Darcy replied. She had no desire to dance with anyone but Jules.

Tanner caught up with the group hoping to dance with Jules. Lucas introduced her to everyone as they welcomed her to their party.

"They're having a shag contest during the next set," Rachel informed the group. "I need a good partner."

"I can Carolina Shag," Tanner said, "if you don't mind dancing with a woman."

"I don't mind if you don't." Rachel surveyed the attractive detective. "Maybe we should do a slow dance first. Just to see if we work well together."

"What the hell just happened?" The look of surprise on Lucas's face as he watched Tanner dance away with his date made Jules laugh.

"I'm not sure your date is a straight shooter," Darcy said.

"You're a great shag dancer," Lucas said to Jules. "Why don't you dance with her?"

"I'm sure Detective West is an excellent dancer," Jules commented as she watched Tanner skillfully maneuver Rachel around the dance floor. "Besides, I want to dance with my date."

Jules turned to Darcy. "From the way you danced at the convention, I bet you can do the Carolina Shag."

"You haven't shagged until you've shagged with me." Darcy pulled Jules into her arms, and they moved onto the dance floor.

"Are we still talking about dancing?" Jules said, her eyes twinkling with delight.

"That too." Darcy pulled her partner closer as the music segued from the two-step to the shag.

Jules surrendered to the strong, confident arms around her, and the two danced as if they had rehearsed for years. By the time the dance was over, everyone had cleared the dance floor and was simply enjoying the sexy show orchestrated by the two women. As the dance ended, Darcy twirled Jules across the floor, and the two collapsed into each other's arms, laughing with abandon.

The applause and wolf whistles pulled them from a world where only they existed.

Rachel glared at Darcy as she and Jules rejoined the group.

"Whew, that took my breath away," Jules exclaimed. "I think we should head home. I have to return to work tomorrow and I'm tired."

Rachel caught Darcy's arm. "Just one dance with me?"

Silence settled over the partiers. "I'm with Jules, and I understood you were with Lucas." Darcy's no-nonsense tone seemed to stop time. "We have no business dancing with anyone but our respective partners."

Tanner West was silent as she watched the interaction between Darcy Reed and others in the group. *I know her from somewhere,* Tanner thought. *Damn, she's beautiful. I can see why Jules is enamored of her.*

Chapter 18

Darcy lay on her back. Jules's head rested on Darcy's shoulder and her leg was thrown over the blonde. Her steady breathing told Darcy she was in a deep sleep.

Darcy tried to organize her thoughts, but her mind kept returning to the thrill of making love to Jules. She had never met anyone as responsive and demanding as Jules, and she loved it. It was probably a good thing Jules had to leave for two weeks. *Maybe I can get my head on straight.*

Darcy didn't want to go to New York for the awards ceremony. She needed to avoid face-to-face contact with everyone until she could contact the real writer of the Darcy Lake novels. She hadn't heard from her in over a month and things were getting out of hand.

Darcy wasn't returning phone calls or answering emails, because she never received them. They went to the novelist. Darcy had never been required to do anything but show up and look beautiful. Everything else was taken care of by someone Darcy had never met.

When Jules moved in her arms, Darcy feigned sleep. Although her heart was more than willing to make love to the woman she was holding, her body wasn't up to it. Jules was exhausting. Fortunately, Jules simply snuggled into her and continued sleeping. Darcy soon followed her into dreamland.

##

"I can drive you to Dallas and then go to Waco," Jules said, kissing Darcy as she handed her a cup of coffee.

"You would be adding over two hours to your trip." Darcy watched Jules as she moved about the kitchen preparing breakfast. "I've already called an Uber driver to take me."

"Mmm," Jules hummed as Darcy slipped her arms around her from behind. "But it would mean I could spend two more hours with you before I head to Waco."

"I can think of a better way to spend two hours than running up and down the highway." Darcy turned her lover to face her and kissed her with all the longing of one who was about to be left behind. "I'll miss you. Will I see you this weekend?"

"No. I need to pack my belongings and arrange to store my furniture until I decide what to do with it. I've lived there for the past five years, so I have a lot of things."

"Two weeks!" Darcy groaned.

"Don't be such a baby." The kiss Jules placed on her lips was the sweetest Darcy had ever known. "You need to eat your breakfast. It's getting cold.

##

"Call me when you reach your apartment," Darcy said. She kissed Jules goodbye and walked out the front door to get into the town car waiting for her.

Jules followed Darcy and leaned into the car to kiss her one more time before letting her go. "See you in two weeks," she murmured against the blonde's lips.

Jules watched the car until it disappeared then returned to the house. It seemed lonely without Darcy. It was funny how the woman had made the Manse warm and happy again.

She went to Nana's office and turned on the computer. Tanner had called her twice during the weekend, asking for Nana's business contacts—editor, proofreader, publisher, promoter, etc. Jules knew none of the information but was certain she could find it in the computer.

A folder titled *Nom de guerre* was on Nana's desktop. Jules clicked on it, and it requested a password.

Before she could type in the password, emails began to flood into Nana's Outlook folder. Jules opened the screen and watched as hundreds of emails from publishers, proofreaders, and editors loaded. As she watched, she realized the electronic messages were loading into an account for Darcy Lake. Puzzled, she opened the email from Agent and read it.

"Dammit, Darcy, I don't care if you do have a gorgeous wife to take care of, you better answer my emails. I've had it with you ignoring me." The email was signed "Cat."

"What the . . . ?" Jules read email after email addressed to Darcy Lake and signed by women she had met at the book convention.

Jules stared at the computer monitor in disbelief. As the numbness left her mind she stumbled to the bookcase and pulled open the doors, revealing all the Darcy Lake novels. She removed one at random and flipped through the pages. They were red with proofreader marks. The final page in the book had PROOF stamped across it. She pulled several books from the shelves and checked the last page in each book. They all contained the word PROOF.

Nana didn't just own every book Darcy Lake had written; she owned the proof copies.

Oh my God! Nana is Darcy Lake!

Jules pinched the bridge of her nose. Some of the love scenes from Lake's novels flashed through her mind. "Oh, God," she moaned out loud.

She returned to Nana's computer and clicked on the folder *Nom de guerre. French for assumed name*, Jules thought. It was so like Nana to hide something in plain sight. She typed the password Nana always used.

As the folder opened, it revealed subfolders for each of the novels written by Darcy Lake. Forty-five folders were labeled with the names of the published Darcy Lake books. There were an additional fifteen folders with titles Jules had never heard of. She clicked on one of the unknown titles, *Dying to Kill*. It was in folder forty-six.

A manuscript opened and Jules began to read. The novel was incomplete, having only forty chapters.

Jules clicked her way through the other new books and found all of them in various stages of completion. *Dying to Kill* was the most complete book

Jules found a new flash drive in Nana's desk and downloaded the *Nom de guerre* folder. *I'll read these as soon as I have time.*

Moving with the ease of one who knew her way around computers, Jules made screenshots of the settings on all of Nana's email accounts. She planned to set up the accounts on her laptop so she could respond to the many questions that had been sent to Darcy Lake.

As she closed the computer and laptop and stood to leave the office, the ABBA song on the doorbell echoed through the Manse. Jules checked the time and wondered where it had gone. Four hours had passed since she'd turned on the computer, and she was still stunned and confused.

By the time she reached the door she knew her visitor was Tanner. Tanner's perfect body was silhouetted by the setting sun. *Another place, another time, and I could fall in love with Tanner West*, she thought.

"Jules!" A pleased expression danced across Tanner's face. "I'm so glad you're still here."

"Is something wrong?" Jules asked.

"No. Um . . . I just wanted to see you before you returned to work."

"Come in. I was about to make a bite to eat. Have you had dinner?" Jules asked as she led Tanner to the island in the kitchen. Nana had been a gourmet cook, and Jules had inherited her love of cooking. She winced as she offered to fix tomato soup and grilled cheese sandwiches for their dinner.

"I would cook something more imaginative," she added, "but I'm leaving for Waco in an hour. I'm already a couple hours behind schedule."

"I understand," Tanner said. "That meal sounds great to me. Much better than the greasy burger and fries I was planning to eat."

Jules prepared the food with ease as she deliberated on whether to share her findings about Nana with Tanner. She decided to keep the information to herself for now.

"So, you're going to marry Darcy Reed?" Tanner asked. "Have you set a date?"

"Oh, heavens no." Jules glanced at Tanner. "I have so much going on with Nana's estate and moving back here. I couldn't—"

"You're moving back?" Tanner couldn't hide her joy at the thought of Jules living in her hometown.

"Yes. I plan to live here, and I want to provide you all the information I can on Nana's publishing contacts. I've started to wade through the information on her computer. It's voluminous.

"I know I'm slowing you down, but please don't confiscate her computer. She has it set up on an internal server so all her information is here in the house. Nana never trusted the cloud. She used to laugh and say, 'Americans are crazy. We scream and yell about our privacy, yet we upload everything we know onto the cloud where total strangers can access it.'"

Tanner ignored the pang of guilt she felt at not properly doing her job and agreed to let Jules search for any information that might be on the computer.

"At least let me be present when you go through it," Tanner mumbled.

"I've made a list of the people involved with publishing Nana's books. It's in her office. I'll get it," Jules said, leaving the room.

"Her publisher is Rattigan and Jarvis," Jules said as she handed Tanner a list of all Nana's contacts with the publishing company. "This is information for her editor, proofreaders, and agent. Her agent can probably help you more than I can."

Tanner's hand brushed Jules's as she took the note. She ignored the warmth that spread through her body.

"Jules, please be careful. I have no idea who murdered Daphne or why anyone would want to kill her. I don't know if you're in danger or not, so I worry about you."

Jules bowed her head, avoiding Tanner's eyes. "I must be going," she said. "I don't like being on the road after dark."

"I'll let myself out. I know you're in a hurry to get on the road. Thanks for dinner."

Tanner stopped midway to the door. "Darcy! I knew she looked familiar. Darcy Reed is also Darcy Lake, the lesbian novelist. Did you know that?"

"Yes," Jules said with a shrug. "I'm quite aware of who my fiancée is."

For the first time, Tanner realized she had no chance of winning Jules from the beautiful author.

Chapter 19

Darcy closed the file she had been staring at for over an hour. She had no idea what was in it. Try as she might, she couldn't get her mind clear of Jules Divine.

The attorney closed her eyes, and a vision of Jules jumped from her memory: the way Jules looked when she turned her head, accentuating the little muscle that ran from her jaw to the soft spot at the base of her throat. The spot where her pulse beat faster when she became excited. The spot Darcy loved to kiss.

Dear God, Darcy thought. *I've only spent two days with Jules in my arms, and I can't get her out of my mind. She is consuming me.*

A tap on Darcy's door preceded the entrance of her partner, Lana Weidman. "Darcy, it's Wednesday morning. Are you going to mope around here all week?"

"I'm sorry, Lana, I must be coming down with something," Darcy said. "I don't seem to be able to get my head in the game."

"Could it have anything to do with that gorgeous Divine woman that was in here a few days ago?"

Darcy stared at her partner for a few seconds. She was always amazed at how intuitive Lana was. "Is it that obvious?"

"Yes!" Lana sat down in the chair across the desk from Darcy. "What's going on, Darcy? I've never seen you fall so hard for a woman, not even a beautiful one."

"I haven't just fallen for her," Darcy said, trying to hide the pride she felt. "I've asked her to marry me and she said yes."

"You're kidding me!" Lana's mouth dropped open. "The consummate bachelorette is getting her wings clipped? When's the wedding?"

"We haven't set a date yet. She's in Waco finishing the school year and—"

"I thought she looked older."

"She's not a student." Darcy wrinkled her nose at her friend. "She's an English teacher."

"Oooh, I see," Lana said. "She's over a hundred miles away and you can't get to her."

"Something like that," Darcy grumbled. "She's finishing the school year and packing her apartment so she can move to Kingston at the end of next week. God, Lana, you should see the house she grew up in. I've never been a big fan of houses, but her home has . . . character and warmth and . . . I don't know. It just seems like home."

"Well, you're pretty worthless in your present condition," Lana said. "Why don't you take off next week and go help her? Oh hell, just leave today. I'll pick up your workload until you return."

"Seriously? Are you sure you're okay with that?" Darcy beamed as she grabbed her purse. "I'll make it up to you. I promise."

"You're damn right you will." Lana stood and smiled. "In about nine months I expect you to carry my workload."

"What happens in nine . . . oh my gosh! Are you—?"

"Yep," Lana said gleefully. "I just hope I can get my husband off the ceiling by then. He's so excited."

"Who wouldn't be?" Darcy declared.

"So, go." Lana shooed Darcy from the office. "Forget about this place for a few days. I can't remember the last time you took a vacation."

Darcy wasted no time. In less than an hour she had gone to her apartment, packed her bags, and filled her car with gas. As she drove, she tried to call Jules. Each time her call went to voicemail.

She cursed herself for knowing so little about Jules's place of employment. She knew Jules taught high school English in Waco but had no idea what high school. A request to Siri for a list of the high schools in Waco had resulted in a long list of public and private schools. Darcy wasn't even certain Jules taught in a public school.

She pulled into the parking lot of the first Whataburger she saw and called Waco ISD. After being transferred to three different people, she finally reached a woman who tried to help her. She explained that she was Jules Adair Divine's attorney and that she had papers Jules must sign today.

The woman put her on hold for a long time before returning with the phone number and address of the school where Jules taught.

As she pulled back into traffic she instructed her phone to call the number. A woman answered and informed her that Jules was in class and could not be disturbed. "Call back in an hour," the woman said. "School will be out then."

Thirty minutes later, Darcy strolled into the school's office. She flashed her sweetest smile at the receptionist and asked if she could wait in the office for Miss Divine.

The woman told her she was welcome to wait and gestured toward a chair. An attractive redhead watched Darcy through the window of her office. The blonde looked familiar. Raylene Horton tried to put a name with the beautiful face. A sly grin crossed her lips as she recalled her name.

Raylene entered the reception area and held out her hand to Darcy. "I'm Raylene Horton, principal of this high school. How may I help you?"

Darcy stood and shook the principal's hand. "I don't need help, but thank you. I'm just waiting for someone."

"Would you like to wait in my office?" Raylene offered.

"No, I'm good," Darcy replied.

"Aren't you Darcy Lake?" Raylene asked.

Darcy nodded.

"I would consider it a favor if you would wait in my office." Raylene smiled as she turned to walk back to her office, confident that Darcy would follow her.

Darcy passed the receptionist as the bell rang signaling the end of the school day. "If Miss Divine passes by, please tell her I'm here." Darcy handed the receptionist her business card.

"You're a friend of Jules Divine?" Raylene asked once they were settled in her office.

"Yes." Darcy didn't volunteer any information.

"How do you know Jules?" Raylene asked.

"I autographed some books for her." Darcy didn't like the way Raylene was interrogating her. "Is there a problem with me being here?"

"Oh, no! It's just that we seldom have celebrities visit our teachers."

Suddenly, Darcy connected the name Raylene with Jules's year-long relationship. "How long have you been principal here?"

"Two years," Raylene said.

Jules charged into Raylene's office. "Darcy? Oh, my gosh! What are you doing here? I can't believe you're here. This wonderful!"

"I . . . um, came to help you pack."

A brilliant smile spread across Jules's face as she fought the desire to wrap her arms around Darcy's neck and kiss her silly. They gazed at each other, oblivious to the world around them.

"She's the reason you're resigning!" Raylene declared.

"Yes." Jules's eyes danced as she moved closer to Darcy. "You two have met?"

"Yes," Darcy answered. "Miss Horton was kind enough to offer me a comfy chair while I waited for you."

Darcy watched as Raylene's eyes went to the ring Jules was wearing. "What's going on here?" she asked.

"I've asked Jules to marry me, and she agreed to." A twisted smile played on Darcy's lips. "I'm here to help her pack and move her things."

Darcy cupped Jules's elbow and steered her toward the door. "Right now, I just want to go to dinner. I haven't eaten today."

"Neither have I," Jules said. "Let me check my school in-box then I'm all yours."

"What more could one want?" Darcy muttered as she waved goodbye to Raylene.

"I need to take my car to my apartment," Jules said as they walked to the school parking lot.

"Or . . . I could drive you to school in the morning." Darcy blushed at her own audacity.

"I'd like that." Jules linked her arm through Darcy's. "Very much!"

Despite their exhaustive lovemaking, Darcy's sleep was restless. Jules held her as she mumbled and cried out.

"Baby, wake up."

"What?" Darcy jerked awake and tightened her grip on Jules.

"You're so restless." Jules stroked her cheek. "What's wrong?"

Darcy waited for her eyes to focus and then sank deeper into the arms of the woman holding her. She lay still for a long time, luxuriating in Jules's softness.

"Jules, I don't know what to do," Darcy said, turning on the bedside lamp and leaning back against the headboard. "I can't contact my writer, and when I have personal contact with people like Cat they hound me for the next book. If I go to New York, those barracudas will eat me alive. I'm in a mess."

Jules had been so excited to see Darcy that she'd forgotten to share her findings with her. "Honey, I know who your writer is . . . or was."

"Who?"

"My Nana was Darcy Lake." Jules sat up and turned to face Darcy. "Detective West asked me to search Nana's computer and provide her a list of Nana's business contacts. I discovered all the original manuscripts for Darcy Lake's books plus fifteen unfinished books."

"Daphne Divine was Darcy Lake? The wide-eyed look on Darcy's face mirrored her doubts. "The content and style are so different from Daphne's mainstream novels."

"I know," Jules said.

Darcy narrowed her eyes. "Other than inventing an excuse to be with you, why is Tanner West requesting information about Daphne?"

Jules tilted her head as a darkness settled across her features. "Nana was murdered."

"Murdered?" Darcy's eyes opened wider as she looked at Jules. "How? Why?"

"She was injected with rattlesnake poison."

"What? You mean someone intentionally injected her with a hypodermic needle? It wasn't a snakebite?" Darcy was aghast. "That's unbelievable!"

"The information hasn't been released to the newspapers," Jules explained. "Tanner doesn't want the killer to know we're aware that Nana was murdered."

"Oh, Jules, I'm so sorry."

"You've made it easier to deal with Nana's death," Jules said. "Having you in my life makes everything better."

"I'm glad." Darcy pushed a strand of dark hair behind Jules's ear. "It's my intention to make your life better in every way."

"You do, baby." Jules pressed her lips against Darcy's and slowly, methodically, drove her crazy.

Darcy moaned. "I've never kissed anyone who kisses like you do. When you move your lips against mine like that, it goes straight to my core. I can't think straight."

"That is as it should be," Jules mumbled against the blonde's lips.

"I can't thing with you kissing me," Darcy pulled back from Jules. "We need to discuss this. It's quite a shock."

"Do you have all the contacts for Darcy Lake's publisher and agent? Did you give them to Tanner?" Darcy asked.

"I gave Tanner all the contacts for Daphne Divine," Jules said. "I didn't give her the names and contacts of Darcy Lake's handlers.

"They're the people you already know: Cat, Marta, Roz. To them, you are Darcy Lake. They don't even know Nana existed."

"Why would anyone want to kill Daphne Divine?" Darcy searched her mind for answers to her own question.

"I don't know," Jules said. "I thought I would set up Darcy Lake's email accounts on my Outlook and see who ceases to email her. If she was having steady correspondence with someone and it suddenly stops at Nana's death, it would tell us that person knew Darcy Lake the writer was dead."

"I believe you're a sleuth in disguise," Darcy said with a chuckle.

"If Daphne is dead, that means Darcy Lake is dead." Darcy almost choked on her words. "What should I do?"

"To the world, you *are* Darcy Lake," Jules reassured her. "Can you write?"

Darcy half laughed, half snorted. "Legal briefs, interrogation notes, and contracts but nothing as exciting as Daphne wrote."

"She has fifteen unfinished books," Jules mused. "If you could finish them, you could truly become Darcy Lake. Her next book, *Dying to Kill,* is three-fourths finished. It just needs a climax and ending. You could do that."

"I could try," Darcy said reluctantly.

Jules pulled the woman of her dreams into her arms. "You do realize we haven't packed a thing tonight?"

"I can't keep my hands off you." Darcy's voice was low and sexy. "Why don't we consider the time we're together our time, and I'll pack while you're at school?"

"Um, I like the way you think, Darcy Reed."

The next morning, Darcy drove Jules to school and pulled alongside her car in the parking lot. Jules looked around and then leaned in for a kiss.

"That won't hold me until school is out."

"I'll have to work on that," Darcy said, squeezing her hand. "But right now, your redheaded principal is watching us."

"Do you want to go out to dinner tonight?" Jules made small talk to keep herself from climbing into Darcy's lap.

A knowing smile lit Darcy's face as she realized the effect she was having on her lover. "I'll cook," she said.

Jules shook her head, trying to gain control of her emotions. "I better go before I get us arrested." She laughed as she opened the car door.

Darcy watched Jules as she entered the school and was rewarded with a happy wave before the brunette disappeared into the building.

Darcy had lived alone all her life. Out of necessity she had become an excellent cook. A stop at the local grocery market netted her fresh broccoli, orange roughy, and brown rice. She had no trouble finding the ingredients for the glaze she had perfected over the years. She hoped Jules wasn't a bread eater, because Darcy had given up bread years ago. *Another calorie I don't need*, she thought as she passed the bakery.

##

Using the boxes and rolls of Bubble Wrap Jules had on hand, Darcy worked nonstop packing the kitchen. She held out two plates, two coffee cups, two glasses, and silverware for them to use until they left. She texted Jules and asked for a thirty-minute warning before her arrival.

Darcy still found it hard to believe that Daphne Divine had been murdered. She could find no reason why the woman would be killed. No one knew Daphne was the author of the Lake novels. If anyone were trying to extinguish Darcy Lake's career, their target would have been Darcy Reed.

She carried boxes to the extra bedroom where she folded linens and packed them along with videos and CDs. By the end of the day, she had almost packed all of Jules's belongings.

Joy filled her when Jules's ringtone announced a call from the brunette.

"Tell me you're on your way home," she pleaded. "I miss you so much."

"I am." The happiness in Jules's voice was unmistakable. "Do I need to stop by the store or pick up anything for you?"

"No, honey, I've got everything under control. Just hurry."

"See you in thirty," Jules said.

##

By the time Jules arrived, Darcy had showered and was waiting to put the orange roughy on the grill.

"Do I have time for a quick shower?" Jules tiptoed to kiss the lips she had dreamed of all day. "Hmm, I have missed this," she hummed as she pulled Darcy into a deep kiss.

"I'll wait until you shower to put on the fish." Darcy ran her hand down Jules's back and pulled her closer. "You'd better go while you can."

Over dinner they discussed their day. Jules was amazed that Darcy had accomplished so much. "You've packed everything except the essentials we need for the week."

"Next Friday we can pack your toiletries and the few items I haven't packed," Darcy said.

"I had planned to spend the entire weekend packing." A devilish smile played across Jules's face. "Whatever will we do for the next two days?"

Darcy clenched her thighs and tried to hide her eagerness to get the woman into bed with her. She bowed her head, certain her eyes would reveal what she was thinking.

Jules placed her soft hand on Darcy's arm. "That's what I want too."

Darcy lay on her back, fighting to catch her breath. Jules threw her arm and leg over Darcy and pushed tighter against her. "I'm glad you came," Jules murmured into her ear.

"I couldn't stay away," Darcy admitted. "I couldn't work. I couldn't concentrate on anything. I couldn't get you out of my mind long enough to think about anything else."

"Mmm." Jules pushed closer. "I like the sound of that. It wouldn't be right if I were the only one going through that torture."

Jules kissed soft breasts and trailed her hand down Darcy's flat stomach. She chuckled when Darcy sucked in a deep breath. "Tell the truth," Jules whispered. "This is really what you came for, isn't it?"

"Yes." Darcy hissed the word as she exhaled the breath she had drawn in. "I need you."

Chapter 20

Jules sipped her coffee as she watched her lover sleep. She had been with women before, but never had she met someone like Darcy Reed. The woman was gorgeous, intelligent, and the lover most women only dreamed of.

As she watched Darcy sleep, Jules tried to formulate the thought that had been dancing around in her mind since she discovered that Nana was really Darcy Lake.

The literary world only knew blonde, blue-eyed Darcy Reed as Darcy Lake. *What if she can write the Lake novels?* Jules though. *What if she could truly become the author? No one would ever know.*

Darcy stirred in her sleep and reached to Jules's side of the bed. She lay still, wondering where her fiancée was. She sensed that she was being watched and modestly pulled the sheet up to cover her breasts as she turned over and sat up.

"I hate waking up without you beside me," she said, ducking her head and giving Jules her cutest little-girl look.

"Let me get you a cup of coffee, and I'll be right back beside you," Jules said.

"Coffee isn't what I'm wanting."

"Coffee first." Jules laughed at Darcy's pitiful groan. "I have an idea we should discuss."

By the time Jules returned with coffee, Darcy was propped against the headboard leafing through a Darcy Lake novel. "Your grandmother could certainly write a love scene," she commented as Jules handed her the coffee cup, "and an amazing thriller."

Jules settled on the bed facing Darcy. She crossed her legs Indian-style, took a drink of the dark liquid, and cleared her throat.

"This weekend I want you to try writing the ending to the *Dying to Kill* novel," Jules announced.

"No way," Darcy said. "Today and tomorrow have officially been designated as Jules and Darcy time. I promise I will begin working on the novel Monday while you're at school.

"Honestly, I think it will be best if I give it my total attention, which is impossible to do with you close to me. I have nothing to do next week. I've packed everything."

"I understand," Jules said. "So, what should we do?"

"Here, hold my coffee and I'll show you." Darcy chuckled as Jules took both of their cups and placed them on the bedside table.

Jules awoke to find Darcy wrapped around her back. She turned over in Darcy's arms and kissed her lips. "Wake up. I'm hungry."

Darcy tightened her arms around the woman she adored and kissed along her neck. "What would you like to eat?"

"Let's order in a pizza and read what we have of *Dying to Kill*."

"Sounds like the perfect ending to a perfect day." Darcy swung her feet to the floor. "Is it okay if I take a quick shower?"

"Let me order the pizza and then I'll soap your back." Jules gave her a wink as she picked up her iPhone.

##

Darcy stepped from the shower, towel-dried her hair, and slipped on her favorite T-shirt and shorts. As she brushed her hair the doorbell rang. "We couldn't have timed that any better," she said as she grabbed a credit card and headed for the door.

Jules carried her iPad as she settled beside Darcy on the sofa. "Pizza looks great. I've really worked up an appetite."

"I hope you don't mind that I put everything on your coffee table," Darcy explained. "I thought it more conducive to reading and eating."

"Let's eat, and then I'll read the manuscript out loud," Jules suggested. "That's how Nana and I always read the finished book the first time. She said it helped her hear how the book flowed. She made a lot of changes after that first reading."

"You have more experience than I," Darcy said. "Just tell me what to do."

Darcy leaned her back against the sofa arm, and Jules sat between her legs and leaned back against her. "This is much more fun than reading with Nana." Jules giggled and began reading as Darcy hugged her.

"Baby, it's almost two a.m.," Darcy murmured against Jules's neck. "You have to teach today. I suspect it's not good to be exhausted when standing in front of a class of teenagers."

"This book is so good." Jules leaned her head back against Darcy and closed her eyes. "I can't put it down, but you're right. It would be like throwing chum in the water to show up unprepared for a class. They would eat me alive."

Jules stood and yawned as she held out her hand to Darcy. "Promise me you won't finish reading it without me."

"Okay," Darcy said. "What should I do all day?"

"I'll leave you my laptop so you can search through Nana's emails and her works-in-progress folder. There may be correspondence you need to answer."

"I need to check into the office too," Darcy added. "I'm certain Lana has everything under control, but I need to let her know she can call if she needs me."

Jules was asleep as soon as her head touched her pillow. Darcy slipped into bed and snuggled up against her. She couldn't remember ever being as happy as she was at that moment.

##

Darcy wandered through the apartment, double-checking her handiwork. Each box was securely taped closed and had a perfectly lettered list of items inside. She checked with her office and found that everything was running smoothly. She fought the temptation to read the rest of *Dying to Kill* but knew Jules would be disappointed if she read without her.

She checked Jules's pantry for spices and canned goods and then drove to the local market and purchased what she needed to cook the next four days.

Darcy killed an hour making meatloaf and scalloped potatoes. Then she carried Jules's laptop from the bedroom to the kitchen island. Sitting on a stool and drinking coffee, she began the arduous task of wading through Daphne's Darcy Lake emails.

"Jesus, no wonder the women came on to me at the conventions," Darcy muttered. "The old bird shamelessly flirted with them online. They thought it was me."

Then she read through an email exchange between Darcy Lake and someone with the name of Neadi Love. Neadi had started conversing with Lake on Facebook too. She "loved" everything the author posted and made short, flirty comments on Lake's posts.

Darcy scanned through Daphne's personal messages and found the conversations between Neadi and Darcy Lake. She scrolled to the beginning of their exchange.

Their conversation went from harmless flirting to declarations of love from both Daphne and Neadi. Neadi was in her forties and either had been or was married. Darcy read the last message Daphne had received from the woman.

"You broke my heart today," Neadi wrote. "I traveled all the way to Dallas to meet you, to spend some time with you. Imagine my surprise when you showed up with your gorgeous wife. I guess I'm a glutton for punishment because I stayed the entire weekend, watching you touch her and steal a kiss when you thought no one was looking. I was watching, and my heart still dies every time that scene replays in my mind. Goodbye, my beloved, Darcy. I hope your beautiful wife loves you just half as much as I do."

Darcy Reed leaned back and rolled her head around to ease the stiffness in her neck. She had been reading Daphne's emails and Facebook postings for hours. The woman was fascinating. She wondered if Jules had any idea what a genius her grandmother was.

I can't write conclusions to her books, Darcy thought. *I couldn't even write the sexy, witty Facebook posts she wrote.*

As she shut down the computer, her cellphone dinged with a text message from Jules. "Principal called a last-minute meeting. I won't be home until five-thirty."

Good, that will give me time to get dinner ready. Darcy set the oven on preheat and pulled two cans of cut green beans from the pantry. She sliced the potatoes and poured her cream sauce over them. She had just enough time to cook everything before Jules came home.

##

"Home cooking!" Jules's eyes danced as she surveyed the meal Darcy had prepared for them. "All this and you're smoking hot in bed too. How did I get so lucky?"

She slipped her arms around Darcy's neck and flattened her body against the blonde. "Um, have you noticed we just fit?" she murmured.

"In every way," Darcy said, savoring the kiss she had waited for all day.

"Color me breathless," Jules mumbled against lips she craved.

"Go change for dinner while I make tea I can't wait to tell you what I learned today."

Over dinner, Darcy told Jules about the online affair Daphne had carried on with Neadi Love. "She said she went to the book convention in Dallas and was heartbroken that I had my gorgeous wife there and kissed you in public."

"Do you think she would have killed Nana in a fit of jealousy?" Jules asked.

"I don't know, but shouldn't we give this information to Detective West?"

"I don't think so," Jules replied. "If she saw you at the convention and knew you were Darcy Lake, she wouldn't kill Nana. Nana looked nothing like you. Besides Nana was already dead at that time.

"No, I think whoever killed Nana knew they were killing Daphne Divine. Nana was already dead when Neadi Love sent her the last message."

"That makes sense," Darcy said.

After dinner, they assumed their positions on the sofa and Jules began to read *Dying to Kill*. Darcy couldn't stop kissing the back of Jules's neck and whispering indecent proposals into her ear.

Jules let her iPad slip to the floor as she succumbed to her partner's suggestions. She turned over to lie on Darcy's stomach. "You are so gorgeous," she said as she nibbled at the blonde's lips. "So desirable."

"Obviously there is no desire on my part," Darcy teased as she slid her fingers beneath Jules's blouse and unfastened her bra. "No desire at all."

Later Jules rested her ear over Darcy's heart and smiled knowing that she was the reason it was beating double time. "You could give a girl a coronary," Darcy said, gasping.

"It's not like you didn't beg for it," Jules reminded her.

"Umm, so worth it," Darcy mumbled.

They held each other a long time. Finally, Jules broke the sweet silence.

"Are you awake?" she whispered.

"Yes, I thought you'd fallen asleep."

"No, I'm just lying here loving the feel of you. I don't even know the words to tell you how much I love you and how you make me feel."

"I'm certain I know," Darcy said. "The feeling is mutual.

"Want to finish reading your grandmother's book?" Darcy asked as she massaged Jules's back.

"Um, as much as I hate to move, I would like to know what happens in the book. You must promise not to seduce me while I'm reading."

Darcy laughed. "I'm making no promises."

##

"That's it? That's all we have?" Darcy squealed when Jules closed her iPad.

"That's it. You'll have to finish it."

"Honey, I'm not sure I can." The frown on Darcy's face convinced Jules she was serious. "Your grandmother was an incredible writer with the most unbelievable imagination. I could never fabricate those twists and subtleties she weaves throughout a story.

"I mean. . . how would you end this story? I still have no idea who the killer is."

"Nana always said to think of a story you would love to read and write it. That's what she did."

"I can't believe someone killed all that talent," Darcy scowled.

##

Friday came quickly, and Darcy was no closer to writing an appropriate ending to *Dying to Kill* than she had been the first time Jules read the manuscript to her.

How did Daphne write like that? she thought as she crumbled the sheets that were still warm from the printer. *This sucks! A fifth-grader could write better than this.*

A text message dinged into her cellphone. She smiled, sure it was Jules. To her surprise the message was from her partner, Lana Weidman. "Are you up to defending a murder case?"

Darcy hated defending murderers, rapists, and child molesters. She refused to do it unless she was positive they were innocent.

"Is the accused innocent?" she responded.

"Not sure."

"Then, no," Darcy answered.

"Should I turn away the business?" Lana was all about the bottom line of their law firm. Darcy was all about integrity, morality, and cases they could win in court.

"Please do."

"Your call," Lana texted back. "Would you at least come to the office and meet with him?"

"Monday, ok?"

"Thanks. See you Monday." Lana ended the exchange with a smiley face emoji.

Darcy stared at the blinking cursor on her screen. *My mind can't make the flights of fantasy that Daphne could conjure.*

A text from Jules lit up her screen. "I am on my way to you."

"God, I've missed you," Darcy responded. "Movers picked up everything this morning. It should be in storage by now. Everything else is packed and ready to leave."

"Can't wait to see you," Jules answered.

"FYI. I suck as a writer," Darcy texted.

Chapter 21

"It is so good to get back home," Jules said with a sigh as she opened the massive entryway door and allowed Darcy to enter.

"Nana's car and SUV are still parked in the other garage," Jules explained. "You can leave your car in the courtyard until I make arrangements to do something with her vehicles."

Darcy nodded and began helping Jules unload her personal things from the two cars. "Let's unload everything and then have dinner at that little restaurant you took me to the first time I spent the night with you."

"That seems like ages ago." Jules flashed her a sexy smile as she carried a box into the Manse.

"It does seem as if you've always been a part of my life," Darcy said. "The best part of it."

"I promise you it will only get better." Jules placed her box on the dresser in her bathroom and watched as Darcy placed her box on the loveseat.

"There's no doubt in my mind." Darcy pulled Jules into her arms soft and slow. "No doubt at all." The world around them disappeared as their lips met and their tongues engaged in a sensuous duet that both knew would end in lovemaking.

##

Jules rolled onto her side and traced Darcy's lips with her fingertips. "Do you believe I love Darcy Reed the woman?" she said softly.

"Yes." Darcy caught her hand and kissed her fingertips. "No one could make love the way you do if it weren't real."

"We should shower if we're going to mingle with others." Jules continued to trace the lines of Darcy's beautiful face. "So gorgeous."

"Or we could order Chinese and stay here," Darcy suggested as she caressed Jules's back. "Restaurant personnel get so upset when I fondle you."

Jules rolled onto her back and laughed out loud. "I love the silly side of you."

"I'm glad, because you make me feel like a teenager." Darcy's open appraisal of Jules's breasts made both blush.

"If you want Chinese, we need to order it now. They close at ten. I'll order the delivery. Why don't you let me see what you've written on Nana's story?"

"It isn't good," Darcy said as she pulled on an oversized T-shirt and running shorts. "Honey, I don't think I can write, make public appearances, and practice law too. Honestly, I make a lot of money from my law practice. I've no idea what Daphne made from the sales of Darcy Lake books."

As they waited for the deliveryman, Jules read Darcy's attempt at finishing the book. "You're right, baby, you're no fiction writer."

Darcy accepted the criticism good-naturedly. "I told you. It's awful."

Both jumped when the doorbell announced the arrival of the deliveryman. "What's going on down there?" Darcy asked as she paid him.

"Dunno," he grunted as he followed Darcy's gaze. "Bunch of cops and an ambulance. Everyone's running around like a chicken with its head cut off."

"Honey, come here for a minute," Darcy called to Jules as the man lumbered toward his car. "Isn't that your friends we met at the Founders Day festival?"

"Yes. And it's the second time in a month that an ambulance has been at their house. Do you think Ashley fell down the stairs again?"

"The police are there too," Darcy pointed out. "Were they called last time?"

"Not that I know of." Jules watched as a white, unmarked vehicle backed into the driveway. "Who is that?"

"A coroner's van," Darcy whispered as if the officials below them would hear. "Almost all departments are changing to unmarked coroner's vans."

"That means . . ."

"Yeah," Darcy whispered. "I wonder what happened."

They watched as a body bag was wheeled from the house and placed into the back of the white van. An unmarked car pulled into the driveway beside the van and a woman got out. Jules recognized the confident walk of Tanner West. The detective spoke at length with the driver of the van and then sauntered toward the house.

Before she entered the murder scene, Tanner glanced up the hill to see if lights were on in Jules's home. She smiled when she saw that they were. She frowned when she spotted two women standing in the courtyard.

Darcy looked out the window as she sipped her coffee.

"Must you go to work tomorrow?" Jules hugged Darcy from behind and pulled her tight against her stomach. "After being with you continuously, I'm having withdrawal pains just thinking about you leaving."

"I'll be back in time for dinner." Darcy leaned into the softness behind her as she watched a squirrel scale the wall behind the Manse. "I can see why you love it here. It's a haven from the rest of the world."

"Yes, and having you here makes it perfect." Jules kissed across Darcy's shoulder and up her neck. "Let's make the most of tonight before you leave in the morning," she murmured in her lover's ear.

Chapter 22

Tanner West watched through the one-way glass as her partner questioned Roy Craft. Craft had returned home from work to find his wife badly beaten and dying. He had called 911 and then tried to revive her, wallowing in blood as he gave her mouth-to-mouth resuscitation. By the time the ambulance and police had arrived, Roy was covered in Ashley's blood and had compromised the crime scene.

Angry at the man for being so stupid, Tanner had arrested him on the spot as a suspect. She was certain he hadn't murdered his wife, but he'd certainly made it impossible for forensics to determine who had. Thanks to Roy, the Forensic Pathology Panel Report was useless when it came to identifying DNA.

She scanned the FPPR the medical examiner had just handed her. Ashley had been beaten to death. Only Roy's DNA was smeared all over the crime scene. Roy's salty tears, his saliva, and even his vomit had contaminated everything else. She wished she could pin the murder on the idiot.

Medical Examiner Shannon Freeman's handwritten note caught her attention. "She had consensual sex prior to dying."

Tanner closed her eyes to think. Unfortunately, the battered face of Ashley Craft floated in her mind. Beaten to death! Tanner wondered if the average Joe even realized what an atrocious act of violence that was; what it took to beat the life from another human being; how angry the assailant had to be to inflict such damage. Breaking a nose didn't do it. Crushing cheekbones didn't do it. Kicks to the torso didn't end a life. It was a culmination of all the violence that climaxed when a final kick was delivered beneath the chin, severing the windpipe. Tanner knew all too well.

Ashley Craft had died violently, killed by someone in a rage. Someone with the strength and size of her husband. Tanner was rethinking her appraisal of Roy Craft. Maybe she could pin the murder on him.

Tanner returned her focus to the interrogation and watched her partner, Detective Pat Patterson, lean over the table, his face inches from Roy's. Roy shrank back, obviously intimidated by the burly detective. *Hell, I'm intimidated by Pattie*, Tanner thought as she watched Patterson leave the interrogation room.

A minute later, Pattie joined her in the observation room. "I don't know, Tanner. The fecker' may have killed her."

Tanner hid her amusement at Pattie's Irish accent. He was the only man she knew who could get away with profanity in any situation.

"Let's send him home and put a tail on him. Maybe we can figure out what he's up to."

Pattie nodded. "I questioned the neighbors, and they all said Mrs. Craft was hospitalized a couple of weeks ago. Said she fell down the stairs. I'm going to see what I can find out from the hospital."

"Good idea. Did you question the woman in the house on the hill?" Tanner asked.

"Jules Divine? Nah" Pattie couldn't hide his blush. "It was late and she'd just lost her mother and all. I thought I'd interview her today. She's single, you know."

Tanner nodded as she studied Pattie. "You like her?"

"What's not to like?" A huge smile spread across Pattie's face. "She's gorgeous . . . legs that go on forever and real nice. Do you think she'd go out wit' me?"

"I believe she's with someone." Tanner grimaced as she admitted to herself that Jules was off the market.

"Really?" Pattie grimaced. "Who? I mean, is it anyone from around here?"

"No, a lawyer from Dallas."

"What's his name?"

"Her name is Darcy Reed." Tanner tried to appear noncommittal. She reached out and closed Pattie's gaping mouth.

"She's a lesbian?" Pattie made a choking sound.

"How long have you lived in this town?" Tanner asked.

"All my life," Pattie answered with pride in his voice. "Second generation American. My Granda and Granny came to America on their honeymoon and stayed."

"I guess you don't attend the First Baptist Church?" Tanner said, chuckling.

"Irish Catholic," Pattie declared.

"Then you don't know about the Reverend Divine and his daughter Jules?"

"I thought Daphne Divine was her mother." Pattie frowned.

"Legally, she is, but by birth she's the daughter of Reverend Warren and Martha Divine. They disowned her when she declared she was a lesbian."

"Oh." Pattie shook his head slowly. "What a waste."

"There are those who would argue with you about that," Tanner said.

"You've only been here seven years," Pattie pointed out. "How do you know so much that I don't?"

"I pay attention," Tanner said with a shrug.

Pattie assimilated his newly acquired information, as he walked to the door. "I'll just go kick Craft loose."

Tanner watched Pattie as he spoke to Roy Craft. Pattie was handsome. At six-two and 195 pounds, he was a great backup to have in a fight. A favorite of the ladies, his curly strawberry-blond hair made him look like an angel. Although the women climbed all over him, he had specific things he was looking for in a woman. That she be a lady was the main requirement.

Long after Pattie took Roy away, Tanner sat in the darkness of the observation room. Two murders had been committed in her quiet little town, and she had no leads on either of them. There was no evidence to tie anyone to the killings. Both murders had taken place in the shadows of the house everyone called the Manse.

Pattie's voice interrupted her thoughts. "You want to get some lunch?"

"Sure," Tanner said as she held up the FPPR. "Let's stop by Shannon's first. I need to ask her something."

Pattie's grunted reply reminded Tanner how much the younger detective hated the morgue. *You need to get used to dead bodies if you're going to survive in this profession*, she thought.

Shannon Freeman was the epitome of dedication. Although she was one of the youngest members of the police organization, her credentials were impressive. To Tanner's knowledge, Shannon had never missed a clue on a body or at a crime scene.

The petite ME was standing on a stool so she could look down on a body. A smile broke the solemnness of her pretty face as she spoke to Pattie and Tanner. "What brings you to my domain?" She noticed both detectives had on the blue booties required to enter the autopsy room. "Thanks for putting those on."

"I have a question about your note on Mrs. Craft's forensic report." Tanner noticed how Pattie gave Shannon the once-over. *You could do worse*, she thought. "You said she had consensual sex before she died."

Shannon nodded.

"Was it with a male or a female?" Tanner asked.

"Female," Shannon said as she climbed down from the stool. "She had consensual intercourse with a female about two hours before she died. There was no tearing and no semen."

"How do you know it was a female?" Pattie asked. "Could have been a man wearing a condom."

Shannon glared at him. "Depth of penetration. Slight abrasions on soft tissue inside. I'm saying fingernails. There are several differences between a male penis and fingers, Detective Patterson.

"Condom manufacturers use substances known as exchangeable traces, which comprise particulates, lubricants, and spermicide. There was no trace of that, so I'm certain no condom was used."

Pattie shrugged. "You're the forensic pathologist, Doc. I was just asking for my own information. It's good to know these things."

"Because you do a large number of autopsies," Shannon huffed.

Tanner gave her partner a "shut up" look and asked another question. "Can you give us a time of death?"

"Around 6 p.m."

"Roy called 911 after eight," Pattie noted. "He said he had just gotten in from work."

"Check his garage and see if his employees will vouch for his whereabouts." Tanner said. "I'm going to pay Miss Divine a visit and see if she saw or heard anything."

Chapter 23

Jules made her third cup of coffee and then returned to Nana's computer. She sent an email to Neadi Love but received no response. She found several emails from Darcy's beta reader, Marta Wayne. Nana flirted with Marta as if she were as young and beautiful as Darcy Lake. Marta flirted back. No wonder the beta thought there was something special between her and Darcy.

Marta's last email had given Nana a date of May thirty-first to receive the *Dying to Kill* manuscript. The email was after Nana's death. Marta didn't know the Darcy Lake author was dead.

A text dinged into Jules's phone, and Darcy's face filled the screen. She couldn't stop smiling when she realized the woman she loved was reaching out to her. She opened the text.

"In a boring meeting. I miss you so much. Having a terrible day without you. Can't wait to get home to you."

Jules fought the urge to call her but settled for a text message since Darcy was in a meeting. "Can't wait until you're home in my arms, kissing my lips and . . ."

"Umm, you're killing me." Darcy had attached her avatar that looked like it was in severe pain. Jules laughed out loud.

"I love you so much," she responded.

"Love you more," Darcy replied. "I'll be home as soon as the meeting is over."

"Hurry."

Jules drained the last bit of coffee from her cup and returned to the kitchen to make more but decided on a small can of cold Dr. Pepper instead. She wandered onto the patio and settled into the soft cushion of a chair facing the pool.

She closed her eyes and Tanner immediately crossed her mind. Tanner was so confident everything was black and white. Jules knew she should give her the information about Nana and Darcy Lake, but something stopped her.

It was Nana's secret. The thought hit her like a bolt of lightning. Nana had defended Jules as a lesbian, but had chosen to hide the fact that she was one. *Or was she?*

Although Nana had written the Darcy Lake novels, Jules had found nothing that would indicate that Nana had ever been involved with a woman. If she was, Nana had gone to great lengths to hide it. *No, I won't out her to the world.*

Jules could see her father's smirking face if he learned that Nana was a lesbian. "That explains why she insisted on taking in Jules," he would say with an expression that indicated something sordid and evil.

"I won't let anything sully Nana's name," Jules said out loud.

The Manse's door chime began playing Abba's song. *That's what I get for leaving the gate open for Darcy,* Jules thought. *We must sync her car with the gate opener.*

Reluctant to have her reverie disturbed, Jules ignored the chime. It rang again. She walked into the house and recognized Tanner's tall frame shifting from one foot to the other outside her door.

"Hello, Tanner." Jules smiled at the detective as she stepped back to allow her entrance into the house. "What's going on at Ashley and Roy's?"

"You haven't heard? Ashley was murdered yesterday."

It felt as if an icy hand had gripped Jules's heart. She staggered to the sofa and slumped into it. "Who would want to kill Ashley? She was one of the sweetest people I've ever met."

Tanner tilted her head and studied Jules for several seconds. "So was Daphne," she said.

Jules seemed to crumble. She buried her face in her hands and sobbed. "Tanner, what is going on in our town?"

Tanner sat down beside Jules and pulled her into her arms. "I'm sorry," she murmured into Jules's hair. "I could've broken that to you a little more gently."

Jules's sobs slowed as she leaned against Tanner's shoulder. It felt safe in Tanner's arms. *I wish Darcy would hurry home. I belong in her arms.*

Tanner released Jules as she pulled away from her and stood. "I'm sorry," Jules said as she walked into the powder room to get a box of tissues.

Tanner walked to the window overlooking the pool. She breathed deeply. She couldn't quell the dull ache Jules had aroused in her. She couldn't drive the softness and fragrance of the woman from her mind.

"I didn't mean to fall apart like that," Jules said as she joined Tanner by the window. "I was having a cold drink on the patio. Would you like to join me?"

"Yes, thank you."

Jules headed for the kitchen to get Tanner a soda, and the two moved to the patio.

"It's nice outside," Jules said as Tanner settled in a chair across from her. "I hate to see such gorgeous weather go to waste."

"Jules, I've spoken to all of Daphne's contacts at her publishing company. All of them were at a book conference in Dublin when Daphne died. Most of them thought Daphne was supposed to attend the affair. I checked airline and hotel reservations. I found no evidence that your grandmother planned to attend the conference."

"I haven't found anything to indicate she was planning a trip." Jules frowned as she recalled the invitation to the Dallas book convention. Nana hadn't planned to go to that either. She hadn't made hotel reservations.

It suddenly occurred to Jules that it was strange that Nana had received the complimentary ticket to the lesbian literary convention. *Who knew Nana was a lesbian or thought she was?*

Suddenly, Tanner pulled her back to the present. "Jules, how long have you known Darcy Reed?"

"I was introduced to her when I was twenty," Jules said, twisting the truth. In a way, she had always known and loved Darcy.

"It just seems strange that she showed up so quickly after Daphne died," Tanner said.

A spark flashed in Jules's eyes. "She was Nana's attorney and handled her will," she snapped, coming quickly to Darcy's defense. "She had nothing to do with Nana's death. To even imply that she might have is . . . . You should leave." Jules jumped to her feet, her drink sloshing on the table.

"Jules," Tanner said, moving quickly to catch Jules by the arm and spin her around. "I didn't mean anything by that comment. I was just being—"

"An ass," Darcy said as she suddenly appeared in the doorway. "Detective West, I believe you have your hands on someone that belongs to me."

Tanner and Jules stared in stunned silence as Darcy marched over to Jules's side. "I'll show you out," she said to Tanner.

As soon as the two women were out of sight, Jules hurried to her bedroom and slammed the door. She was furious. She didn't belong to anyone. She needed to think. The dark look of fury on Darcy's face was both terrifying and spellbinding. A soft knock a few minutes later told Jules the woman was at her door.

"Come in," Jules croaked swallowing hard against the lump in her throat.

Darcy entered before Jules could make her voice work again. "What's wrong, honey?"

Jules backed away until she stood against the wall. Darcy advanced slowly as a scowl wrinkled her forehead. Jules could tell by the look on Darcy's face that she was genuinely concerned, but a hint of anger still lingered in her eyes.

"Jules, what's wrong?"

"I don't belong to anyone," Jules said, her voice squeaking.

Darcy placed her hands on the wall on either side of Jules's head, trapping her without touching her. Jules held her breath. Darcy slowly lowered her lips to Jules's as softly as a butterfly's kiss.

Jules exhaled slowly, and the sweetness of her soft breath seemed to ignite desire in Darcy. She pressed her body against Jules's as she deepened the kiss. Lips moved against each other as soft strokes heightened passion. Tongues caressed, retracted, and then possessed each other.

Jules lost track of time and place. She was only aware of the way Darcy was possessively moving her hands over her body, touching her, inflaming her, owning her.

"Please," Jules whispered.

Ignoring her plea, Darcy continued to trail fingertips down Jules's body as her other hand deftly unbuttoned Jules's blouse. Jules moaned as Darcy's soft lips left hers and moved hungrily down her body, setting fire to every part they touched.

She threw her head back, hitting the wall, as Darcy used her tongue to draw circles around her nipple and her hands roamed Jules's body. There seemed to be no place her lover was leaving untouched. She set fire to every inch of Jules's being.

"Please, Darcy, please," Jules' begged as she dug her nails into Darcy's back. She found the zipper to Darcy's dress and pulled it down. In seconds the blonde was almost naked.

"Bed," Jules gasped as Darcy continued to stroke and tantalize her. In one smooth motion, Darcy picked up her lover and carried her to the bed. She gently placed Jules on the comforter and then stood looking down at her.

"You know what I like," Jules murmured, her eyes black as onyx as she writhed on the bed. Darcy left the room and returned in minutes.

"Yes." Jules's breath escaped slowly as Darcy settled between her legs and began to rub her hands up and down her thighs. She leaned forward, touching where Jules needed her most, as she sucked and caressed breasts taut with need.

"Darcy, please." Jules fisted blonde hair and pulled her lover down on her. "Please."

"Why?" Darcy asked.

For a moment, the haze of desire cleared as Jules realized what Darcy was asking.

"Why, Jules? Why should I do this to you?"

"Because you own me," Jules cried. "Because I belong to you. Because I love you more than life itself."

"And no one else can put their hands on you." Darcy's voice was deep and demanding as she continued to stroke and caress Jules.

"Only you," Jules cried as she arched toward Darcy, trying to get what she craved. "Please don't tease me anymore. You know I belong to you."

"Don't ever forget it," Darcy murmured into her ear as she lowered her body and covered Jules from head to toe with searing-hot lust, an emotion so powerful nothing could stand in its way.

"I . . . I can't get enough of you." Jules begged for more as Darcy's strong arms held her tight against her and she moved to please her.

##

"Are you okay?" Darcy's lips moved against her skin, barely a whisper, yet the words thundered in Jules's mind.

"I'll never be okay again," Jules whispered. "I'll never be whole without you."

"You'll always be safe with me." Darcy kissed her lips.\ "I'll never let you down or disappoint you. I love you, Jules Divine. With every breath I take I love you more. You're mine and I belong to you heart and soul."

They lay together, whispering promises and words of love, reveling in the silky softness of each other, knowing that they completed each other in every way. They dozed, made love, and slept again.

Dawn heralded the sun's full arrival as Jules pushed closer to the woman in her bed. A twinge of soreness reminded her of their night of amorous lovemaking. She clenched her thighs together, trying to quell the rising desire pooling below her stomach. As if reading her needs, Darcy placed a hand on her and gently stroked her as she slid her other arm under Jules's waist and pulled her closer.

"Does someone in this bed belong to me?" Darcy whispered in her ear. Her warm breath and soft lips sent shockwaves through Jules's body.

"Oh God, yes," Jules moaned.

Later, Jules lay with her head on Darcy's shoulder. She let her fingers trail sensuously across Darcy's stomach and up to her perfect breasts. "Do you have to go to the office today?"

"No, I plan to spend the day indulging in you," Darcy said with a chuckle. The words sent tremors down Jules's body.

"What happened last night with Tanner?" Jules asked. "I've never seen you like that."

"Nothing has ever affected me like that," Darcy said. "It was an emotion I've never experienced in my life."

"What?"

Darcy paused for a minute, deep in thought. "Jealously. I was consumed with jealousy when I saw Tanner's hands on you. It was a horrible feeling."

"It is an emotion you need never experience again." Jules kissed her. "As you proved last night, I'm yours."

Darcy breathed deeply and stroked Jules's back.

"Let's go skinny-dipping," Jules said, eager to lighten the mood. "Last one in has to cook breakfast."

They hit the floor running, streaked through the great room, out the patio door, and dove into the pool. Neither of them saw Renee Baxter standing at the kitchen island.

Jules pushed Darcy against the pool wall as they disappeared behind the waterfall. "Have you ever been fu…"—urgent kisses cut her off— "…in a swimming pool?"

"No, but I'm willing." Darcy tossed her head to get the hair out of her eyes. "I'll do anything you want."

"I'm going to like belonging to you." Jules's mouth melded with her lover's.

An hour later they emerged from the pool. Darcy looked around for towels. "We can't track water through your house," she said, scowling.

Jules caught her hand and led her to a door at the side of the house. "Pool bathroom," Jules explained as she keyed in a code that unlocked the door.

They laughed and kissed as they dried each other. Then Jules pulled two pairs of cargo shorts and T-shirts from the closet. "I believe I hit the water first," she said, casting a steamy look at Darcy. "You can cook breakfast or . . ."

"Breakfast it is." Darcy threw her head back and laughed. "You're killing me, woman."

They looked at each other as the smell of coffee brewing and bacon frying greeted them when they entered the great room.

"About time you got up," Renee said as she handed them both a cup of coffee. "I need to get started on cleaning the house."

Jules made the introductions. "Renee took care of the house for Nana and now she helps us."

Darcy gave Renee her best smile. The one that lit up a room and made anyone close to her want to kiss the little dimples on each side of her lips.

"Sit," Renee commanded as she placed plates of bacon and eggs in front of the two. "Do you like butter on your toast, Darcy?"

"Yes, please." Darcy placed her hand against the small of Jules's back and applied pressure as the brunette leaned into her touch before moving forward to sit on the island stool.

"Have you eaten breakfast?" Darcy asked

"No, I was running late this morning." Renee looked down, hoping they wouldn't see the smile playing at the corner of her lips. "I just arrived."

"Please join us," Darcy insisted. "We'll be out of your way soon. We have a few errands to run."

The three visited over breakfast, laughing and talking. The conversation soon took a solemn turn as they discussed the death of Ashley Craft.

"She was so sweet and kind to everyone," Renee said.

"Did you know her well?" Jules asked.

"Yes, I kept house for her too. Although I think she needed me more for the company than the housework. You know, Roy wouldn't let her work and didn't like it if she went out without him."

"We met them at the Founders Day festival," Darcy said. "She was quiet. In fact, I don't think she said a word."

"No, she wouldn't." Renee frowned. "She hasn't spoken since she miscarried their baby."

Darcy shook her head. "That's a real shame. Did they have any children?"

"No," Renee replied. "I cleaned their house the day before she was murdered. My son, Brandon, helped me rehang a drape that had been torn down. I still can't figure out how they pulled it down."

Darcy stacked Jules's plate on top of hers and carried them to the sink.

"Don't take my job," Renee said, laughing. "Leave the dishes. You two have things to do, so scoot."

"Would you start with the other side of the house, first?" Jules requested.

Darcy followed Jules into the bedroom to get their shoes. Jules locked the door behind them.

"I'm beginning to recognize that look." Darcy flashed her dimples, destroying any thread of control Jules had.

"Then you know what I want," Jules murmured, her voice low and sexy.

"What about Renee?"

"She won't hear a thing. This house is virtually soundproof."

"Don't scream out my name." An impish grin danced on Darcy's face. "I don't want her to think I'm doing something carnal to you."

"But you're going to, aren't you?" Jules looked up at her through long dark lashes.

"Of course I am."

Chapter 24

"Where are we going?" Jules asked as Darcy pulled her car from the driveway.

"I don't like all the violence in your neighborhood." Darcy glanced at her lover. "I'm not trying to move in, because I know how you feel about U-Haul romances, but I would feel better if I'm with you at night. Just until they catch Daphne and Ashley's killers."

"Is that the only reason you want to be with me at night?" Jules played with the blonde hair at the nape of Darcy's neck.

"What do you think?" Darcy grinned. "But, seriously, I am concerned about you. I can't figure out what's going on."

They discussed the emails from Marta Wayne and the unknown woman, Neadi Love.

"Obviously a phony name," Darcy said.

"Yes. Marta kept emailing Nana after her death, but Neadi stopped communication after the convention in Dallas.

"Tanner said Nana entertained a woman in her house the night she died," Jules added.

"Have you told Tanner about Nana's lesbian email pals?"

"No." Jules frowned. "If Nana was a lesbian, she went to great lengths to hide it. I'm not going to expose her if I can help it."

"If it begins to look like someone from our community killed her, you'll have to," Darcy said.

The smooth motion of the car and exhaustion from their all-night activities quickly lulled Jules into a deep sleep. Darcy rested her hand on Jules's leg and tried to focus on the road. She was content.

Jules was still asleep when they reached Darcy's condo. "Wake up, Sleeping Beauty. We're here." Darcy brushed her lips against Jules's.

Jules's eyes fluttered open as Darcy's lips increased their pressure and kissed her deeply. "I'm just going to pack my toiletries and pick up a few dresses to make it through the week," Darcy explained as she opened the car door.

Jules followed her into the lobby of one of Dallas's most elite condo-home complexes.

"I knew you'd live in a place like this," Jules said as she looked at the building. Everything around her screamed money.

Darcy nodded as the impeccable doorman greeted them. "Good afternoon, Miss Reed." His surreptitious glance at Jules did not go unnoticed.

"Afternoon, Paul." Darcy placed her hand on Jules's back and steered her toward the elevators. "Don't grope me," Darcy warned as the elevator doors closed. "There are cameras everywhere."

The elevator went to the top floor and opened into Darcy's penthouse.

"You own the penthouse?" Jules's eyes widened as she touched expensive paintings and vases.

Darcy was pleased that Jules was impressed. It was important to the attorney that Jules knew she was wealthy too. She never wanted money to be an issue between them.

##

They discussed their future on the way back to the Manse. Darcy would divide her time between her Dallas office and establishing an office in Jules's hometown. She would help Jules settle all the legal aspects of Daphne Divine's estate.

"It is a simple matter to change the IRS and banking forms on Amazon since you have the password for the account. I'll handle that for you," Darcy said. "Daphne put everything else in your name when I drew up the will for her, so that is already handled."

"What should I do about Darcy Lake?" Jules asked.

"I'm not certain," Darcy said. "We don't know if your grandmother's murderer intended to kill Daphne Divine or Darcy Lake. For the time being, let's keep Darcy Lake alive."

When they arrived at the Manse, Jules was surprised to see her gate open. Then she noticed a landscaping truck across the street with the motto "Take a Chance on Me" written across the side. Beneath that was the name of the business—Chance Landscaping—a phone number and website address. She smiled as she thought of the young woman Nana had helped.

"This closet is huge," Darcy declared as she hung up her dresses. "While attending college, I lived in houses smaller than this."

"Like you,"—Jules gestured toward the heels Darcy was placing under each dress—"Nana coordinated everything: purses, shoes, dresses, you name it."

"We award-winning authors have to present a certain image." Suddenly, Darcy seemed lost in time. "That's what Daphne taught me."

"We need to sync your car with the gate and garage door openers," Jules declared as they walked down the long hall to the kitchen. "Knowing Nana, she has a file somewhere titled, *Instructions*. It's probably in her file cabinet."

Darcy wandered toward the back window as Jules entered Nana's office.

"Honey," Darcy called, "there's an Amazon in our backyard."

Jules chuckled as she slipped her arm through Darcy's. Together, they watched Chance stroll across their yard, her muscles straining against her T-shirt as she bent over to examine something in the grass.

Darcy's face was an open question as she looked at Jules for an answer.

"Nana's yard service," Jules said, suppressing a smile. "You aren't going to be jealous of her too, are you?"

Darcy kissed Jules with such fervor that it took her breath away. "I'm guessing that since you're with me, you don't go for that type."

"Um, you guessed right," Jules said.

They jumped when their gaze returned to the window to find Chance peering in at them. She smiled and motioned for them to come out on the patio.

Jules introduced Darcy to Chance.

"Wow, you're gorgeous," the young woman said.

Darcy failed miserably in her attempt to hide the blush that crept up her neck and onto her cheeks.

"I'm sorry," Chance said. "I didn't mean to be so forward. It's just that you took me by surprise."

"Thank you." Darcy looked down, obviously embarrassed by the scrutiny of the other woman.

Jules laced her fingers through Darcy's. "Darcy is my fiancée," she said, beaming with pride.

"Again, I meant no disrespect," Chance said.

Darcy took control of the situation. She liked the young woman and wanted to put her at ease. "It's no problem. By the way, you do a splendid job of keeping the grounds looking perfect."

"Thanks." Chance flashed her smile, showing off beautiful white teeth. "I need to spray insecticide today. It isn't harmful to humans, but if you have a small dog you probably want to keep it inside until the spray dries completely. They tend to get it on their feet and lick it off."

"We're going to Sabello's for an early dinner," Jules informed Chance, "so, do whatever you need to do. We won't be in your way."

##

"How did Daphne happen to hire Chance?" Darcy asked as they slid into their favorite booth.

Jules related the story with pride. "I'm finding more and more people who Nana helped. She never mentioned them to me, especially you."

"Yes, I guess I was quite a surprise." Darcy chuckled.

"Does Chance take care of many yards in your neighborhood?"

"Twenty, I think." Jules tried to recall the conversation she'd had with Chance. "Including Roy Craft's yard."

"She should be proud," Darcy said. "She's come a long way from rotting in jail to owning her own company. Judging from the equipment truck she was driving, I'm guessing she's very successful."

Jules waited until the waitress took their order to broach the subject that had been haunting her all day. "I know we've only known each other a little over two months . . ." She hesitated, took a deep breath, and plunged forward. "But I would like you to move in with me."

"Are you sure?" Darcy studied Jules's face for any sign of doubt.

"You know I adore you," Jules assured her. "Even the thought of spending one night away from you makes me hyperventilate."

Darcy suppressed a laugh at the thought. "You know I can't stay away from you," she said. "So, yes, I would love to move in with you."

They sat in silence as the waitress returned and placed their order on the table.

"Did you hear?" the waitress whispered. "Tanner made an arrest in the Ashley Craft murder."

"Who?" Jules asked.

"That dyke Chance Howard."

Darcy cringed at the woman's choice of words and felt Jules stiffen beside her.

"Chance?" Jules was astounded. The young woman was so nice and was a hard worker. Chance's words flitted across her mind: *"I service most of the single women . . ."* But Ashley wasn't single and certainly wasn't a lesbian.

"That's surprising," Darcy said as soon as the waitress walked away. "Although Tanner tends to put her hands where they don't belong, I think she's an outstanding investigator. She wouldn't make an arrest without good cause. Still, I'm surprised she's arrested Chance."

"Do you mind if we go by the jail when we finish dinner?" Jules asked.

"Not at all," Darcy replied. "I'd like to know what's going on."

##

They found Tanner standing behind the police department's service desk. "Jules, what brings you here?"

"We heard you arrested Chance Howard for the murder of Ashley Craft." They approached the service desk.

"Yes, we found her fingerprints all over Ashley's bedroom. We're running a more in-depth forensic panel on the prints to see what we find.

"Why don't we take this conversation into my office?" Tanner led the way down a narrow hall into a cramped office. There was just room enough for a desk and three chairs. She motioned for them to sit down.

"I can't share most of what I know," Tanner said, "but I'm fairly certain she is the killer."

"And Daphne's killer?" Darcy asked. "Is she tied to Daphne's death too?"

"I don't know yet," Tanner said. "We're interrogating her now. Hopefully she'll come clean and solve both murders." She shuffled through the folders in her lap drawer and withdrew Chance's file.

"Does she work for you?" the detective asked Jules.

"Yes, and she seems like a wonderful person, a very hard worker."

"How long have you known her?"

"I met her right after Nana's funeral. She keeps the grounds at Nana's house."

"Now your house," Tanner said casually. "But you never met her when you visited your grandmother?"

"No."

"Who is representing her?" Darcy's tone was matter-of-fact.

"The courts will assign her a public defender," Tanner answered.

"May we speak to her?" Jules asked.

"No, we're not through processing her yet," Tanner replied.

Darcy opened her purse and pulled out a business card. She handed the card to Tanner. "I'm her counsel. I want to see my client."

"If you'll wait in interview room three, I'll see if I can get someone to bring her here." Tanner stopped short of gritting her teeth when she spoke.

"I think you made her angry," Jules whispered once they were alone in the room. "Are we being recorded?"

Darcy looked around the room. "I don't think so. The cameras don't appear to be on."

Without warning, the door opened and Chance was escorted inside.

"Jules! Darcy!" Chance sobbed. "Thank you, thank you, so much for coming. I don't know what's going on. They think I murdered Ashley. I could never do that. I loved her."

Darcy held up her hand, stopping the flow of conversation as she pushed the door closed. "They left it open on purpose," she said. 'Legally, they can eavesdrop if we aren't smart enough to close the door.

"Start from the beginning," Darcy said. "You and Ashley were having an affair?"

Chance bristled at the inference. "Not an affair. We were in love. My business is successful enough that I can support a wife. She was going to leave Roy and marry me."

"How long has this been going on? And did Roy know?" Darcy asked.

"No, Roy didn't know. We were very careful." Chance bowed her head, and tears fell on the interview table. "Roy was abusive. He beat her and pushed her down the stairs. He didn't want children, so when Ashley got pregnant he shoved her down the stairs to make her miscarry. That's why she lost the baby. But I don't know why he pushed her down the stairs this last time. She said he just gave her a shove for no reason at all. Oh God! This is a nightmare. I can't believe she's gone!"

"Did you see her the day she died?" Darcy asked.

"Yes. I mowed her yard. Just as she always does, she invited me in for a cold drink. I showered and we made love. Mowing her yard was the highlight of my week."

"I began doing other things the yard needed—edging, pulling weeds, cleaning flowerbeds, trimming hedges, and any other excuse I could find just to see her."

"They probably have hair from the shower with your DNA on it," Darcy thought out loud. "Did you touch anything in the house?"

"God, yes," Chance moaned. "I used her towels. We drank iced tea and left the glasses in the sink. Ashley said she could straighten up after I left. She wanted to . . ."

"Make love," Jules whispered.

Chance nodded. "I swear I wouldn't harm a hair on her body."

I touched the doorknob. She always made me lock the door, just in case Roy came home unexpectedly. I'm sure my hand and fingerprints are all over her headboard where I gripped it for . . ."

"Leverage," Jules said. It was so easy to relate to what Chance's feelings for Ashley.

"Yes." The misery in Chance's eyes was heartbreaking. "This sounds so awful, so tawdry, but it wasn't. I loved her with everything in me."

"Did you ever rendezvous at your house?" Darcy asked.

"Occasionally," Chance mumbled.

"Please tell me you don't have anything in your home with Ashley's blood on it?"

"Of course not." Chance looked appalled. "Why would I?"

"Sometimes couples like—" The fury in Chance's eyes stopped Darcy.

"No, she didn't like rough sex," Chance declared. "I could never do anything that would hurt her."

"That is one thing in our favor," Darcy said. "Right now it sounds like all they have is circumstantial evidence that can be explained away by the fact that you're her yard service."

"What about her fingerprints on the headboard?" Jules said.

"That could be a little tricky."

"I did help her turn her mattress recently," Chance offered. "Actually, Roy called me to help him turn it. We ended up moving the furniture in the bedroom."

"That'll blow their case out of the water," Darcy said, her eyes twinkling. "Court opens at eight in the morning. I'll file for a bail hearing and try to get you released on your own recognizance. Failing that, I'll fight for the lowest bail possible.

"Chance, you might have better luck with a local attorney. I've never worked in this court before."

Chance shook her head. "I'll find a way to pay you. I trust you."

"You don't need to pay me," Darcy said. "This will certainly get my name out in the community. Do you own a dress?"

"A couple," Chance grumbled. "Why?"

"Can someone let us into your house? You'll do better in front of a judge in a dress." Darcy looked around the room. "They're already calling you a dyke and acting like you raped and killed Ashley. The narrative from the prosecuting attorney won't be nice."

Chance propped her head on her hands. "Just tell me what to do."

It was two in the morning when Darcy finished downloading and filling out the forms she needed to get Chance out on bail. Jules stood behind her, massaging her shoulders.

"You're so tense, baby."

"That feels good." Darcy leaned back into hands that were gentle and strong. "We'd better get to bed. Seven comes early."

Although they were naked, they didn't make love. Both were exhausted and were content to simply lie in each other's arms. *This is what it's all about*, Jules thought. She felt Darcy's body curve around hers as she pulled Jules's buttocks into her stomach. She felt as if she were encased in a silky, warm shell of love.

Chapter 25

Chance had been dashing in a pair of jeans and a T-shirt, but she was model-beautiful in a dress that hugged her curves then flared out from the waist. Darcy was surprised at how gracefully she walked in a pair of heels.

"Lower your eyebrows, Counselor," Chance chided her. "Everyone will think you've never seen a woman in a dress before."

When the bailiff called Chance's name, Darcy and Chance walked in front of the judge. They stood patiently as the judge looked over Darcy's filing. He laid down the papers, removed his glasses, and stared at Chance.

"Did you kill Ashley Craft?" The judge's voice was a low rumble but filled the silent courtroom.

"No, Your Honor, I did not," Chance replied.

"Defendant is released on her own recognizance." His eyes drilled into Chance. "You understand that you cannot leave town and that you must appear in court on the date given you by the court clerk?"

"Yes, Your Honor."

##

Darcy sat down on the bed and removed her heels. She was pleased with the way she had been treated in the county criminal court and felt she had made some good contacts. *This might be a better place to practice law than Dallas*, she thought.

She wished her rapport with Tanner was better. The detective was dedicated and good at her job. She didn't want to go against Tanner with a guilty client, but she was certain Chance was innocent.

The sound of Jules moving around in the kitchen made her smile. Jules didn't just complete her, Jules made her. She was still surprised at how quickly the other woman had become the focal point of her life, her reason for living. She hung up her dress and slipped on something Jules would really like. Then she pulled on her loose-fitting sweats and a soft T-shirt.

Jules sensed Darcy before she saw her. She waited for Darcy to slip her arms around her and kiss the back of her neck. Darcy never disappointed her.

"Mmm, you smell divine, Jules Divine." Darcy nuzzled her nose into the silky dark hair resting on Jules's shoulders. The fragrance was enough to bring her to her knees. Her hands slid around Jules's body to cup soft, full breasts. Jules's sharp intake of breath and slight tremor told her all she needed to know.

Darcy kissed along her neck then slowly turned her around. Jules's kisses were always an earthquake for her. They rocked her from the top of her head to the soles of her feet. It was as if someone had filled her body with hot molten liquid. She had to fight for control, to keep from taking Jules too quickly.

"I don't need foreplay," Jules whispered against her lips. "I've been aching for you ever since I watched you in court. Damn, you're hot, Counselor."

In one quick move, Jules lifted Darcy's T-shirt over her head and caressed her breasts through her bra. She pulled the straps down and slid her hands behind Darcy to unfasten her bra. "Dear Lord, you're gorgeous," she whispered as she lowered her mouth to capture one of Darcy's breasts.

Darcy was thankful for the kitchen island. It was the only thing that kept her from falling when her legs turned to jelly. She stopped Jules's hands as they tried to pull down her sweats. "Not yet, honey."

Jules moaned when Darcy continued kissing her as she unbuttoned the silk blouse Jules wore and let it fall to the floor. Her skirt and bra soon joined the blouse. Darcy's hands and lips were everywhere, stroking her, kissing her, sucking her, driving her mad.

"Darcy," she whimpered, "the things you do with your mouth are . . ." Lost for words, her voice trailed into a soft moan of pleasure.

Still kissing her, Darcy moved her to the sofa and nestled between her legs. "I've thought about doing this to you all day," Darcy whispered in her ear, knowing her soft sounds and warm lips would drive her lover crazy.

"Please," Jules moaned, tugging at Darcy's sweatpants. "Please, you know what I like."

Darcy continued to stroke her and touch her, kissing every inch of her. Jules was in a lust-driven frenzy when Darcy slipped off her sweatpants. Moaning and pleading for relief, Jules gasped when Darcy pushed against her.

Jules' eyes opened wide as she realized what Darcy had brought to the party. "When did you slip into this?" she whimpered.

"When I changed." Darcy's voice was a deep guttural growl. "I want you so badly, Jules."

"Then take me. You know I belong to you."

Jules lay on her back, cuddling Darcy's face between her breasts. Ten minutes had passed since the culmination of their passion had sucked the breath from their bodies. Her breathing had almost returned to normal.

Darcy moved her head, snuggling deeper into the space between Jules's breasts. "I love it here," she murmured. "The very first time I saw you, this is where I wanted to be."

Jules giggled. "The first time I saw you, this is where I wanted you to be." A tremor ran through her body as she thought about the way Darcy made love to her. "I liked the way you surprised me."

"I thought you might." Darcy's lips moved against her breasts. "That's why I did it."

Darcy pulled the soft throw from the back of the sofa and covered their naked bodies with it. "Are you cold? Do you want to go to bed?"

"I'm perfect," Jules said with a sigh as she kissed the top of Darcy's head. "Just perfect.

##

Jules awoke slowly, momentarily confused about where she was. A lazy smile spread across her lips as she recalled how sweetly Darcy had made love to her. She got up, pulled the throw around her shoulders, and went to find Darcy.

The sound of fingernails clicking across a keyboard caught her attention. She headed for her office and found Darcy, still dressed in the clothes she'd worn the night before. *I've never seen anybody type that fast*, Jules thought.

"Good morning," Jules said as she approached Darcy. "What are you working on so hard?"

Darcy swung around in the desk chair. A look of happiness mingled with desire covered her face as she gazed at Jules. "I thought you would never wake up."

"Do you need me for something?"

"I do. I can't find paper for the printer." Darcy wrinkled her nose in an impish manner.

Without a word, Jules walked to the drawer beside the desk and pulled out a stack of paper. "What are you printing?"

"I'm filing this as soon as I can." Darcy gestured toward the monitor. "It's a request for both the exculpatory and inculpatory evidence the prosecutor has in Chance's case."

"Exculpatory evidence . . . I'm familiar with that term," Jules said. "It's evidence that is favorable to Chance. Inculpatory, I'm not positive about."

"Evidence that proves Chance's guilt," Darcy said, her hungry eyes roving over Jules.

"I want to know everything they have that makes them believe Chance committed Ashley's murder. I want to discover. . .what is under this blanket." Darcy raised her eyebrows as she pulled the throw from Jules's shoulders.

"Nothing new," Jules said. "Just the same thing you had last night."

"Umm, and that's what I have for you." Darcy inhaled sharply as Jules straddled her and lowered herself onto her lap.

"I have no words for the way you make me feel," Jules murmured against Darcy's lips.

They showered, dressed, and headed for the police station. Darcy was looking forward to meeting the prosecutor on the case. She hoped the assistant DA would be as professional and accommodating as the court employees she had met yesterday.

Jules waited in the reception area as Darcy was led into the prosecutor's office.

"ADA Anthony Cancelli." The dark-haired, handsome man in his early forties stood as Darcy entered his office. "It's a pleasure to have you practicing in our county, Ms. Reed."

"Thank you." Darcy appreciated his warm welcome.

"What may I do for you?" Cancelli's smile was kind and friendly.

"I'm representing Chance Howard," Darcy explained as she slid the information request across his desk.

"I'm surprised that a woman as beautiful as you would defend a dyke." Cancelli flashed his smile again.

"You think that dykes should only be represented by ugly attorneys?" Darcy raised a perfectly arched brow. "Or perhaps they deserve no representation at all?"

Cancelli tilted his head to one side and studied her. "I think I was crude," he said. "Please forgive me."

Cancelli picked up Darcy's filings. His forehead wrinkled as he examined the date stamp. "You've already filed these with the court clerk." Darcy heard a hint of disapproval in his voice.

"Yes." Darcy gave him her little-girl look—the one that accentuated her dimples. "Isn't that the proper procedure?"

"My office usually handles that," Cancelli explained. "It looks like you did an excellent job."

"How soon can I expect the information?" Darcy got to the point. "I need to know why my client is being charged."

Darcy waited as Cancelli undressed her with his eyes. She was aware of the effect she was having on him. *He's going to start drooling any minute*, she thought.

"I have the arrest warrant, if you'd like a copy," Cancelli said.

"What about exculpatory evidence?"

"I'm afraid I've found nothing that will exonerate your client," Cancelli answered.

"I'll take what you have," Darcy said, "but you still have to provide me anything you find later."

"Of course," Cancelli said, chuckling. "Would you like to join me for lunch? I'll be happy to answer any questions you have."

"Isn't that fraternizing with the enemy?" Darcy teased.

"I doubt that a woman as beautiful as you has many enemies," Cancelli said. "Certainly not me."

"I'll take a rain check. Now, about those copies?"

##

"Just as I suspected," Darcy declared as she showed Jules the arrest warrant. "They only have circumstantial evidence."

Jules closed the file folder as the waitress took their order and walked away. "I'm starving," she said. "Skipping breakfast for time with you leaves a girl weak in several ways."

"And breathless." Darcy stole a quick kiss. "You leave me breathless."

Darcy pulled the folder in front of them so they could read the warrant together. "I can probably keep this from going to court. The most incriminating evidence they have is Chance's fingerprints on the headboard. When Roy tells the police about Chance helping him turn the mattress, that will explain why the prints were there.

"I'd like to ask Tanner to accompany me to question Roy," Darcy added. "That way, we can make it official and enter his testimony into evidence."

"Let's go by Tanner's office and talk with her," Jules said. "The sooner we can resolve this, the better. Chance is losing customers right and left. At this rate, she won't have a business when this is over."

##

Tanner listened to Darcy's request to interview Roy Craft. "We grilled him for three hours," she said. "I don't think you'll get anything out of him that we didn't."

"I'm looking for different information," Darcy informed her. "You were looking at him as a suspect. I'm looking at him as someone who can verify my client's statements."

Tanner shrugged. "Okay. You want me to have him picked up or do you want to go to his place of business?"

"Let's visit him at his office," Darcy said. "He'll be more at ease there."

Tanner turned her attention to Jules. "You should go home. Too many of us showing up at his garage would only upset him. Darcy can ride with me, and I'll drop her off at your house when we're finished."

Jules agreed and Darcy walked her to the car.

"I'll be home as quickly as possible," Darcy said, leaning in through the window to kiss Jules goodbye. "Why don't you see if you can track down the accountant who handled Daphne's Darcy Lake books?"

##

"What kind of information are you looking for?" Tanner asked as she pulled her car from the police lot.

"I just need to verify some statements," Darcy said. "Get some timelines straight. That kind of thing. I don't like to go into court without knowing the answers to the questions I need to ask."

Tanner laughed. "Never ask a question you don't know the answer to, eh?"

"Something like that."

"Look, Darcy, I think you and I got off on the wrong foot. I apologize if I did anything out of line. It wasn't my intent. I'm just concerned about Jules's safety."

"I probably overreacted," Darcy admitted. "Honestly, I've never been in love before. I'm experiencing a lot of emotions that are new to me."

Tanner nodded. "Truce?"

"Truce," Darcy said with a chuckle.

##

Roy Craft was underneath a car on a lift when the two women entered his auto repair business.

"What can I do for you?" He wiped his hands on a blue towel as he moved from under the vehicle. He didn't have the demeanor of a guilty man.

Tanner shook hands with the man and then introduced Darcy.

"How can you defend a woman who would rape and murder another woman?" Roy said as he squinted at Darcy. His question seemed sincere. "Ashley never hurt anyone."

Darcy was certain that now was not the time to tell him that the sex had been consensual, so technically they were only searching for a murderer.

Darcy noticed Roy's employees trying to overhear their conversation. "Is there somewhere we can speak privately?" she asked.

Roy led them to his office, closed the door, and motioned for them to sit down.

"Did you know Chance Howard very well?" Darcy's tone was casual and nonconfrontational.

"No more than anyone knows their yard service personnel." Roy seemed indignant that Darcy thought he might socialize with the hired help.

"Was she helpful? I mean, did she do odd jobs around the house?" Darcy continued.

"Yeah, she was. She was always willing to help out." Roy wrinkled his brow. "She was probably only trying to find reasons to be around my Ashley."

"Did she do repairs, help you move furniture, that sort of thing?" Darcy held her breath. She had finally asked the question she needed the right answer to.

Roy thought about it for a minute. "Yeah. She helped me move some furniture a couple of weeks ago. Ashley wanted the bedroom rearranged. Chance helped me move the bed and dresser."

Darcy blew out a soft breath. She had just destroyed the prosecution's case against Chance. "I know this is difficult for you, Mr. Craft, and I appreciate you talking with us."

"I have one more question for you," Tanner said. "Where did you say you were at the time of Ashley's murder?"

"Working." Roy rolled his shoulders and rubbed the back of his neck.

"Were you here at the garage?"

Roy looked around. "Yes. Uh, no. I had gone out to change a flat for a couple."

"Could you give me the customer's name?" Tanner pulled a small spiral notepad from her pocket.

"It was someone passing through." Roy cleared his throat. "No one I know."

"A credit card receipt?" Tanner asked.

"They paid cash," Roy countered. "I told you they were travelers, a man and his wife."

Tanner snapped the pad closed and returned it to her pocket. "Thanks, Roy. Again, I'm so sorry for your loss."

Once they were in the car, Darcy queried Tanner. "That pokes holes in his alibi, doesn't it?"

"Nah," Tanner snorted. "He didn't kill his wife, but he is up to something. I just wanted to rattle his cage."

Darcy turned in her seat to face the detective. "Tanner, you do know that his saying Chance helped him move furniture kills the evidence the ADA is using to prosecute a case against Chance."

"Humph. Cancelli has more than that."

"What?" Darcy's asked in disbelief. "I have a copy of the arrest warrant. Everything listed on it is purely circumstantial."

"I think Anthony is trying her more for being a lesbian than a real killer," Tanner explained.

"That's ridiculous," Darcy growled. "Tanner, you know that girl didn't murder Ashley Craft."

"Cancelli is running for district attorney. He wants to try a splashy case that will generate a lot of media coverage." The disapproval was obvious in Tanner's voice. "He thinks he has a winner. You know, local lesbian murders lover. He's searching for a way to tie Chance to Daphne's murder too. It's like a circus in the DA's office, and Cancelli is the head clown. If he finds out you're a lesbian, he'll have a field day with that."

Darcy sat in silence. Maybe it was time to alert Tanner about Daphne's ties to the lesbian literary world. But that would play into Cancelli's narrative. She decided to discuss everything with Jules. They always worked things out together.

##

From the Manse's study window, Jules had a clear view of the street leading into the cul-de-sac. She frowned in frustration because she couldn't find any reference to an accountant handling the Darcy Lake funds.

In the past she'd helped Nana gather tax forms to take to the CPA to file her tax returns. She knew there was always a 1099-MISC form from Amazon.

She located the user name and password for the Darcy Lake account on Amazon and logged into the tax forms section. She opened the forms and printed the last 1099-MISC available.

"Holy. . . ." She fell silent as she looked at the seven-digit figure shown as royalties for the Darcy Lake books.

Jules's heart skipped a beat when she saw Tanner's car turn onto her street. She pushed a button and the gate slid open as the vehicle approached. Jules was waiting and opened the passenger side door before the car came to a complete stop in the courtyard. *I think she's happy to see me too*, she thought as she caught sight of Darcy's brilliant smile. Darcy slid from the car into Jules's arms, and the two exchanged a breathtaking kiss.

"Let's take this inside, honey," Darcy said, a hint of a smile on her face. "Then I can show you exactly how much I've missed you."

Tanner didn't bother getting out of the car. It was obvious the two were only interested in each other. She backed up, waved goodbye, and drove down the driveway.

"You will never believe how much Nana made a year off the Darcy Lake books," Jules cried as she pulled Darcy into the study.

Darcy studied the IRS form as a low whistle escaped her lips. "This is certainly a motive for murder, but the only one who stood to inherit all of this was you. How could anyone else hope to benefit from Daphne's death?"

They talked until after midnight, trying to sort out the best plan of action. They both agreed to keep Nana's Darcy Lake affiliation to themselves.

Darcy told Jules what Tanner had said about Cancelli wanting to convict Chance because she was a lesbian. Jules was shocked to learn that Anthony Cancelli was homophobic. "How can he possibly hope to be elected DA with an attitude like that?"

"I don't know, honey, but I've never hidden the fact that I prefer women. I don't flaunt it, but I don't hide it."

"Neither do I," Jules said. "Why don't you slip into something comfortable while I get dinner on the table?"

She laughed at the sultry look Darcy gave her. "Save that for later. I have something I want to show you after dinner."

##

"Sit here,"—Jules patted the space between her legs—"and lean back. I'm going to read you something."

Darcy did as she was told and thrilled to the soft warmness of the other woman as she leaned back against her.

Three hours later, Jules read, "The End."

Darcy didn't move.

Jules held her breath, waiting for her lover to comment. "Well, what do you think?"

"Where did you find that?" Darcy asked. "That was an awesome ending to *Dying to Kill.* I would've never guessed she was the killer."

"I wrote it," Jules admitted.

Darcy tilted her head back to look at Jules. "Honey, that was incredible. I had no idea you could write like that."

"Neither did I," Jules said. "I sat down at Nana's computer, read the last two chapters of *Dying to Kill,* and it just came to me. It just flowed. I . . . I don't know how to explain it."

"Do you know what this means?" Darcy's excitement was contagious. "It means you can become Darcy Lake!"

"I don't think—"

Darcy turned over to face Jules and kissed her. "Right now we don't have to think," she whispered against the brunette's ear. "Right now I just want to make love to you."

"Umm," Jules hummed, "be my guest."

"I love when you begin to breathe harder," Darcy said as she nibbled at Jules's lower lip. "I love the way the desire builds in you and how vocal you are."

"I love how you love me." Jules moaned as she clutched a fistful of blonde hair and devoured the lips that were tormenting her.

Chapter 26

Darcy woke slowly, loving the feel of the soft woman draped across her side. She listened to Jules's soft, steady breathing and resisted the urge to hug her tighter for fear of waking her.

Jules's uncanny writing ability still amazed her. The woman was just as good as her grandmother, maybe better. The ending she had written to *Dying to Kill* was genius.

Jules stirred in her arms and captured her nipple with her soft lips. A gentle tug on her breast sent a quake through Darcy. She pulled Jules closer as the brunette had her way with her.

"Baby, please don't start something I can't finished," Darcy whispered. "You wore me out last night. I need a day to recuperate.

"We have a lot to do today." Darcy gasped. She trembled as Jules placed kisses down her body. "But nothing that can't wait."

Afterward they lay in each other's arms, lips touching. "Let's email the manuscript to Cat and see how she reacts," Darcy said.

"And you need to come up with an idea to save Chance," Jules added.

"The main thing I have to do is prevent this from becoming a national media feeding frenzy," Darcy replied. "The last thing we need is the walking vagina group showing up in their ridiculous costumes to protest against Cancelli. That always turns public opinion against us. It might fly in Washington and New York, but it doesn't play

well in the Bible Belt. More than anything I need to find
the real killer."

Darcy sat at the kitchen island while Jules made
coffee. "I know you like to have coffee by the pool," Darcy
said, "but can we have it in the TV room today? I want to
catch the local news."

"There's a TV on the patio," Jules said, wrinkling her
nose in that cute way Darcy had come to love. "You really
should take the time to learn the many wonderful things
Nana's house has to offer."

She handed Darcy a cup of coffee and walked toward
the patio door. Darcy slid from the stool and followed her.

"How did I miss that?" Darcy exclaimed as Jules
pushed the button that turned on a large flat-screen TV over
the outdoor fireplace. They settled on the patio couch as a
cable news station announced that demonstrators were
preparing to march on behalf of a lesbian yard worker who
was being railroaded for murdering her client.

Darcy nearly strangled on her coffee. "How the hell
did they get that?"

"We have Anthony Cancelli, the Assistant District
Attorney prosecuting the case, with us on a live feed from
Cleburne, Texas," the news anchor announced. "Mr.
Cancelli, can you give us the facts in this case?"

"Well, as you know, Ashley Craft was raped and
murdered—"

"That lying SOB," Darcy growled. "He knows she
wasn't raped."

". . . Chance Howard will be arraigned for the vicious
murder tomorrow morning at 8 a.m."

"That's just great." Darcy jumped up and began to
pace. "He told the world before I was informed. God, I
hope Chance isn't watching this."

Darcy grabbed her cell phone and pushed a button.

"Who are you calling?" Jules asked. Darcy held up her
finger for silence.

"Hello, Norm. This is Darcy Reed. I need your help."

Darcy spoke with the man for several minutes as she paced up and down the patio. "Today! Norm, that would be great. Thank you so much."

She gave Norm their address then hung up the phone.

"Norman Holt is a detective who works for my firm," she explained to Jules. "Tanner thinks Roy is hiding something, and I believe she's right, but the police aren't following up on it. Norm will find out what it is."

"We need to call Chance and make certain she's okay," Jules said, biting her lower lip.

Darcy groaned. "Please don't do sexy things when I'm trying to concentrate."

"I didn't . . . Oh, sorry. I wasn't trying to be sexy."

"That's just it; you don't even have to try."

##

Darcy spent the entire day working with Chance, telling her what to expect at the arraignment and how to react. "Ignore the crowd outside the courthouse," she told her. "They've probably been flown in just to embarrass us."

"But they're protesting the injustice being done to me," Chance argued.

"No, they're not," Darcy huffed. "They've been flown in to turn public opinion against you. They'll wear ridiculous hats and carry offensive signs that will agitate the citizens and make them think all lesbians are crass, sex-crazed fiends."

Chance paced the length of the great room and stopped in front of Jules's portrait hanging over the fireplace. She stared at it for a long time. "So, are you two getting married?" she asked without moving her gaze from the portrait.

Jules and Darcy exchanged looks. "Eventually," Darcy answered. "Why do you ask?"

"It's good to see a healthy relationship between two women." Chance turned from the portrait and smiled. "You two are perfect together."

Chance wiped tears from her eyes with the back of her hand. "Ashley and I were perfect together too. I bought a new home, one she was proud of. She didn't care. She said she would be happy in a shack as long as she was with me."

Jules's heart went out to the young woman, and she moved to console her. Chance had to bend down to cry on Jules's shoulder. She clung to Jules as if she were a lifeline.

"You need to go home and get a good night's sleep," Darcy instructed. "Has the forensic team searched your house yet?"

"No." Chance frowned. "Why? Are they going to?"

"I'm surprised they haven't already," Darcy said. "Someone has slipped up, but that's not our problem. We'll pick you up at seven in the morning. Hopefully we'll arrive before the circus starts."

Chance nodded, and Jules walked her to her car, still consoling her.

As Chance pulled out of the driveway, Norman Holt pulled in. Darcy walked into the courtyard to greet her friend. She caught Jules's hand.

Norm got out of his car, wide-eyed. He let his gaze wander over the Manse and the gorgeous grounds that surrounded the stately home. "Wow!" he muttered before turning his focus on Jules. "And you must be Rapunzel."

"I beg your pardon?" she said.

"You know, the princess at the top of the tower." Norm laughed.

"You'll have to forgive Norm." Darcy grinned. "He's been reading fairy tales to his three-year-old twin girls."

Darcy made the introductions as Norman offered Jules his hand.

"It's a pleasure to meet someone woman enough to harness Darcy," Norm said with a smile as he teased his friend.

Harness? Oh, Norm, you have such a way with words, Darcy thought.

"Come in and let's get started." Darcy led the way into the Manse as Jules scrutinized the handsome, thirty-something detective and found she liked him.

"I'd prefer the local police know nothing of your investigation," Darcy said. "So don't draw any attention to yourself.

"I'm sending pictures of Roy Craft and his car to your cell phone now. The last photo is his license plate." She scrolled her phone and tapped the screen. "The address is his place of business, an automotive repair shop. He lives in the house next door. He's Jules's neighbor."

"On my way," Norm said. "It was a pleasure to meet you, Jules."

"I'm going to work in the study," Darcy informed Jules as she pulled her laptop from her briefcase. "I'm going to file for a change of venue. Maybe I can convince Cancelli to call off the circus performers if he thinks I'm moving this out of his jurisdiction."

"I'll be in Nana's office." Jules hugged Darcy and then headed down the hallway. A wolf whistle echoed behind her.

"God, I love the way you walk," Darcy said as she watched the shapely brunette sashay away from her.

Jules's laughter filled the Manse. She loved the way Darcy made her feel.

Jules checked Nana's phone to if she had a text from Cat. She laughed as she opened Cat's email and a celebration GIF image filled her screen.

"WOW! Just wow!" Cat wrote. "This is your best one yet. It's as if you got a shot of adrenaline. Awesome ending. When can I run with it?"

"Marta needs to read it," Jules responded. "Then my editor. It should be all yours in a month."

"Rush it," Cat typed back. "I want to get it out before you receive the award in NY."

"I'll try," Jules replied.

She'd forgotten about New York. She needed to talk to Darcy and discuss how they would handle Darcy Lake's future.

Jules emailed the manuscript to Marta, closed the computer, and went to find Darcy.

##

Darcy was staring out the study window, watching Roy pull into his garage. She smiled when she saw Norm's nondescript Ford parked at the end of the block. She rolled her shoulders, trying to release some of the tension that had settled there while she drafted the change of venue request.

Soft hands began to massage her shoulders and neck. She leaned into Jules's touch as her body trembled. She wondered if Jules would always affect her like that. She was certain she would.

Chapter 27

Jules cringed when she turned the corner and saw the crowd of people marching in front of the courthouse. "What in the name of God . . . ?"

"I warned you," Darcy said. "They are not here for Chance."

Chance dragged her hands down her face as they drove by two women carrying a sign that read, "Hey homophobe, I get more pussy than you do."

Chance gasped. "This is offensive to me. I hate to think what others are thinking. Where did these women come from?"

"Is that woman actually wearing a vagina costume?" Jules cried out. "And what in the world do they have on their heads?"

"Drive to the back," Darcy directed Jules. "Let us off at the wheelchair entrance. Maybe we can avoid the TV cameras and keep Chance from being shown next to any of them."

Jules did as Darcy asked and then drove back around the courthouse to park. She headed for the steps and looked around before walking up them. *Darcy is right. This is a circus.*

"Hey, pretty mama, whatcha' doing here? This ain't no place for straight girls." A tattoo-covered woman with a Mohawk haircut blocked her way.

"What makes you think I'm straight?" Jules demanded. "You aren't from around here, are you?"

"No, but I could be for a looker like you," the tattooed woman said, grinning salaciously.

"Where are you from?" Jules asked.

"California," the woman said proudly. "They bused us in last night. Pretty good gig—free food, a hotel room, and a hundred bucks a day. Hey, you need a place to stay?"

"Why are you here?" Jules asked.

"Dunno. They just gave me this sign and told me to march in front of the courthouse."

Jules was livid. Paid protesters were handing Anthony Cancelli a guilty verdict. Chance didn't have a snowball's chance in hell of getting a fair trial.

"What the hell do you have on your head?" Jules yelled at another protester. "It looks like you have your head stuck up your—"

"You better come with me." A firm hand cupped Jules's elbow and steered her up the courthouse steps.

"Tanner, can't you arrest these people?" Jules asked when she realized who was holding her arm.

"Unfortunately, they have a right to protest." Tanner pulled open the door and ushered her into the courthouse.

"They aren't even from here," Jules said. "Can't you arrest them for vagrancy or something?"

"Nope."

Loud arguing greeted them as they entered the courthouse.

"You can't do that!" Cancelli screamed. He clenched his fists a she shoved his face in front of Darcy's.

Darcy didn't flinch. "I can, and I will. You've turned this into a three-ring circus. You aren't trying Chance for murder. You're trying her for being a lesbian."

"One crime is as bad as the other," Cancelli screeched.

For a second Darcy was speechless. She couldn't believe anyone in today's world would feel the way Cancelli did, especially an elected official.

"Either get rid of those ridiculous people, or I'm filing right now," Darcy said. "If they aren't gone by the time the judge enters the courtroom, I will file for a change of venue, and I promise you I will get it."

Cancelli's face turned dark purple as he stomped out of the courthouse. Darcy followed him and watched as he spoke to a group standing at the top of the courthouse steps. Within minutes the protestors began moving the crowd away from the building. They walked a block and loaded into waiting buses.

"I got your exchange with him on video," a young woman with a camera resting on her shoulder said as she approached Darcy. "I'm with Channel 4, and I'd love to do a quick interview with you."

Darcy looked around. She smiled when she spotted Jules and motioned for her to join them. "I'd be glad to give you an interview."

The three women found a quiet hallway and the reporter began asking questions. Darcy explained Cancelli's role in busing in protestors to cast a bad light on Chance.

"Those protesters didn't help my client," Darcy said. "Their sole purpose in being here was to make Chance Howard look bad. Their lewd signs and stupid costumes were meant to offend the citizens of this town so they would associate Chance with that kind of behavior. Too often things are not what they appear to be. This is one of those times."

"Thank you," the reporter said as she handed Darcy her business card. "I've got to run. I want to get this on the nine o'clock news tonight."

Jules waited outside the courtroom as Darcy handled the arraignment. Tanner sat down beside her.

"This will take a while," Tanner said. "Would you like to get a cup of coffee? There's a nice coffee shop across the street."

Jules was tempted, but she wanted to be there when Darcy was finished. "No, I want to make sure everything goes okay."

"I don't know if this will help or hurt your case," Tanner said, "but I just received the forensic report showing the same brand of wine in the stomach content of both Ashley and Daphne. Cancelli could use that to accuse Chance of killing both women. She was their groundskeeper."

Jules looked heavenward. "Darcy needs to know that."

"Jules, you're not going to like what I'm about to say, but please hear me out before you tear my head off."

Jules turned toward Tanner, giving the detective her full attention.

"I know the book convention you attended in Dallas was an assembly of lesbian book aficionados and authors. How did you know about it?"

"I received a complimentary ticket through email."

"You received the invitation?" Tanner asked.

"No, it was sent to Daphne Divine, but I used it."

"Was Daphne in the habit of attending that convention?"

"No, to my knowledge she never attended the lesfic conventions."

"How did you tie up with Darcy?" Tanner's said.

Jules told Tanner the entire story of attending the convention in hopes of meeting the beautiful author. She didn't tell the detective that Daphne Divine was the writer of the Darcy Lake murder mysteries.

"Don't you think it's odd that Daphne was invited to the lesbian author's convention for the first time, and Darcy Lake just happened to bump into you in that club?"

"I don't—"

"Hear me out." Tanner held up her hand. "Then Darcy Lake and Darcy Reed, the attorney who handled your grandmother's will, turned out to be the same person."

"Has it occurred to you that Darcy Reed knew the fortune you were about to inherit and set you up for an accidental meeting?"

Jules tried to hide her anger at Tanner's accusation. If the detective had taken the time to check, she would know that Darcy Reed was a wealthy woman in her own right. Noise in the courtroom pulled her attention away from Tanner.

The courtroom doors swung open and Darcy and Chance walked toward them. Jules stood and slipped her hand into Darcy's, making it clear to Tanner that she trusted Darcy and resented Tanner's efforts to make her doubt her fiancée.

"The trial begins next Monday," Darcy informed them. "Chance is free until then. The judge seems to be aware of Cancelli's tricks. That's in our favor."

Jules was unusually quiet as she fixed dinner. Darcy was on the phone with Norm, taking notes as he reported his findings.

"Norm visited the hospital today and met a very friendly nurse." Darcy smiled as she picked up the plates. "Want to eat on the patio?"

"Fine," Jules replied.

"Fine?" Darcy turned to look at her. "You know fine means 'I couldn't care less'?"

"I'm sorry." Jules faked a smile. "I'm just tired. This murder business is upsetting. What were you saying about Norm?"

"He talked a nurse into letting him see Ashley's files. During the past five years she's been in the hospital several times for broken bones and black eyes. It appears good old Roy is a wife abuser. Ashley always covered for him. She swore all her injuries were accidents."

Jules nodded but said nothing.

"Honey, tell me what's wrong." Darcy had been with the brunette over three months, but she had never encountered the mood Jules was in tonight.

Jules pressed the remote, bringing the TV to life. "In local news today, we have an exclusive interview with Darcy Reed, the attorney representing accused lesbian killer Chance Howard."

"They could have prefaced that better," Darcy huffed.

They watched as the conversation between Darcy and Cancelli played. It made Cancelli look like the fool he was.

"That should lose him the LGBT vote in this county," Jules commented.

Darcy brushed her teeth and then joined Jules in their bed. She was surprised to find Jules wearing pajamas that covered everything but her head, hands, and feet. "Are you okay?" she asked.

"I'm exhausted," Jules muttered. "I don't feel well."

"Is it the curse?"

"No. Just tired."

"Goodnight, then." Darcy leaned over and kissed her. Jules couldn't keep from kissing her back.

"Good," Darcy murmured against her lips. "I was afraid you were upset with me." She pulled the sheet up to her chin and quickly fell asleep.

Jules lay awake, fretting about her conversation with Tanner. *Damn, Tanner. She's just trying to cause trouble between us.* Jules knew that if she weren't so in love with Darcy, she would be attracted to Tanner.

The thought that Darcy might be after her money was ludicrous. Darcy was a wealthy attorney. She didn't need Jules's money.

God, these pajamas are suffocating me, Jules thought as she slid off the pajama bottoms. *No one in Texas wears pajamas in the summer.* She unbuttoned the top and dropped it on the floor.

Darcy was just inches away, her back to Jules. A minor shift in bed and she would touch soft, silky skin. Jules wrapped around the other woman, slipped her arm around her waist, and snuggled into her back.

"That's more like it," Darcy said without moving. "Get some sleep. We have a big day ahead of us."

"Mmm," Jules hummed as soft lips kissed her neck and slowly moved down to the pulse point in her throat. "You certainly know how to wake up a woman," she whispered.

Darcy continued touching her, kissing from her throat to the space between her breasts. Jules inhaled deeply and then slowly released her breath as she fought for control.

It's useless, Jules thought. *I would rather die than pull away from her.*

After they made love, Darcy held her tightly and caressed her back. "Are you going to tell me what's wrong?"

"Nothing, now." Jules kissed her soundly. "Absolutely nothing."

"But there was something," Darcy said, cupping Jules's buttocks and pulling her tighter against her. "I love the way you just fit me. I'm not letting you go until you tell me."

"What makes you think I want you to release me?" Jules mumbled. "Okay, I do have something to tell you. While you were in court yesterday, Tanner said Nana and Ashley's stomach contents showed they drank the same wine just before dying, and Cancelli might try to pin both the murders on Chance."

Darcy pulled back from Jules, leaving a cold emptiness that cut through the brunette like a knife.

Erin Wade
LIVING TWO LIVES

"And you just now decided to share that with me?" The shocked look on Darcy's face was disconcerting. "It could cause real problems for Chance if Cancelli can do that."

"Oh, baby, I'm so sorry," Jules said as she tried to pull Darcy back against her. "I should have shared that information with you right away."

"No." Darcy held her away from her. "Tell me everything. I know you well enough to know when something is wrong. What else did Tanner say?"

Jules related her entire conversation with Tanner. Darcy lay on her back and stared at the ceiling.

"Say something," Jules pleaded.

"You gave credence to Tanner's hypothesis," Darcy said. Her voice was low and toneless.

Jules's stomach twisted as she thought about doubting Darcy . . . even for a brief second. As the woman beside her stiffened, she realized how much she had hurt her.

"Oh baby!" Jules moved to lie on top of Darcy. "No, I never for a moment doubted your love for me. I'm no fool. I know Tanner is just trying to get into my head."

"She wants to be in my place," Darcy said. "She wants to be in your arms. She wants to be the one doing this to you."

Darcy's lips touched Jules's, hesitating as if asking permission to go further. Firm hands grasped the back of Darcy's head and pressed their lips harder against each other. The kiss was slow and searing. As if in slow motion, Darcy continued to kiss her as she rolled Jules onto her back and rose above her.

Strong hands stroked and caressed Jules until she thought she would scream. "Please," she begged shamelessly. "Please make love to me."

"I must," Darcy whispered in her ear. "I must have this from you, Jules."

Chapter 28

The wail of a firetruck siren pulled them from a sated sleep. Then another joined the scream of the first. "A two-alarm fire," Jules mumbled as she slowly awoke.

Jules's phone began to ring, and then Darcy's did the same. They scrambled to answer the calls.

"Oh my God!" Jules exclaimed. "Are you okay?"

"We're on our way," Darcy said into her phone.

"Chance's home is on fire."

"I know," Jules said as she pulled jeans and shirts from her closet for them.

Darcy's car was still in the courtyard. "You drive, honey," she instructed. "I'm going to contact Norm and see what he knows. He surveilled Roy all night."

Firetrucks and news teams made it impossible for Jules to drive close to the burning house. She parked down the block and followed Darcy as she sprinted across the street to where Tanner and Chance were standing.

Chance fell into Jules's arms and began to sob uncontrollably. "I've lost everything, Jules. Everything. My business, my home, the woman I love. Oh God."

Jules tried to console the distraught woman as she cried against her shoulder. Tanner and Darcy were in an animated conversation, but there was too much noise for Jules to hear what they were saying.

A few minutes later, Darcy moved to Jules's side. "What happened?" she asked Chance.

"I . . . I don't know." Chance sniffled. "I was sleeping. I took a sedative last night, so I was pretty out of it. My little dog was frantically licking my face trying to wake me.

That's when I smelled the smoke. If he hadn't . . . Oh God, that would be me burning in that fire."

Chance stopped talking and looked around. "Rabbit? Where's Rabbit?" she yelled, wringing her hands.

"Your dog's named Rabbit?" Jules said.

Chance shrugged. "It's a long story. Where is he?"

Chance whistled—an ear-piercing shrill—and a tiny bundle of fur ran toward her and leaped into her arms.

"Thank God I didn't lose you too," she cried as she hugged the wiggling dog to her chest.

The three watched as Tanner walked toward them. "I don't have any information," she informed them. "It will be a couple of days before we know anything. The good news is your insurance agent is already here assessing the damage. In a town this small, everyone knows your business almost as soon as you do."

"Where will you stay until your home is rebuilt?"

"I—"

"She can stay with us for the time being," Jules said, ignoring Darcy's surprised expression.

"Yes, she will be safe with us until she can make other arrangements," Darcy added.

"What about Rabbit?" Chance wiped tears from her eyes with one hand as she clutched the dog to her with the other. "He's house-trained."

Jules and Darcy nodded in unison as Jules laced her fingers with Darcy's, letting her fiancée and Tanner know how strong the bond was between them.

"You're lucky you didn't pull your truck into the garage last night," Tanner noted. "At least you still have transportation."

Darcy watched Jules and Chance play with Rabbit on the patio. Jules laughed as the small dog snuggled into her arms. *Lucky dog*, Darcy thought as she placed a pitcher of iced tea and sweetener on a tray with three glasses of ice and carried it outside.

"Tanner's on her way," Jules said as she placed her cell phone on the table. "She has the arson investigator's report and wants to go over it with Chance."

Darcy sat down next to Jules and touched her arm in a way that let the brunette know she loved her. Their eyes locked momentarily as they reconnected.

"You do know that doorbell is obnoxious," Darcy said, laughing as she got up to open the door for Tanner,

"Nana loved it. I can't bring myself to change it."

No doubt about it, Darcy thought as she crossed the great room. *Daphne Divine was eccentric in many ways, but she raised a hell of a good woman.*

"Any surprises?" Darcy asked as she led Tanner to the patio.

"Depends on how one looks at it," Tanner replied.

Darcy brought another glass from the kitchen and poured Tanner some tea.

Tanner greeted Jules and Chance and then cleared her throat. "The fire was arson. Accelerant was poured over the garage floor and up the wall that was common to your bedroom. Unfortunately, the damage was so severe the investigator couldn't tell if someone entered through the garage window. That would indicate premeditated murder."

"What else could it be?" Jules demanded.

Tanner bowed her head. "Chance could have set the fire herself."

"Are you nuts?" Chance shrieked.

Jules placed a calming hand on the woman's arm. "Tanner didn't say she believed you set the fire. She said you could have or someone could have gotten into your garage through the window."

"Yeah." Tanner frowned as Jules put words into her mouth. "There's no conclusive evidence either way.

"There were an inordinate number of gas cans in your garage," Tanner continued, looking at the report.

"Hell, yes," an agitated Chance replied. "I mow frickin' yards for a living. I keep fuel for my equipment in my garage."

"There was no equipment in your garage," Tanner pointed out. "It looks like you removed anything of importance from your house."

"I keep my equipment in the storage building I rent so the people who work . . . worked for me could access it."

Darcy calmly watched the scene play out in front of her. "So that's it. An inconclusive arson report, circumstantial evidence against Chance in a murder case, and I have to deal with an ADA who thinks political correctness is suppressing his urge to scratch his privates in public."

Silence fell over the four women, and then Jules burst into laughter. "Your description of Cancelli is so perfect."

The others joined her merriment, happy to find something to laugh about. Darcy was pleased that she had been able to make Jules laugh.

"I will file for a continuance," Darcy said. "I'm sure Cancelli will fight a postponement, but I believe any judge would grant us one under the circumstances."

"No," Chance snapped. "I want to get this over with as soon as possible. I can't live like this."

"A continuance would be in your best interest," Darcy pointed out. "It would give us time to investigate—"

"Please," Chance said. "I want this nightmare to be over."

"There are three ways this could end." Darcy leaned forward and gazed into Chance's eyes. "You could be acquitted, you could get life in prison, or lethal injection. You need to give me the time to do the best job I can do for you. I don't like losing a case, especially a murder case."

No one moved as Chance considered her options.

"Okay, tell me what to do."

"Why don't you find an apartment you can rent until your house is rebuilt? The rebuild will probably take six to nine months." Darcy wanted to keep Chance's thoughts positive.

"Honey, I need to set up an office outside our home. I don't like everyone traipsing through here. Do you have any ideas?"

"Yes, Nana owns . . . uh, I own an office building on Main Street. I think there's a vacancy right now. Let me call Sherry Martin. She manages Nana's properties. I need to have a meeting with her anyway."

"I need to get back to work." Tanner stood and held a copy of the arson report out to Darcy. "I can see myself out. Keep the report to yourself. Cancelli is bound by law to provide you a copy, but he'll take his sweet time doing it."

Chance retired to the guest bedroom and Darcy followed Jules into Nana's office to find the number for Sherry Martin.

##

Sherry Martin wasn't a typical real estate agent. Petite and pretty, she was a bundle of energy with no filters. Her chatter and good looks belied her age of forty-nine. She could easily pass for thirty-five.

"It was a personal tragedy for me to lose Daphne," she said as Jules and Darcy followed her into her office. "She was one of my biggest supporters. I think she had a crush on me, and I adored her."

Jules didn't reply. She wasn't sure the woman was wrong. She always held her breath for fear an unknown woman would pop out of the woodwork and declare herself Nana's lover.

"Do we have a vacancy in Divine Plaza?" Jules asked.

"Yes, we do." Sherry's heels clicked on her tile floor as she walked to the file cabinet. "Here we go. Yes, the best

spot we have just became available, a four-office suite."
She settled at her desk with the file folder. "Clay Simmons
just retired and closed his accounting business. My
goodness, he was in that space for eight years, a prime
space. Let me see what that rents for."

"No rent," Jules said.

"Yes, I'll pay rent," Darcy insisted. "For the time
being, we need to keep our business separate."

Sherry squinted as she examined the two women. "Are
you lovers?" she blurted out.

"Yes," Jules responded without hesitation. "Are you
usually so blunt?"

Darcy gave Jules a look of pure adoration. She loved
how open she was about their relationship.

Sherry was at a loss for words, surprised to find
someone as straightforward as she was. "I . . . I"—

"There is a lot to be said for tact," Jules continued.

"I didn't mean to be rude," Sherry said. She had
forgotten that Jules Divine was now the owner of her most
lucrative rental properties. "I sometimes let my mouth take
off before my brain cranks up."

"Please provide Darcy a contract at the same rate Mr.
Simmons was paying. Let's replace the carpet and repaint
the entire suite. Do whatever it takes to make it pristine."

"I can have the space ready in a week," Sherry
promised. "It was a pleasure meeting both of you, and don't
worry, I'll keep your secret."

"What secret?"

"That you're lesbians" Sherry could tell by the angry
look on Jules's face that she had put her foot in her mouth
again.

"It's no secret." Jules's voice was low and ominous.
"We're not ashamed of who we are."

"May I have a key so we can look at the space?" Darcy
asked. "I need to see what furniture I'll need."

##

They spent the rest of the day putting things in place to set up Darcy's office. Darcy loved the space. One office had a window that overlooked the courtyard fountain. "I love splashing water," Darcy said. She hugged Jules as they checked out the view.

They spent four hours at a furniture store in Fort Worth selecting the furniture for Darcy's new office.

##

Chance was mowing the Manse lawn when they pulled into the driveway. She turned off the mower and sauntered to their car as it rolled to a stop.

"I was about to send the posse to search for you," she said, laughing.

"We spent the day taking care of my office," Darcy informed her. "After next week I'll have a legitimate place of business."

Jules beamed at Chance. "The grounds look wonderful, but you didn't have to work all day on our place."

"It's the least I can do for you," Chance said. "You've done so much for me. I don't know where I'd be without you two. Probably rotting in a jail cell."

"Why don't you put away your equipment and take a shower while I make dinner," Jules said. "We'd love for you to join us."

"Do you know how to make Salisbury steak?" Darcy asked as she draped her arm over Jules's shoulder.

"I do," the brunette replied. "Do you like brown gravy or the tomato sauce recipe?"

A broad smile crossed Darcy's face as she leaned down for a kiss. "Surprise me!"

##

"Oh my gosh?" Chance moaned. "That is the best thing I've ever eaten. I'm not much of a cook, but Ashley is an awesome . . . was . . ." She looked away as tears ran down her cheeks.

"Have you been able to salvage any of your former clients?" Darcy asked, trying to change the subject.

"A few," Chance mumbled as she regained her composure. "Most want to wait and see if I'm guilty."

Jules walked to the cabinet and picked up the instruction book for the gate opener. "Why don't you and Chance see if you can sync the button in your car to the Manse's gate opener while I clean up the kitchen?"

"Good idea," Darcy said as she pushed back from the table, "but first we'll help carry the dishes to the kitchen."

Jules finished loading the dishwasher and went out to check on Darcy and Chance. She watched as they laughed and teased each other when the gate failed to open after several tries.

"Which one of you read the instructions?" she asked, looking around for the booklet.

She could tell by their sheepish expressions that neither woman had bothered to read a word of it.

"That's what I thought," Jules said. "Did you follow the instructions in this paragraph?"

Darcy took the book and read the short paragraph. "Well, Kemosabe, we missed an entire step." She laughed as she pitched Chance the instructions. "Let's try adding that step and see if it works."

They followed the instructions and held their breaths as the gate silently slid open.

"All we needed was a beautiful supervisor." Chance giggled as she pushed the button to close the gate then open it again. "We're on a roll. Let's sync the garage door to your car."

"What are you going to do with Daphne's Jeep and SUV?" Chance asked.

"Lucas and Trent are stopping by to pick them up. Lucas wants the Jeep, and he has a buyer for the SUV." Jules turned to Darcy. "Then your car will have its own garage."

##

Darkness had settled on the Manse when the bright lights of a car flashed up the cul-de-sac. The car stopped at the Craft drive and threw the high beam onto the three women standing in the courtyard before creeping toward the Manse. It was stopped by the closed gate across the drive.

The driver put the vehicle in park and stepped out of the car. The headlights blinded the three women, but there was no mistaking the voice that railed at them.

"Jules Divine!" Roy screamed. "I can't believe you're harboring Ashley's killer. I thought you were my friend."

Jules stepped toward the car, but Darcy caught her arm. "Don't go down there, honey. He may be dangerous. Let's all go into the house."

They watched from the study window as Roy jumped back in the car, screeched out of the driveway, and headed home.

"I would almost feel sorry for him if he hadn't been so abusive to Ashley," Jules said.

"He was horrible to her," Chance declared. "He belittled her and hit her. I can't believe he was so awful to her, and *I'm* the one accused of killing her."

"Why don't we have a glass of wine on the patio?" Jules suggested. "That always soothes me."

"I'll get a bottle from the wine cabinet," Darcy said as she left the room.

As Chance took two of the glasses from Jules, she let her fingers linger around Jules's. Chance inhaled sharply. Jules's touch was electrifying. Chance held Jules's gaze for a second before pulling away. "I'm sorry," she mumbled.

Jules bowed her head. She felt sorry for the young woman. She knew how she would feel if something happened to Darcy. "Nothing to be sorry for, Chance." She patted the younger woman's arm.

They settled on the patio, and Darcy poured the wine. "A toast," Chance said as they clinked their glasses together, "to the best friends a girl could ever hope for."

"I'll drink to that," Jules said. She jumped as her cell phone rang, smiling as her brother's face filled the screen.

"Hello, Bro," she said. She mouthed an apology to Darcy and Chance and listened for a few minutes before responding. "We'll be here. Tomorrow is fine. They aren't going anywhere. Love you too."

She hung up the phone and let the others know that Lucas had a problem on the job and wouldn't be able to pick up Nana's vehicles until the next day.

Darcy nodded and then turned her attention to Chance.

"I know this is difficult for you," Darcy said, "but could you answer a few questions for me . . . just to give me perspective?"

Chance placed her wine glass on the table. "Of course. Fire away."

"How old are you?"

"Twenty-two," Chance answered.

"And Ashley was what, forty-something?"

"Forty-seven." Chance scowled. "What are you getting at?"

"She was twenty-five years older than you," Darcy pointed out.

"How old did she look to you?" Chance asked.

"Honestly? Until Jules told me she was in her late forties, I thought she was around thirty."

Chance nodded. "Exactly. I had no idea she was that much older than me when I found myself attracted to her. By the time I learned her age, it didn't matter. I adored her." Chance gave a bitter laugh. "I like older women."

"Was she truly a mute, or was she just silent around her abusive husband?"

"At first, she was silent except when we made love." Chance hung her head and blushed. "Then she was very vocal.

"As we grew closer, she confided in me. We talked a lot. She was afraid that I wouldn't want her when I found out her age. It didn't matter to me. She was the most wonderful, beautiful woman I had ever met. I . . ." Chance's voice cracked reflecting the emotion she was feeling.

Darcy sipped her wine as she waited for Chance to get herself under control. Jules scooted closer to the blonde, smiled, and touched her arm. *I really just want to take you to bed*, Darcy thought as she looked at Jules and fought the smile that was toying with her lips.

Then Darcy resumed her questions. "How long had you and Ashley been lovers?"

"About five years." Chance's voice was barely above a whisper.

"Five years? You were underage," Darcy blurted out. "You were still in high school."

"I was old enough to know what I wanted," Chance declared. "I wanted her. I still do. I miss her every minute of the day."

"We must find out who killed Ashley," Jules said. "That's the only way we'll be able to repair the damage to Chance's reputation."

"I wonder if Tanner has learned anything new," Darcy thought out loud. "Let's call her in the morning."

Jules drained the last bit of wine from her glass. "I'm tired. I think I'll take a shower and call it a night."

"Go ahead, honey," Darcy said as she collected the wine glasses and empty bottle. "I need to get my briefcase from my car."

"Do you mind if I walk out with you?" Chance asked as she followed Darcy through the great room.

"Not at all," Darcy said, leading the way.

Chance leaned against Darcy's car while she pulled her briefcase from the back seat. "Please give it to me straight," Chance said with a heavy sigh. "What are my chances of being found not guilty?"

"Very good," Darcy replied with a bravado she didn't truly feel. "The evidence they have against you is all circumstantial.

"But on another note, I'm concerned about you. Whoever set fire to your home was obviously trying to kill you. You need to be careful."

##

Jules was in bed by the time Darcy returned. "What took you so long?" she asked as she watched Darcy undress.

"Chance is worried." Darcy leaned over and kissed her lover. "Let me take a quick shower, and then I'm all yours." She dragged her bottom lip slowly away from Jules's as if hating to end the kiss.

"Hurry," Jules whispered.

Darcy was cool from the shower and the sensation of snuggling into Jules's soft, warm arms was overpowering. She reveled in the feeling of silky skin and soft kisses.

"Mmm, you smell good," Jules whispered into Darcy's ear as she undulated against her.

Darcy moved her hands over her lover's body and inhaled deeply as she cupped Jules's firm breast. "I have waited all day for this," she murmured, her voice low and husky.

Jules moaned loudly as Darcy slipped between her legs.

"Shush, baby," Darcy reminded her. "Chance is hurting. It would be awful for her to hear us making love. No screaming my name."

Jules promised to try but quickly forgot as Darcy's hands worked their magic. She dragged her fingernails down Darcy's back, spurring her on and gasping for breath.

"You can whisper my name," Darcy mumbled against lips that always haunted her thoughts.

"I need more," Jules begged as she pulled Darcy down on her. She buried her face in Darcy's hair as she dug her nails into the blonde's back. "Much more!"

Chapter 29

Jules had fallen asleep sprawled on top of Darcy. She gripped the woman beneath her and moaned when the doorbell rang.

"I'm beginning to like the door chime," Darcy said, snickering as she held Jules in place on top of her. "I guess we must answer it."

"Says who?" Jules kissed her deeply. "Thank you for a most memorable night."

"You're the one that makes our nights memorable." Darcy kissed her again. "I love the sounds you make. I swear, just listening to you could send me over the top."

"Money! Money! Money!" The chime interrupted their moment.

Jules laughed. "I'll get it if you'll release me."

"Reluctantly," Darcy whispered.

Jules pulled on Darcy's Henley and a pair of running shorts and walked barefoot to the door.

"Lucas, what are you doing here so early?" Jules hugged her brother.

"Early?" Lucas looked at his watch. "Since when did ten in the morning become early to a Divine?"

Darcy sauntered from the bedroom dressed similarly to Jules. "Oh." Lucas whistled softly. "Since Darcy came on the scene."

"Come in the kitchen," Jules said as she hip-bumped her brother playfully. "I'll make coffee for everyone."

"And bacon and eggs?" Lucas asked.

"For you, Bro, anything." She caught his hand and tugged him to the kitchen island as Darcy pulled cups and plates from the cabinet.

The three laughed and teased one another as they sipped their coffee and Jules cooked breakfast.

"It sounds like a free-for-all out here," Chance said as she padded into the kitchen.

Lucas got to his feet to greet her. "Chance, I was so sorry to hear about your home. Have they determined the cause of the fire?"

"Nothing concrete." Chance gave Jules a thankful smile as her friend handed her a cup of coffee.

"Sit." Darcy motioned to the empty stool at the counter. "We almost have breakfast ready."

"What can I do to help?" Chance asked.

"Nothing." Darcy placed a plate piled high with bacon on the table as Jules handed Chance a dish of scrambled eggs.

Darcy refilled everyone's coffee cup and settled beside Jules at the island.

"I appreciate you allowing me to continue to care for your yard," Chance said to Lucas as she passed him the eggs.

"No reason not to." Lucas grinned as he piled several slices of bacon on his plate. "I know you're innocent, and I know Darcy will get you off."

After breakfast, Lucas helped clean the kitchen and then followed the women into the great room. "Darcy, if you'll give me your key fob, I'll move your car so I can back Nana's SUV from the garage.

"It's on the entryway table," Darcy said, nodding toward the bowl holding their keys and other odds and ends. "Mine's the red leather one."

"Of course it is," Lucas teased. "What does this button do?" He held up the fob and pointed to a button that looked like a lightning bolt.

"That's the remote start button," Darcy replied. "You can crank the car from right here. Just push that button."

Lucas smiled as he pressed the button.

An explosion rocked the Manse.

"What the hell?" Darcy embraced Jules as she turned to protect the brunette with her own body.

"I don't know," Jules croaked. "An explosion?"

Chance was already trying to unlock the massive front door. She gasped as she pulled it open. "Flames! Your car's on fire!"

"Damn," Darcy mumbled as she stepped into the courtyard.

Before Jules finished her call to 911, the firetruck sirens were screaming through town. It took only a few minutes for the engines to fill the cul-de-sac and begin hosing down the blazing vehicle.

As the water doused the fire, a lone figure scrambled up the steep driveway. "Lucas! Lucas!" Trent screamed as he searched for his friend.

Lucas ran into his arms and they clung to each other, as Trent fired off questions, not waiting for answers.

"Are you okay? Are you hurt? What happened?"

"Yes, I'm fine," Lucas mumbled. "Someone firebombed Darcy's car."

"It looks like Jules's car," Trent noted.

"Our cars are identical," Jules said. She stared at the incinerated vehicle and wondered if the bomb had been intended for her or Darcy.

Chapter 30

Tanner placed the four reports in chronological order on her desk. Nana was poisoned. Ashley was beaten to death. An arsonist set fire to Chance's home, and someone firebombed Darcy's car. All the violence centered around the Manse.

Tanner kept going over the three questions all good investigators ask: who, where and why.

Who? *I have no idea who the culprit is.*

Where? *I know where each offense occurred.* An in-depth report from the pathologist determined the lividity of Daphne's body was consistent with where her bed would have touched her, so she did die in bed.

Why? *I can find no reason for Daphne's murder.*

Roy seems to have a better reason than Chance for killing his wife, if he learned of her affair with their yard woman. He has an alibi of sorts. Killing Darcy in the car fire would have left Chance with no defense attorney so that rules her out.

I know of no reason why Chance would want to kill Ashley.

Chance was present at the site of both fires but was almost the victim of one. If Darcy had gotten into her car and started it, she would have been the victim in the firebombing.

"Damn, I need a break in this case," Tanner said out loud.

"Talking to yourself again?" Pattie said as he held out a cup of hot coffee toward his partner.

"These murders and fires are driving me crazy," Tanner replied. "I've tried looking at them as separate incidents, and I've looked at them as a grand scheme designed toward an end.

"Unfortunately, I have no idea what the end game is but it all seems to be tied together. Several people gained from Daphne Divine's death, but none of them were hurting for money except the Reverend Divine and his wife. Jules walked away with the lion's share of Daphne's estate, but she wasn't aware of the terms of the will and was in Waco at the time of Daphne's death."

"Maybe you should take a closer look at the esteemed Reverend Divine," Pattie suggested. "Anyone capable of putting a fourteen-year-old-girl out on the streets is capable of anything."

"Maybe I will," Tanner said. "Right now, I'm going to visit Jules Divine."

"Need some company?" Pattie waggled his eyebrows.

"I think I can handle her by myself," Tanner said, flashing him a smile as she pulled her service pistol from her desk drawer.

##

Chance was planting new flowerbeds in front of the Manse when Tanner arrived. She held up her hand for Tanner to wait and then hurried inside to push the button that opened the gate.

"Thanks," Tanner said as she got out of her car. "I forget about that gate. I should have called ahead."

"They usually leave it open during the day." Chance flashed her a beautiful smile.

How could anyone as beautiful as this woman be a killer? Tanner thought.

"What are you planting?" Tanner motioned toward the potted plants Chance had set three feet apart in front of the beds.

"Pink caladiums and elephant ear plants," Chance grinned as she slapped the yardstick against her thigh. "They do best when planted three feet apart."

"They're beautiful," Tanner commented. "Are you ready for your day in court next Monday?"

"Darcy says we're ready." Chance smiled again and ducked her head shyly. "I trust her."

"She seems to know her business," Tanner said, reluctant to admit that Darcy Reed was quite capable. "Are they around?"

"Jules is out back by the pool. Darcy is at her new office."

"New office?" Tanner tried to hide her disappointment that Reed had an office in her town.

"Yeah, she moved into Mr. Simmon's old offices. They spruced it up. It looks very impressive. Of course, everything about Darcy is impressive."

Tanner wondered if Chance knew that Darcy Reed the attorney and Darcy Lake the international best-selling lesbian author were the same person. *Probably not.*

"You can go around that way," Chance said, pointing toward the side of the house. "Jules is on the patio."

Tanner nodded her thanks and headed for the backyard.

Jules was unaware the detective was observing her from the corner of her home. She was reading emails for Darcy Lake on her iPad.

Marta had returned the manuscript for *Dying to Kill. I'll make the changes she suggests then forward the manuscript to my editor,* Jules thought.

She jumped when Tanner cleared her throat. "I'm sorry, Jules. I didn't mean to scare you. Chance said you were out here."

"I was just catching up on my emails," Jules said with a smile. "Grab something from the fridge and join me. There are soft drinks, tea, and Shiner Bock."

"Do you have any new information?" Jules asked, turning off her iPad as Tanner returned with a drink.

"Actually, I'm stumped." Tanner took a long pull on her beer. "I have never had a case with so many dead ends.

"The incendiary device used to destroy Darcy's car was a simple contraption designed to detonate when she started the car. Thank God your brother cranked it remotely.

"I don't know if the perp was trying to kill Darcy or you," Tanner continued. "Your cars are very similar."

"Why would anyone want to kill either of us?" Jules asked.

"How evil are your parents?" Tanner said.

"It's not my place to judge them." Jules frowned. "I'm not very objective when it comes to my parents. I'm the daughter they threw out of their home when I was fourteen. Remember?"

Tanner nodded. "Do you think they would be capable of killing Daphne in anticipation of inheriting her millions?"

"No!" Jules's answer was emphatic. "They knew Nana had no use for them. Surely they didn't expect to inherit much from her."

Jules recalled her parents' reaction to the reading of the will. "They were furious that she only left them a thousand dollars. I know they wanted the Manse. My mother has always wanted to live here. They threatened to contest the will, but Darcy stopped that cold."

A whining noise drew their attention to the small dog peeking out the glass door. Jules got up and opened the door, and Rabbit bounced onto the patio and into Tanner's lap.

"He likes you." Jules laughed as she knelt to pet the dog Tanner was holding.

Tanner couldn't stop smiling as she watched the way Jules's eyes sparkled as she ruffled the little dog's fur and talked baby talk to it.

Suddenly, their eyes met. "How do you feel about me?" Tanner asked.

"I . . . I—" Jules's reply was cut off by Tanner's lips on hers.

Jules pushed the detective away and scrambled to her feet. "You need to leave," she whispered as she drew the back of her hand across her lips. "If you were a man, I would file sexual harassment charges against you."

"Jules, I'm so sorry," Tanner said, reaching out to her.

"Don't touch me! Please, just leave."

A loud cracking sound echoed across the yard as Chance unconsciously broke her yardstick in half. Her anger seethed as she watched Tanner West kiss Jules. A wry grin twisted her lips as she watched Jules push the detective away. *Good for you, Jules.*

Chance was standing beside Tanner's car when the detective walked around the corner. "From now on you should call before you come," she said as she opened the car door for Tanner.

Chance closed the gate behind Tanner's car and then walked to the patio. She found Jules huddled on the sofa, her face buried in her hands. "Are you okay?"

Jules looked up at her, tears streaming down her cheeks. "I'm fine."

"Oh, Jules." Chance sat down beside the smaller woman and pulled her into her arms. She rocked Jules as she sobbed against her chest. "It's okay. Everything is going to be okay. I'll never let anyone hurt you."

As Jules regained her composure, she pulled away from Chance's arms. "I'm just a little upset," she said. "Tanner and I had words. Nothing serious."

Chance nodded and stroked Jules's arm. "I know. I saw. I told her to call before she came again."

"That's a good idea."

Jules closed the door to Nana's office and turned on the computer. She tried to clear her mind as she waited for the machine to populate the screen.

Tanner's kiss had surprised her. She considered the detective a friend. Obviously, Darcy was right; Tanner did want to be more than that.

She opened Marta's email and downloaded the corrected manuscript. She was surprised at how clean it was. Even the part she had written had few errors. She spent two hours making corrections and then emailed the manuscript to her editor.

My editor, Jules thought. *Darcy Lake's editor*. She had become Darcy Lake. She fired off an email to Cat informing her that the editor had the manuscript. Then she sent an email to Marta thanking her for the outstanding beta job.

She wondered who her editor was. *I need to research that.*

Jules answered emails and checked Amazon's sales report for Darcy Lake books. Darcy always had two or three books in the top twenty best sellers. As she logged off her computer, she wondered where Darcy was.

As if to answer her question, a message from Darcy lit up her cell phone screen. "Meeting with Norm is running longer than expected. Should be home in 30."

Jules hugged herself as she thought about the feel of Darcy's arms around her.

Chapter 31

"This is the one that will blow your mind, boss." Norm shoved his iPad across the desk to Darcy.

"Seriously?" Darcy stared at the photo Norm had taken. "Oh God, Norm. This isn't a card I want to play."

"It only gets better . . . or worse, however you look at it." Norm shrugged. "Slide to the next photos."

"That lying hypocrite." Darcy blew out the breath she'd been holding as she looked at the other pictures.

"I've got more for you," Norm said, flipping the iPad photos to copies of official-looking forms. "Look at the timeline on these."

Darcy looked at the confidential records of Ashley Craft. "I don't even want to know how you got these," she said.

"Good, because I don't want to tell you." Norm rolled his eyes.

"Boss, I saved the best for last." Norm scrolled to a photo that took Darcy's breath away.

The detective and the attorney sat in silence as they assimilated the information the man had accumulated.

"What the hell is wrong with Tanner?" Darcy growled. "Why hasn't she uncovered any of this?"

Norm's eyes opened wide. "I've been watching her too. I'd bet a month's pay she has the hots for your woman."

Darcy raked a hand through her hair and shook her head. "What a mess I've gotten myself into, Norm."

She sent Jules a text telling her she would be late then gave Norm her full attention.

"Our strategy has to be perfect on this one, Norm. We'll only get one shot at it. Honestly, I'm not certain I can stoop to introducing this into evidence."

Jules was reading the next unfinished manuscript Nana had started, *Color Her Dead*. The gate's beep let her know Darcy was home. She hurried to the garage and waited for her love to pull Nana's SUV into the garage. She was in Darcy's arms as soon as the blonde stepped from the vehicle.

"Wow! What did I do to deserve this?" Darcy giggled as Jules kissed from her lips to her neck and back again.

"I've missed you," Jules said as she inhaled deeply, savoring the soft fragrance that was Darcy Reed. "God, I love you."

"I've never made love in a garage before," Darcy murmured against soft lips, "but I'm willing to."

Jules pulled her into the house and down the hallway leading into their bedroom. "Everything we need is in here," she said, "and the bed is softer."

Jules closed their bedroom door and wrapped her arms around Darcy's waist. As she kissed her, she slipped her hand between them, unbuttoned the blonde's blouse, slid it down her arms and let it fall to the floor.

"You're gorgeous," Jules whispered in Darcy's ear as she unhooked her bra and slowly slid the straps down her arms.

Darcy gasped as Jules kissed from her neck to her breast and captured a nipple between her lips while her hands unzipped Darcy's skirt and pushed it down her hips to the floor.

Jules pushed her fiancée to sit on the bed and dropped to her knees. "I want to undress you. I've been playing this scene in my mind all day."

Jules slipped off Darcy's heels and tugged her pantyhose down her legs, flinging them out of the way. "Lovely," Jules said. She sighed as she pushed the blonde back onto the pillows. "You're so lovely."

##

Darcy rolled over on her back. "Wow! Could you just make a quick note of what I did to deserve that welcome home, so I'll be sure to do it every day?" She chuckled as she pulled Jules against her side.

"My entire day has been segments tied together by missing you," Jules whispered. "How was your first day in your new office?"

"Not nearly as wonderful as my welcome home party." Darcy sighed. "You never cease to surprise me."

"Um, just wait until my inhibitions fall away," Jules said with a grin.

"I hope my heart can stand it."

As their breathing returned to normal, a peaceful stillness filled the room. Jules broke the silence.

"Tanner visited me today," she said.

"What did Tanner want?" Darcy's tone was just short of disgust.

"I . . . I don't know." Jules tried to recall if Tanner had mentioned a reason for her visit. "She kissed me, and I asked her to leave."

Darcy's arms tightened around Jules as she inhaled sharply. "I think she has fallen in love with you, which is understandable, but she knows you're my woman."

"Yes, I made that clear. I told her I would file sexual harassment charges against her if she touched me again."

Jules could feel the pounding of her lover's heart against her breast. "She apologized and left. Chance told her to call ahead next time she needed to speak with us."

"Chance was here?"

"Yes, she planted pink caladiums in the front flower beds. They're beautiful." Jules listened for Darcy's heartbeat to slow, but it didn't. "Are you okay, baby?"

"I'm perfect." Darcy shifted so Jules's lips were touching hers. "I have some things to share with you too. Right now, I need a glass of water. I'm dying of thirst."

"Me too," Jules whispered as she wiggled over Darcy and slipped from their bed.

Darcy settled on the sofa and Jules brought cold water from the refrigerator. She snuggled under Darcy's arm and handed her a bottle.

"Anything else happen today?" Darcy asked.

"I received the *Dying to Kill* manuscript from Marta, made the corrections, and sent it to your editor." Jules tilted her head to look at her lover. "You know, we make a pretty good writing team."

"How would you feel about that?" Darcy asked.

"I would love it." Jules beamed. "We could travel together, and you would be much better informed about what was happening in the world of Darcy Lake. I'm afraid Nana often left you in the dark."

"That is the understatement of a lifetime," Darcy noted. "I was always flying by the seat of my pants."

"I would always be with you, so you would always know what was going on and—"

"And I wouldn't have to spend all those lonely nights in strange hotel rooms with no one to talk to," Darcy added.

"I doubt you lacked companionship." Jules elbowed her playfully.

"There was no one whose companionship I desired." One look at Darcy's face and Jules knew the beautiful woman was telling the truth.

She snuggled closer to Darcy. "Would you like to form the Darcy Lake writing team with me?"

"I'd like that very much," Darcy said. She pressed her lips to Jules's—one of those smoldering kisses that sent heat spreading through their bodies.

Jules reluctantly broke their kiss and leaned her forehead against Darcy's as she tried to catch her breath.

"Where's Chance?"

"In her bedroom, I think," Jules said. "I heard her showering. She worked in the flower beds all day. She's probably exhausted.

"You still haven't told me about your day," Jules said, moving the conversation away from Chance. "Come into the kitchen and I'll put dinner on the table."

Darcy watched Jules as she moved around the kitchen. In short order, chicken salad on a bed of lettuce and a fruit cup appeared in front of her. "When did you have time to do this?" Darcy asked. "Your energy always amazes me."

"I can't sit in front of a computer all day," Jules said. "I walked around the block and then made this for our dinner. I hope you like it."

"It's incredible," Darcy mumbled around a bite of chicken salad. "I can cook too, you know."

"I was home. You were at work." Jules placed her hand on Darcy's arm. "I like to do things for you. Now, are you going to tell me about your day or not?"

"I took on a new client today." Darcy ducked her head and gave Jules a coy smile.

Jules laughed. "You don't have to be modest with me. I love how cocky you are."

Darcy threw back her head and laughed. "How can you know me so well?"

Jules's answer was simple and honest. "I love you."

"You know the auto manufacturing plant opening between here and Cleburne?"

"Yes."

"They've hired our firm to represent them in all their plant negotiations—land purchases, steel purchases, you name it. We'll be handling contracts and litigation for them."

"Won't that require more people?" Jules asked.

"Definitely," Darcy said as she carried their dishes to the sink, rinsed them, and placed them in the dishwasher.

"There is something I want to discuss with you." Darcy refilled their iced tea glasses and led Jules onto the patio.

Jules was a little wary of the serious tone in Darcy's voice. They sat on the sofa and Darcy turned to face her.

"I want to marry you," she said. "Will you marry me?"

"Yes, of course." Jules caught Darcy's face between her hands and placed a sweet kiss on the blonde's lips.

"When?" Darcy asked.

"Whenever you want." Jules tittered. "Tomorrow?"

"Do you want a big church wedding?" Darcy asked.

"Heavens no! A simple ceremony performed by the justice of the peace will be sufficient. As long as it's binding, I'll be happy."

"How about Friday?" Darcy asked. "We can get the license Tuesday and get married Friday."

"Isn't there a required waiting period?"

"Seventy-two hours," Darcy proudly informed her. "I checked today."

"Yes! Yes! I'd love to marry you Friday."

"I want you to be my wife when we go to New York," Darcy added. "I mean, *really* be my wife."

"I really want to be your wife."

##

Darcy awoke slowly, aware of the woman in her arms, legs entwined with her own. She relished the sensation of silky skin pressed against her. The fragrance of Jules's hair filled her nostrils as the brunette turned her head to rest comfortably on Darcy's shoulder.

How did I get so lucky? Darcy asked herself as she held Jules. *Jules Divine. The name fits her. Everything about her is divine.*

Darcy could feel her body temperature increase as her desire for Jules grew. It would only be a matter of seconds until Jules would respond or roll away from the heat. In a deep sleep, Jules turned over, releasing her hold on Darcy.

Darcy slipped from the bed and quietly entered the en suite. She suppressed a laugh as she recalled her own happiness at Jules's agreement to marry her. *Life just can't get any better than this,* she thought.

She shampooed her hair and luxuriated in the feel of the hot shower strumming her back. She wrestled with how to tell Jules what Norm had discovered. It was something she wanted to avoid but knew she couldn't.

She brushed her teeth and returned to their bed. Jules was still asleep.

Chapter 32

Darcy was surprised when her receptionist announced Chance Howard was there to see her. "Send her in," Darcy replied as she slid the marriage license she and Jules had gotten earlier into her desk drawer.

"Thank you for seeing me," Chance said, her usual confident manner subdued. "I know I should've made an appointment, but I was debating whether or not to discuss this matter with you."

Darcy gestured toward the chair in front of her desk, and Chance took a seat. "Go ahead," Darcy said.

Chance shifted in the chair, trying to get comfortable. "I was working in the flowerbeds at the Manse when Detective West visited Jules."

Darcy waited in silence for the woman to continue.

"I saw her kissing Jules."

"Yes, Jules told me." A smile flashed across Darcy's face when she recalled the other things Jules had said to her.

"She did?"

"We tell each other everything," Darcy admitted.

"I'm glad," Chance said. "I'm not trying to cause trouble between you and Jules. I just thought you should know."

"I appreciate that. So, are you ready to go to trial next Monday?" Darcy said, watching Chance's eyes.

"I am. I feel very confident with you handling my defense. I know you'll get me off."

"Do you have any idea who killed Ashley?" Darcy asked.

"No," Chance answered after several seconds of silence. "Ashley was sweet and kind. I can't imagine . . ." A tear ran down Chance's cheek. "I don't want to talk about it."

The momentary silence was interrupted by Darcy's receptionist. "You have a call on line two," she announced over Darcy's intercom.

"I have to take this call," Darcy said. "I appreciate you coming by to talk with me."

Chance nodded as she got to her feet. She opened the door and looked back over her shoulder. "I hope you know how lucky you and Jules are to have found each other." She closed the door behind her.

I'm the luckiest woman in the world, Darcy thought as she picked up the receiver. "Darcy Reed."

"When will you be home?" a sexy voice hummed over the phone.

"I don't know," Darcy teased. "It depends on what I'll find when I get there." She gathered her laptop and purse as she spoke.

"I have it on good authority that there is a very aroused woman in your bed."

Darcy continued to play Jules's game as she waved goodbye to her receptionist. "Be careful. My future wife is around there somewhere."

"It was her idea to call you," Jules said, her voice low and seductive.

"Did she tell you what she wants from me?" Darcy started the car and pulled from the parking lot as Jules's reply made her head swim.

They stayed on the phone—Jules whispering her expectations and Darcy zipping through traffic, grateful to miss most of the red lights—until Darcy screeched to a stop in the driveway.

"Oh my gosh, you're here!" Jules squealed as the garage door went up. "Hurry! Tomorrow is our wedding day. This is the last night we can have casual sex."

Darcy laughed into her phone. "Believe me, there has never been anything casual about sex with you."

##

"Both of you look stunning," Lucas said to Darcy and Jules as he opened the door for them to get into the back seat of his car.

"We're honored that you asked us to stand up with you," Trent added as Lucas started the vehicle.

They drove the short distance to the sub-courthouse in nervous silence. Darcy clasped Jules's hand in hers. "Do you have our rings?" she asked Lucas.

"Right here." Lucas patted the breast pocket of his suit jacket.

The ceremony was performed by the justice of the peace with little fanfare. They exchanged matching wedding bands and kissed. "Hello, Mrs. Divine," Jules murmured against Darcy's lips.

"You're taking Jules's last name?" Lucas was dismayed. "But, you're Darcy Lake!"

Darcy smiled. "Darcy Lake is a pen name. Darcy Divine. I think it's a divine name."

##

They spent the weekend much like they'd spent every other day since their declaration of love for one another: making love, waking to talk and plan their future, then making love again.

"Have you heard from our editor?" Darcy asked as they settled on the sofa to read Nana's next half-finished book.

"Let me check my email." Jules propped her feet on the ottoman as she tapped the email app on her iPad.

"Yes, she's finished editing it. I just need to look it over and make certain I agree with her edits. She says it's extremely clean. I'll go over it tomorrow," Jules said. "Right now, I want to read *Color Her Dead* to you. I think you're going to like it."

Darcy stretched out on the sofa, resting her head in Jules's lap. Jules played with her wife's long blonde hair as she read out loud.

"Don't stop now. It's getting exciting," Darcy pleaded when Jules finally stopped reading.

"That's all Nana wrote," Jules informed her. "We have to take it from there."

"Judging from Cat's reaction, you're a natural at this," Darcy reminded her wife.

"I'll make the corrections on *Dying to Kill* and send it to Cat. What I've gleaned from correspondence between Nana and Cat is that the agent deals with the publisher and handles whatever needs to be done to get the book released. It will be out of our hands.

"Then I'll start on *Color Her Dead*."

Chapter 33

The trial started the same day the medical examiner released Ashley's body for burial. Attending the trial and handling funeral arrangements proved to be too much for Roy, who asked to be excused from the proceedings.

The presiding judge, Dorthea Young, called the attorneys into her chambers. "I don't like to see these things drag on," she explained, "but let's give Mr. Craft a chance to bury his wife, and then we'll proceed with the trial."

Cancelli grumbled but agreed.

Even though Warren Divine was officiating the services for Ashley, Jules wanted to attend. She asked Darcy to go with her.

"I'm not certain how the community will react to me attending," Darcy noted. "After all, I am defending the woman they believe killed Ashley. Cancelli tried to get the judge to incarcerate Chance to keep her from attending the funeral. Fortunately, the judge is a proponent of 'innocent until proven guilty' and refused to arrest Chance."

"Please?" Jules brushed her lips across Darcy's. "Lucas and Trent will go with us."

"Okay," Darcy said with a sigh. "I am so weak where you're concerned."

Most of the town attended Ashley Craft's funeral. It was a closed-casket service. Roy and Reverend Warren Divine greeted attendees as they entered the church.

Chance, Darcy, Jules, Lucas, and Trent entered the foyer of the church, signed the guest book, and took a funeral program. As they walked down the aisle to be seated, four church deacons, accompanied by Rev. Divine, blocked their way.

"You're not welcome here," Warren said to his daughter in a loud voice before turning his gaze to Darcy. "Neither are you." He made a point to stare at their matching wedding rings. "You aren't welcome in this town either.

"There is no place in God's house for homosexuals. Women who marry women are an abomination to the Lord." Rev. Divine's self-righteous venom filled the sanctuary.

Darcy glared at Jules's father and opened her mouth to speak. Jules's gentle hand on her arm stopped her. "This was a bad idea," Jules said in a soft, sad voice. "I thought this was a house of God, but I was wrong."

As the five turned to leave, Rev. Divine spoke again. "You can stay."

Jules turned to face her father. Perhaps miracles did happen.

"Not you!" The pastor snorted. "I was speaking to my son."

Lucas stared at his father in amazement and shook his head. "I'm no son of yours," he said, his voice filled with despair. He took his sister's elbow, and the five of them walked from the church.

Darcy was furious. Warren Divine's cruel treatment of his daughter was ghastly. Any humane feelings she might have had for the man were now nonexistent.

She listened as Lucas and Trent tried to console a sobbing Chance, but the look on her wife's face was what wrenched Darcy's heart.

Bring on the trial, Darcy thought. *I'll crucify the bastards.*

Chapter 34

The first two days of the trial were spent on jury selection. Cancelli kept selecting jurors who believed lesbians were an abomination, and Darcy would strike them. Darcy would select jurors who were intelligent and believed consenting adults had the right to love whomever they pleased. Cancelli would strike them. In the end the jury was split fifty-fifty.

ADA Anthony Cancelli's opening statement bordered on discrimination, telling the jury they should find Chance guilty because she was an admitted lesbian. He made incendiary statements designed to agitate the jury and fire up their rage against gays. He immediately withdrew the ridiculous statements every time Darcy objected, but the damage had been done. No one has ever been able to unhear something they just heard.

A sneer settled on Cancelli's face as he turned the jury box over to Darcy.

"Mr. Cancelli has painted a picture for you of vile, immoral creatures who spend their time participating in depraved debauchery. Nothing could be farther from the truth. Lesbians are no different from the rest of you, except for the fact that they find women more attractive than men.

"Lesbians are excellent school teachers and educators. They are loving and caring parents, doctors, nurses, and veterinarians. They are lawyers, law enforcement officers, and firefighters. They are prevalent in every segment of society. So don't let Mr. Cancelli trick you into thinking they are an anomaly in our universe.

"Chance Harper is a hardworking young woman who has pulled herself up by her bootstraps. She started with nothing and worked night and day to build a successful lawn care business."

Darcy looked from juror to juror. "Many of you contracted her to maintain your yards and never had a single problem with her or her employees.

"Look at her." Darcy gestured toward Chance, who held her head high. "She's the epitome of a good citizen. She hasn't a blight on her record.

"She's a hard worker. She pays taxes. She had a lovely home until someone burned it to the ground.

"Don't judge her as a woman. Don't judge her as a lesbian. Judge her as an individual who is innocent of the horrendous charges that have been leveled against her. I believe that when you see the lack of evidence against Chance Howard, you will find her not guilty."

The silence that had fallen over the courtroom was broken as someone in the galley began to clap. Soon, more observers were on their feet and applauding Darcy's opening statement.

Cancelli growled as he got to his feet. "May we adjourn for lunch, Your Honor?" he asked in an obvious effort to distance the jury from the mood Darcy had set.

The judge looked at her watch and nodded.

Jules watched from the last row in the courtroom as Darcy spoke with Chance before the two walked out the side door. Jules caught up with them at the elevator reserved for bailiffs and at-risk defendants.

"That was some opening speech, Counselor." Jules smiled at Darcy. "It's a shame we can't poll the jury right now."

"Yes," Darcy huffed, "but that's why Cancelli wanted a lunch break. He wants to put my opening statement out of their minds before he starts presenting his nebulous evidence."

Jules touched Darcy's arm as they got on the elevator. "That was an amazing presentation. I was impressed with you at the RAW convention. You're a superb orator. Now I know why."

As they ate lunch, visions of Darcy in the jury box continued to excite Jules. Darcy didn't just speak to the jury; she owned them. *She owns me too*, Jules thought as the memory of Darcy's hands on her body took her breath away. She shivered.

"Are you okay?" Darcy asked.

"I'm just fine." Jules pressed her thigh against Darcy's. Darcy couldn't mistake the twinkle in her wife's eye. She knew exactly what was wrong with her.

The blonde leaned down and whispered in Jules's ear. "Later."

##

"Prosecution calls Mr. Roy Craft." Anthony Cancelli strutted to the witness box and gave the jury his best benevolent smile. He waited until Roy was sworn in and turned to him.

"I know how difficult this must be for you, Mr. Craft, and I will try to be as kind as possible. Could you describe what happened on the night of your wife's death?"

"Yes." Roy took a deep breath and bowed his head for a few seconds before facing the jury. "I returned home from the garage a little after eight that night. I walked into the living room and was surprised that Ashley wasn't in the kitchen. I called her name and began to look for her when she didn't answer."

Tears began to stream down Roy's face. The courtroom was silent as he regained his composure.

"I . . . I found her in our bedroom. She had been brutally beaten. I tried to save her. I tried to give her mouth-to-mouth resuscitation. She was so cold." Roy's sobs echoed through the courtroom. "I couldn't . . . couldn't get her mouth open. Oh God. It was so horrible."

Cancelli handed Roy a tissue and waited for him to stop sobbing.

"What did you do when you realized you couldn't revive your wife?"

"I called the police. They arrived with an ambulance."

"Did you have any idea who killed your wife?"

Darcy stood. "Objection! Counsel is leading the witness to supposition, not facts in evidence."

"Were you surprised when the police arrested Chance Howard for Ashley's murder?" Cancelli asked.

"Yes, she has worked for us for about five years. She has always been a great groundskeeper."

"So, you weren't aware that your wife was having an affair with your lawn woman?" Cancelli sneered.

Darcy got to her feet and objected again. "Permission to approach the bench, Your Honor?"

The judge waved both attorneys forward. "What seems to be the problem, Ms. Reed?"

"My client has a name, Your Honor," Darcy said. "Please instruct ADA Cancelli to use her name when referring to her instead of work-related descriptions he believes are derogatory."

"That is a fair request," Judge Young said. "Mr. Cancelli, in the future you will refer to the defendant by her name, Chance Howard or Ms. Howard."

Cancelli snorted again. The judge had taken away one of his weapons, but he had plenty more tricks up his sleeve.

Cancelli returned to his position in front of the witness box. "Mr. Craft, how did you feel when you were told your wife had been sleeping with another woman?"

"Objection!" Darcy stood again. "Mr. Craft's feelings about his wife's affair have no bearing on the case.

"Your Honor, if Mr. Cancelli has hard evidence to present to the jury, please ask him to do so."

"I'm through with this witness," Cancelli said, turning to Darcy.

"I have no desire to cross examine at this time, Your Honor," Darcy said. "Defense does reserve the right to recall this witness."

Cancelli called Larry Wrenn, the lead forensic investigator on the case.

"Mr. Wrenn, please tell the jury whose fingerprints you found at the crime scene and where you found them."

"We found Chance . . . uh, Ms. Howard's prints all over the house. Especially in the bedroom. They were on the bedroom door and doorknob. They were on the dresser and in the bathroom."

"Where else did you find them?"

"On the headboard of Mrs. Craft's bed," Wrenn replied.

Cancelli swaggered to the prosecution table and picked up a yardstick. "Pretend this yardstick is the headboard," he said as he held the three-foot stick up for the jury to see. "Show us how the fingerprints were placed on the headboard.

"Like this." Wrenn curled his fingers over the top of the stick. "Where my fingertips are is where the backside of the headboard would be. Ms. Howard's fingerprints were there."

Jules inhaled. She was quite familiar with the position Wrenn was describing. She looked at the faces of the jury. Most of them clearly understood too.

"What else did you find that would link Ms. Howard to the crime scene?" Cancelli said with confidence, as if he had already won the case.

"Ms. Howard's hair was in the shower and bathroom drain. Her blood was on the floor, and like I said, her fingerprints were everywhere."

"Thank you, Mr. Wrenn." Cancelli looked at Darcy and smirked. "Your turn, Counselor."

"I would like to question Mr. Wrenn," Darcy said, "but first I want to question Mr. Craft to clarify a few things."

A low rumble went through the crowd as Roy Craft made his way to the stand.

"Mr. Craft, I won't keep you here long. I know this is difficult for you." Darcy walked to the defense table, picked up a stack of papers, and flipped through them as if looking for something. "Ah, yes. Here it is," she said.

"Mr. Craft, when Detective West and I visited you at your place of business you told us that Ms. Howard had helped you rearrange your bedroom furniture a few weeks prior to Ashley's death. Do you remember that?"

"Yes," Roy said.

"Could you tell us what furniture you moved?"

"We moved the bed and the dresser. I needed Chance's help, because we had to remove the mattresses and disassemble the bed frame to move it. She's strong. She moved the headboard and side rails while I moved the footboard and slats."

Darcy turned toward the jury. "So, Chance would have gotten her fingerprints all over the headboard?"

"Probably," Roy mumbled.

"I'm sorry, I didn't hear what you said."

"Yes. Yes, she did pick up the headboard." Roy closed his eyes and hung his head.

"Thank you, Mr. Craft. I have no more questions for this witness."

Roy glanced at Cancelli as he walked past the prosecutor's table.

"Defense would like to recall Mr. Larry Wrenn to the stand." Darcy stepped back to allow him to pass.

"Mr. Wrenn, you have just heard Roy Craft's testimony," Darcy said in a respectful manner. "Do you think the fingerprints you found on the headboard of the

Craft bed could have been put there when Ms. Howard helped Roy Craft move the furniture?"

"Yes, of course," Wrenn replied. "We have no way of knowing how long the prints have been on the headboard, just that they were there."

"Thank you, Mr. Wrenn. I appreciate your expertise in this matter. I have no further questions for this witness, Your Honor."

"Court is adjourned for the day," Judge Young announced. "We will reconvene at eight in the morning." Then the judge requested that the attorneys join her in her chambers.

Darcy and Cancelli followed Judge Young into her office and stood quietly as she removed her robe and sat down behind her desk.

"Mr. Cancelli, do you have any additional incriminating evidence?" the judge asked.

"Her fingerprints and DNA are all over everything." Cancelli's indignation was laughable. "What more do you want?"

"Motive, murder weapon, eyewitness, physical evidence . . . you know, those things that prove a murder case." Judge Young wrinkled her brow. "Chance Howard has admitted that she was Ashley Craft's lover. Of course her fingerprints and DNA are all over everything. If I get even an inkling that you are railroading this poor girl for murder just because she's a lesbian, I will have you disbarred. Do I make myself clear?"

"Yes, Your Honor." Cancelli slammed the door as he left the office.

"Darcy Reed," Judge Young said, smiling. "You look surprisingly like one of my favorite authors."

"I hear that a lot." Darcy laughed, her dimples flashing. "See you in court in the morning, Your Honor."

Chapter 35

"Wow, Darcy, you're really something," Chance exclaimed as Jules pulled the car from the courthouse parking lot. "You are going to get me off, aren't you?"

"That's my intent." Darcy chuckled as she reached over to rest her hand on Jules' arm. "I just want to get home and kick off these heels."

"Yeah, those fuck-me heels are killers," Chance said a bit too exuberantly.

"Um, Chance, that's a little out of line." Jules frowned at the younger woman's lapse in good manners.

"Oh, I'm sorry," Chance said. "I'm just so damn happy. I won't be blamed for killing Ashley."

"It's not over yet," Darcy pointed out. "I don't trust Cancelli. He'll do anything to win this case."

As they entered the Manse, they sniffed a delightful aroma. Renee met them in the great room. "I thought you might be hungry," she said. "I've roasted a hen and have veggies and salad already on the table for you. Go wash your hands and get comfortable."

"Yes, Mother," Jules teased the older woman. "That smells delectable. I'm starving."

Darcy closed their bedroom door and leaned back against it. They stood still just admiring each other.

"You were remarkable in that courtroom," Jules said, nibbling on her bottom lip. "I can't even begin to tell you what a turn-on it is to watch you."

"I can't tell you what a turn-on that lip thing you just did is." Darcy slowly pulled Jules into her arms. "Maybe you can tell me after dinner . . . or show me."

"Mmm," Jules murmured as soft lips captured hers.

The trial was the topic of discussion at dinner as the three women gave Renee a blow-by-blow description of the proceedings.

"You have to see Darcy in action to believe how incredible she is," Chance gushed.

"I must agree," Jules added, her eyes twinkling. "Of course, I'm prejudiced."

Darcy's phone rang as they were eating, but she chose to ignore it.

"Aren't you going to answer that?" Chance asked.

"No. I never let my cell phone interrupt dinner with friends," Darcy said. "Whatever it is, it'll wait until we're finished."

The phone rang again as they were clearing the table.

"I suppose I should answer that." Darcy sighed as she pushed the button that brought Cat Webb back into her life. As she listened she walked into their bedroom.

"What are you doing after you're finished here?" Chance asked Renee as they cleaned the kitchen."

"Heading home," Renee replied. "The boys have football practice until after dark."

"Want to go to the movies?" Chance asked with a hesitant, shy smile.

Renee studied the young woman for several seconds. "Sure. Why not?"

Jules locked the door behind Renee and Chance and walked into the bedroom. Darcy, still on the phone, patted the bed, motioning for Jules to sit beside her.

"That is unbelievable, Cat," Darcy said. "I'll check it right now. I'm sorry. I don't mean to ignore you." She finished the call and gaped at Jules.

"Cat shopped *Dying to Kill*," Darcy said as she placed her phone on the nightstand. "She has the best contract she has ever negotiated for a Darcy Lake book. It calls for a strenuous talk show tour, and the publisher wants the movie rights too."

"Sounds good to me," Jules said as she stretched out on the bed. "You have other commitments you need to tend to first."

"She says she needs the contract signed and in her hands by eight a.m. tomorrow," Darcy mumbled as Jules pulled her down beside her.

"Surely you can complete your commitments by eight in the morning." Jules's eyes danced as she slipped her hand beneath her wife's T-shirt. "Unless you don't want to make love to—"

Warm, demanding kisses silenced the brunette's teasing.

Something jerked Jules awake. She lay still, listening, but heard nothing. *I must have been dreaming*, she thought. A glance at her bedside clock told her it was two a.m. She snuggled deeper into the strong arms wrapped around her. Darcy fit her like a glove. Everything about her wife was perfect for her.

Even though their lives had been a whirlwind of activity since their meeting in Dallas, Jules was always at peace within herself. She knew that Darcy had a lot to do with that. She thought about how naturally their friendship had evolved into a loving relationship. Darcy Reed was so much more than the pretty face of Darcy Lake novels. She wondered how traveling and a movie would affect Darcy's law practice. They would have to discuss everything before signing any contracts.

There! A sound! Nothing frightening, just a little noise in the house. Probably Chance in the refrigerator.

Jules gently untangled herself from Darcy's arms and slipped from their bed. She pulled on a pair of sweats and a T-shirt and then tiptoed from their room.

A quick check of the kitchen proved no one was there. She walked to the glass wall and looked out at the pool. None of the motion-detector lights were on, so there was no one outside.

Wide awake, Jules pulled a Dr. Pepper from the refrigerator and walked toward Nana's office. She was surprised to see a faint glow of light from the office doorway. Silently, she stepped through the entrance.

Chance was sitting at Nana's computer. She appeared to be searching for files. She cursed softly as the password she entered failed to open the computer.

Jules flipped the light switch, flooding the room with overhead lights. Chance jumped up so quickly that she turned over the chair she was sitting in.

"Shit! You scared the hell out of me," Chance growled.

"What are you doing at Nana's computer?" Jules demanded.

"Nothing. I couldn't sleep so I came in here to get a book. The computer was on, so I sat in the chair while I closed the system. I'm sorry if I woke you. I was trying to be quiet."

"Darcy must have left it on," Jules said. "Did you find a book?"

"A book? Oh, yes." Chance set the chair upright as she looked around the room. "I thought I would read the latest Darcy Lake novel."

Jules picked up the newest book and handed it to Chance. "Here you go. Enjoy it."

Chance's hand closed around Jules's as she accepted the book. Their eyes locked for a moment, and then Jules pulled away her hand. "Good night, Chance." Jules's tone was firm and apprehensive.

Chance turned on her heel and came face-to-face with Darcy. "Everything okay in here?" Darcy asked. "I heard a loud noise."

"I knocked over a chair," Chance said as she stepped around the blonde and left the room.

"Why are you up?" Darcy asked her wife.

"I couldn't sleep," Jules said. "I thought I would print the contract from Cat so you could look it over in the morning. Then I could put the Darcy Lake electronic signature on it and return it to Cat."

Darcy took the cold can of Dr. Pepper from Jules's hand and drank from it. "Why don't I sit with you while you print it? Then we can go back to bed and read the contract together."

"I'd like that," Jules said. "I'd like that a lot. But you need to get your own Dr. Pepper."

Darcy laughed as she headed for the kitchen.

##

Darcy settled against the headboard and pulled back the covers for Jules to slip into their bed. Jules snuggled into Darcy's side and let her hand rest on her wife's thigh as she leaned in to read the contract Darcy held so both could see it.

"You can leave your hand there," Darcy said, "but don't start moving it and caressing my thigh. I need to concentrate on this contract. Okay?"

"You're no fun," Jules mumbled.

"I will be fun after we read this contract. There aren't enough hours in the day for all we need to do."

"I know. We need to discuss that when we finish with this contract," Jules said.

Darcy finished reading the contract. It was a high-seven-figure offer for the publishing and movie rights to the book. She knew that once Hollywood discovered the Darcy Lake novels, there would be more contracts for movie rights. She also knew that *Color Her Dead* would land the same offers, only higher, as moviemakers became aware of how good the murder mysteries were.

Darcy had been amazed at the ideas Daphne Divine had for the Darcy Lake novels. Jules was a natural at perfecting them. Darcy knew that by the time her wife finished writing the books her grandmother had started, she would be able to write Darcy Lake novels from start to finish.

Darcy had scraped and scratched her way through law school. She enjoyed practicing law. She also enjoyed being Darcy Lake and Jules Divine's wife. She wondered how she could reconcile the two careers.

"What do you think, honey?" Darcy said.

When she received no answer, she knew her wife was sound asleep. She eased away from Jules and settled her head on the pillow.

It can wait until morning, Darcy thought as she turned off the light.

Chapter 36

"We're questioning Tanner this morning," Darcy informed Jules and Chance as they pulled into the courthouse parking lot.

"Cancelli is also calling some of Chance's customers who will testify that Chance made passes at them."

Chance yelped. "That's insane! I'd never come on to my customers."

"What about Ashley?" Jules asked.

"She initiated our relationship," Chance said. "She kissed me."

Just as Darcy expected, Tanner testified to finding Chance's blood in Ashley's sink. Darcy countered with a statement from a doctor that he had sutured Chance's hand where she had cut herself on a gardening tool. Chance still had a healing scar from the cut.

The hair in Ashley's shower was explained away by Chance's statement that she often showered there before being with Ashley.

Darcy glared at Tanner. "Detective West, why did you arrest my client?"

"I was told to," Tanner said.

"By whom?"

"ADA Anthony Cancelli."

"Isn't that a little unusual?" Darcy turned to face the jury. "Don't you usually make the arrest before you take the case to the district attorney's office?"

"Yes," Tanner said.

"Why did Mr. Cancelli initiate the arrest?"

Cancelli jumped to his feet. "Objection, Your Honor!"

"Overruled," Judge Young said.

"Let me repeat my question," Darcy said. "Why did ADA Anthony Cancelli initiate the arrest?"

"You'll have to ask him," Tanner replied. "I have no idea."

"Would you have arrested Chance Howard based on the evidence you had?" Darcy asked.

Cancelli objected again.

"I want to hear Detective Tanner's reply," Judge Young said, glaring at Cancelli. "Overruled."

"No." Tanner's voice was loud and clear. "No, I would not have arrested Chance Howard on circumstantial evidence that was easily explained away. At the time that was all we had."

"Do you think ADA Cancelli has a personal vendetta against lesbians?" Darcy asked.

"Objection! Counselor is asking for an answer the witness has no way of knowing." Cancelli threw his pen onto the desk.

"Sustained." Judge Young looked over the top of her glasses at Darcy. "You know better than that, Counselor."

Darcy walked back to her desk. A slight smile played on her lips. She had planted the thought in the jury's mind. That was what mattered.

##

After lunch, Cancelli paraded in twelve women and seated them directly behind the prosecution's table.

"Who are they?" Darcy asked Chance.

"They're former clients," Chase answered. "All are married."

"Did you sexually harass them in even the slightest way, even teasing?" Darcy kept the expression on her face pleasant and relaxed. Inside, she was praying Cancelli had no surprise up his sleeve.

"No! I wouldn't do that," Chance said.

The rest of the afternoon was spent listening to woman after woman accuse Chance of sexually harassing them. It was obvious that each woman had been carefully coached in her testimony. Each one told the exact same story.

After each testimony, Darcy stood and said, "Defense reserves the right to recall this witness."

At five o'clock, two women were left to testify. "Your Honor, prosecution is willing to forego questioning the last two witnesses. As you can see, Chance Howard's mode of operation was the same in all cases." Cancelli's slimy smile made Darcy's skin crawl.

"Yes," Judge Young said. "Exactly the same. Almost as if each of your witnesses were working off the same script."

"Your Honor," Darcy said as she got to her feet. "Defense requests the right to question the two final witnesses in the morning."

"Request granted." Judge Young slammed her gavel on the stand. "Court is adjourned until eight in the morning."

"That hurt us, didn't it?" Chance said as she got into the car. "Just the sheer number of women testifying that I accosted them has got to make the jury think where there's smoke there's fire."

"I'm afraid so." Darcy's mind was racing. "We need to come back tomorrow with something mind-boggling to make the jury understand the prosecution's case is all smoke and mirrors."

"I'm going to leave that to my attorney," Chance said with a chuckle as Jules pulled the car into the garage. "I'm going to go for a drive and clear my head."

Jules and Darcy stood in the courtyard and watched Chance's truck disappear down the street.

"Does this mean we have some time alone?" Darcy laced her fingers with Jules's as they walked into the house. "We could go skinny-dipping."

Jules laughed out loud. "Let's make certain Renee is gone for the day."

"Um, good idea," Darcy said as she touched her lips against her wife's."

"I wonder how Cancelli convinced all those women to testify against Chance." Jules said a few minutes later as they shed their clothes beside the pool and slipped into the tepid water.

Darcy sank beneath the surface and shot back up, slinging water everywhere as she shook it from her hair. "God, that feels good." She smiled as Jules followed suit.

When Jules broke the surface, Darcy caught her hands and pulled her close. Jules wrapped her legs around her wife's waist. They talked as they bobbed in the water.

"Have you given any thought to the publishing contract?" Jules asked.

"I think it would be delightful to go on tour with you." Darcy nuzzled her neck. "We could make love in at least nine countries."

Jules giggled. "That settles it. I'm signing that contract and returning it tonight."

"Have you decided what to do tomorrow to counteract the stunt Cancelli is pulling?" Jules asked, curious about what her wife had up her sleeve.

"When we get out of the pool, I'm going to make a few phone calls," Darcy said. "But right now, I just want to enjoy you."

"Be my guest," Jules murmured against her wife's lips.

##

"Are you going to stay all day?" Darcy asked the next morning as they headed inside the courtroom.

"I wouldn't miss this for the world." Jules winked as she followed Darcy and Chance into court.

The judge entered, and the proceedings got underway.

"Prosecution wishes to call Mary Latham," Cancelli bellowed.

A timid-looking woman, her thin, gray hair in a bun piled on top of her head, walked to the witness box. Cancelli paced while she was sworn in and then address her in a loud voice. "Mrs. Latham, did Chance Howard ever work for you?"

"Yes," Mary whispered.

"I didn't hear you." Cancelli glared at her.

"Yes," Mary repeated louder.

"Is Ms. Howard in the courtroom?" Cancelli's smarmy smile made Darcy want to barf.

Mary pointed a shaky finger at Chance.

Chance bowed her head and shook it.

"Could you tell us what she said to you?" Cancelli asked.

"Yes, she said my lawn needed a lot of extra attention." Mary eagerly repeated the words she had been given.

"Your lawn?"

"Yes." Mary blushed. "But she didn't really mean my lawn. She meant . . . you know."

"I don't know," Cancelli said, frowning. "Please enlighten us."

"She meant that I should shave my . . . um . . ." Mary's eyes brightened as if she'd had an epiphany. "My lady parts."

The people in the gallery snickered.

Darcy could tell from Cancelli's smug expression that he thought he'd accomplished his goal.

Darcy stood and walked over to Mary.

"Mrs. Latham, thank you for coming forward." Darcy's voice was kind and sincere. "Tell me how it made you feel to have someone tell you to shave your lady parts."

"Uh . . ." Mary made a choking sound.

"Did Chance say, 'You need to shave your lady parts,' or did she say, 'Your lady parts need shaving?' I'm curious about how she would even know that."

"Well, umm . . . uh, she didn't say it in exactly those words." Mary looked down at her hands folded in her lap.

"Were you naked when she said that to you?" Darcy was going for the shock factor now. "Were you naked in front of her?"

"Objection," Cancelli croaked. "Counsel is badgering the witness."

"Overruled," Judge Young responded. "I'd like to hear Mrs. Latham's answer."

"She didn't say those exact words," Mary blurted out. "She just said 'your lawn needs mowing.'"

"And you took that as sexual harassment?" The incredulous expression on Darcy's face caused the jurors to chuckle.

"I have no more questions for this witness," Darcy said in disgust.

The judge directed Mr. Cancelli to call his next witness.

A heated, whispered argument ensued between Cancelli and the woman, a fiery redhead named Lucile Pimbrook.

"I have no further witnesses," Cancelli said.

"Ms. Reed?" The judge looked at Darcy.

"Defense would like to call Lucile Pimbrook," Darcy answered. "We request that Mrs. Pimbrook be shown as a hostile witness."

"I told you, I don't wish to testify," Lucile said, glaring at Cancelli.

"You have no choice," Darcy informed her. "Your name is on the witness list. I have the right to call you to the stand."

"You said she wouldn't cross-examine me." Lucile's loud whisper—meant for Cancelli—was heard by the jury and spectators.

"Mrs. Pimbrook, please take the witness stand," Judge Young instructed.

Lucile glared daggers at Cancelli before she walked to the witness stand. Darcy stood with her head bowed as the woman was sworn in. She turned to stare at Lucile as the bailiff said, ". . . the whole truth and nothing but the truth."

Lucile hesitated and then said, "I do."

Darcy smiled at Lucile Pimbrook as she approached the stand. "Mrs. Pimbrook, you do understand that you are under oath, and any false information you give will be considered perjury. Perjury is punishable by a fine or jail time. The jail time can be from one to ten years, at the judge's discretion. So please, for your sake, answer my questions as truthfully as possible. Do you understand?"

"Yes," Lucile croaked.

"Has Chance Howard ever worked for you?"

"Yes."

"Has she ever said anything or done anything that was disrespectful toward you?"

"No!" Lucile mumbled as a titter ran through the crowd.

"Did someone put pressure on you to falsely testify that Ms. Howard was forward or sexually harassed you?"

Lucile looked up but didn't utter a word. It was obvious she was struggling with how to answer.

"Mrs. Pimbrook, you must answer the question," Judge Young said.

"Yes," Lucile blurted out. "Yes, Mr. Cancelli said I should accuse Chance of making passes at me, but Chance has always been a perfect lady in all of our dealings."

A roar came from the spectators, and the judge took a moment to silence the crowd.

"Were the other ladies that paraded up here yesterday also pressured to provide testimony against Ms. Howard?"

"I believe they were," Lucile said, causing the gallery to go crazy.

"Objection! Objection!" Cancelli was screeching over the noise. "This entire thing has gotten out of hand."

"I have no further questions, Your Honor," Darcy said before taking a seat beside Chance.

"You did it," Chance whispered. "You proved this whole thing is trumped up."

Judge Young quieted the court spectators and jurors. "Court is adjourned for the day. We will meet back here at eight in the morning. Counselors, be prepared to give your closing arguments.

"Mr. Cancelli, may I see you in my chambers?"

As they walked from the courtroom, one of the witnesses from the prior day grabbed Darcy's arm and pulled her into a corner. "I must speak with you," she said.

"Oh my God! You really kicked some butt in there today," Chance crowed as Jules pulled the car into the traffic.

"You made Cancelli look like the ass he is and have probably cost him his job." Chance's glee was uncontrollable.

"You truly are something." Jules beamed. "Nice job, Counselor."

Jules was pleased by the sight of Renee's car in the courtyard of the Manse.

"Renee was kind enough to fix lunch for us," Jules said, "Then we have the rest of the day to do whatever we want."

Darcy tried to suppress the blush that was moving up her neck to her cheeks. She was pleased to catch the shy little smile that flitted across Jules's lips.

An hour later, they were putting away the dishes when Norm called. "I need to take this." Darcy held up the phone so Jules could see who was calling. She walked outside and sat down beside the pool.

Jules watched her wife as she gestured with her hands. She smiled at how animated Darcy was when she talked. That was just one of the many things she loved about her.

Chance moved to stand behind Jules. She placed her hands on Jules's shoulders. "She certainly gets excited, doesn't she?" she whispered into Jules's ear.

Jules moved away from Chance's hands. "Yes, she does." The brunette turned to gaze at Chance. "You really shouldn't put your hands on other women. That may be coming back to haunt you."

"I . . . I didn't mean anything sexual by it." Chance's sincere apology convinced Jules she had no nefarious intentions.

"I think I'll go for a drive," Chance said. "Give you two some time alone."

As Chance went out the front door, Darcy entered the back door. "Baby, I need to run to the office for a couple of hours," she informed Jules.

Jules moaned softly. "I need to send that contract to Cat and start writing an ending for *Color Her Dead*. I'll find plenty to keep me busy until you return."

Darcy reached for her, holding Jules's gaze with her own. "I love you so much more than I ever imagined loving anyone," she said.

##

Jules placed the electronic signature on the contract and emailed it to Cat. Then she made a call to her accountant and left a message to cancel all donations to Warren Divine's church. "Arrange for that money to be donated to the women's shelter," Jules instructed.

She opened *Color Her Dead*. Her fingers were dancing on the keyboard as she added to the story her grandmother had started. She jumped when Nana's phone rang.

She waited until the caller left a message and then played back the voicemail. "Darcy, thanks for the contract. Trying to get book printed before your NY appearance. Cover attached for your approval."

Jules saved the cover photo to the cloud.

"Your cloud is full," Nana's iPhone notified her.

She was surprised that Nana had uploaded anything to the cloud. Jules knew her eccentric grandmother hadn't trusted the cloud and refused to upload her novels to it for fear someone would steal them.

"Let's just see what was put on the cloud," Jules mused out loud as she downloaded the contents to Nana's computer.

She scrolled through some photos and then opened a video. She watched in horrified silence as the video played. "Oh my God!" she sobbed. "Oh, dear God!"

She sent the video to her iPhone and powered off the computer. *Tanner. I must get the video to Tanner.*

Jules grabbed her purse and fob and ran to her car. She had to get to Tanner before Darcy returned. She knew what she had to do.

She instructed her car phone to dial Tanner's number.

"Detective Tanner West," the strong vibrant voice said.

"Tanner, this is Jules. I must see you. Where are you?"

"I'm on a stakeout," the detective said. "I'm with Pattie in his unmarked car. Go to the Exxon station on Main Street. We'll meet you there."

"I can only talk to you," Jules said, nearly choking on her words.

"We'll be there by the time you arrive," Tanner assured her.

Tanner and Pattie were parked beside the service station when Jules pulled up. Tanner left the car and sprinted to Jules.

"Are you okay?" the detective asked as she slid into the passenger seat of Jules's Lexus.

"I didn't know what to do," Jules sobbed. "You've got to see this." She cued the video, pushed the Play button, and handed the phone to Tanner.

"Dear God," Tanner gasped. "Where's Darcy now?"

"She said she was going to her office." Jules frowned. "I don't think I should go with you."

"No, that would be a problem," Tanner said. "We have to handle this just right, or it will blow up in our faces.

"Send that video to my phone. I don't want anyone to know how I got it. Don't tell Darcy you gave it to me."

"I don't . . ."—Jules took a deep breath—"I can't . . ."

"It's imperative that Darcy know nothing about this," Tanner reiterated.

Darcy was home when Jules returned. "Honey, I was just about to call you," she said as Jules entered the Manse.

"Where were you?"

"I missed you, so I went to your office," Jules said, "but you had already left."

"We probably passed in the night." Darcy pulled Jules into her arms and kissed her forehead. "We'd better get some sleep. Tomorrow will be a big day."

Jules nodded and followed her wife into the bedroom. When Darcy slipped into their bed after taking her shower, Jules pretended to be asleep.

##

Tanner walked up the steps to the courthouse. She patted the arrest warrant in her jacket pocket. As soon as the trial concluded she would serve it.

Darcy looked around the courtroom. Anthony Cancelli wasn't in yet. She scanned the papers she planned to submit to the judge. To Darcy's surprise, ADA Linda Patton entered the room.

"Where's Cancelli?" Darcy asked.

"Judge Young took him off the case," Patton replied. "She's moving to have him disbarred."

Everyone stood as the judge entered the courtroom. Judge Young looked around the room, a slight smile on her lips. As soon as the echo of "The court is now in session" had died, Darcy got to her feet.

"Your Honor, in view of the fact that ADA Cancelli tampered with witnesses and waged his own personal battle against gays, I move that a mistrial be declared."

"The prosecution has no objection," Linda Patton replied.

"So ordered." Judge Young brought down her gavel.

"I'm free," Chance squealed. "You did it. I'm free."

"Yes," Darcy said, smiling.

Darcy turned to look for Jules among the spectators. Her smile turned to a frown as she saw Tanner and Jules walking toward her.

Tanner didn't waste words. "You're under arrest for the murder of Ashley Craft and Daphne Divine. You have the right to remain silent . . ." She Mirandized Chance as she fastened the handcuffs around the young woman's wrists.

"You can't do that!" Chance screamed. "I can't be tried twice for the same crime."

"You won't be," Tanner said. "This hearing ended in a mistrial, so technically you haven't been tried for Ashley's murder.

"You are also under arrest for the murder of Daphne Divine." Tanner turned Chance over to two officers waiting to take her to jail. "You won't be getting bail this time," she called out as they led Chance away.

Tanner held out her hand to Darcy. "Thanks. It's an honor to have you practicing law in our town."

Darcy grinned and shook the detective's hand. News teams crowded around the three as Jules, Darcy, and Tanner made their way down the courthouse steps. Tanner pulled a file from her notebook and turned to Darcy. "These were left at my precinct last night."

As Tanner held out the folder, a reporter fell into her, knocking the folder from her hand. It flew open and photos scattered over the courthouse steps. Reporters snatched the pornographic photos from the steps and rushed to their vehicles, each trying to be the first to report on the trial and the photos that showed the Reverend Warren Divine engaging in sex with ADA Anthony Cancelli.

Chapter 37

"Cat says *Dying to Kill* will be printed and ready for distribution at the convention in New York. Preorders are out of sight," Jules informed her wife as she walked into their bedroom with the airline tickets. "I've printed our tickets, and Lucas is going to take us to the airport. He's making a wonderful home for Rabbit. He fell in love with that little fuzzball."

"Sounds like you're even more efficient than Daphne." Darcy caught Jules's hand and led her to the loveseat.

"I just got off the phone with Tanner," Darcy said. "Chance got the death penalty. The death penalty is appealed automatically to the Texas Court of Criminal Appeals, which means she'll have another day in court. Fortunately, the attorney who represented her in the recent trial must represent her in the appeals court, so I won't be pulled into that mess. She'll probably end up serving life without parole. Killing Ashley could be presented as a crime of passion, but murdering your grandmother was premeditated."

"I'm glad the trial you handled ended in a mistrial," Jules said. "If you'd let it go to the jury, she would have walked away scot-free."

"That's why I requested a mistrial." Darcy bowed her head. "I have a confession to make," she said. "Norm left the anonymous envelope on Tanner's desk. That's where the photos of your father and Cancelli came from. Tanner had already figured out the timeline, that Ashley's hospital visits coincided with dates Roy was out of town, and Chance was the one abusing Ashley.

"The abuse began when Ashley confided to Chance that she was pregnant. The anger management counseling Daphne paid for to help Chance didn't solve Chance's anger issues. She had been cavorting with Ashley for almost a year when Ashley became pregnant. Chance was furious that she was still having relations with Roy, and Ashley wanted to end their affair. Chance pushed her down the stairs, causing her to miscarry.

"Tanner had also matched the fingerprints on the wine bottle in Daphne's trash to Chance." Darcy took a deep breath. "Are you okay, honey? I know this is a lot to process."

"Yes," Jules said. "I want to hear all of it."

Darcy continued. "Roy told Tanner he knew something was wrong, because Ashley kept getting hurt and making excuses like falling down the stairs or running into a door. It never occurred to him that Chance was her lover and her abuser.

"The woman that pulled me aside the day before closing statements swore to me that Chance had raped her. She was so sincere; it made me stop and think," Darcy said.

"The fire marshal felt that Chance torched her own house to destroy any blood evidence that might be there. She admitted beating Ashley in her home.

"Norm had a grainy video of Chance tampering with my car. He was surveilling Roy and accidently shot the video of Chance."

"Chance admitted bombing my car. She thought that would draw suspicion away from her. No one would believe she would try to kill her defense attorney. She thought my death would cause you to turn to her for consolation. She became obsessed with you after your first meeting and had stalked us all over town.

"The video Daphne made through her telescope of Chance beating Ashley so badly she had to be hospitalized was what got her killed. Your grandmother confronted

Chance and told her she was going to notify Roy and the authorities. I don't know how Tanner got that video, but it sealed Chance's casket.

"Tanner had located a rattlesnake breeder who provided records and a security video of Chance purchasing the venom. When Tanner confronted her with the evidence, she admitted she killed Daphne to keep her from telling the authorities and Roy that she was abusing Ashley."

"I know it isn't exactly kosher for a defense attorney to help convict a client, but I couldn't be responsible for putting her back on the streets. I never looked at the evidence Norm had collected against Chance. I just told him to anonymously give all the evidence he'd found to Tanner. She's a good cop. I knew she would find the truth. I did see the photos of your father and Cancelli. I never intended those to go public."

"I'm glad they did," Jules muttered. "He dealt so many people so much misery over their sexuality, and all the time he was the ultimate hypocrite. He deserved to be exposed."

Darcy hugged her wife, smoothing her hair and kissing her forehead. "It's all over now. We can get on with our lives."

"I have a confession to make too," Jules said. "I gave Tanner that video."

Darcy pulled away from the woman in her arms. "Why didn't you bring it to me?"

"I knew that if you were aware of it you would be bound by ethics to keep it from getting into the trial to be used against Chance. So, I took it to Tanner and told her you knew nothing of its existence, which was true."

Darcy laughed. "Sometimes, Jules Divine, you completely amaze me with your knowledge."

"Writers have to do a lot of research to make their books accurate and believable." Jules beamed at her wife's approval. "Writers know things."

A horn honking in the courtyard announced Lucas's arrival.

"Time to take the writing team of Divine and Lake on the road," Darcy said. "I believe my next ten years as Darcy Lake will be much more rewarding than the last ten years."

"What type of reward do you have in mind?" Jules's eyes twinkled as she teased her wife.

"I'll leave that up to you. You're the writer with the amazing imagination. I'm just the pretty face who—what did you call it—shills for you?"

"I'll be expecting more from you than a simple appearance," Jules said. She shot her wife a sultry look and then kissed her soundly. "Much more!"

"Since you'll require more of me, I must insist on a lot of fringe benefits." Darcy laughed.

"I certainly hope so." Jules placed the tips of her fingers on Darcy's lips.

Darcy laced her fingers through Jules's as Lucas honked the horn again. "Ready for our next adventure?"

"I am! What could be more exciting than living two lives with you?" Jules said as they closed the door behind them.

THE END

Learn more about Erin Wade
and her books at www.erinwade.us

**Other #1 Best Selling Books
by Erin Wade**
Too Strong to Die
Death Was Too Easy
Three Times as Deadly
Branded Wives

Erin Wade writing as D.J. Jouett
The Destiny Factor

Coming in March 2018
Living Two Lives
Don't Dare the Devil
The Roughneck & the Lady
Assassination Authorized!

***Following is a preview of
Don't Dare the Devil***

263

Coming Summer of 2018

Don't Dare the Devil

Chapter 1

Eden Daye fidgeted in the hard, uncomfortable chair across from Detective Wayne Rose's desk. She watched as two officers discussed the information she had just given them. She could tell they thought she was demented or—at best—high on some new designer drug.

Eden thought about the information. Maybe they were right. Maybe she was hallucinating or crazy.

Across the room Rose and his partner spoke in hushed tones. "We need to get the chief involved in this," Rose insisted. "This is too coincidental."

"He'll send us all to the shrink," Rose's partner Dozer Davis barked. "Remember how he reacted when we filed that report on Marian Lewis?"

Rose hesitated. "This is . . . look, Eden Daye isn't some nut case off the street. She is *the* Eden Daye, Fortune 500 Daye, heiress to the Clayton Daye oil and gas fortune.

"It has only been six months since her father was brutally murdered. Something's not right in that family."

"The others were ladies of wealth too" Dozer pointed out. "Marian Lewis was also an heiress. We spent six months trying to track her down. You know what we found." Dozer shuttered as if the memory was too horrific to revisit. "We got nothing—no clues, no suspects."

"I say we call in Knight." Rose's tone was the sound one would use to commemorate the dead.

"You know the Commissioner has to approve that." The look of fear in Dozer's eyes was unmistakable.

"Gentlemen," Eden said, raising her voice over the hum of their heated discussion. "Will someone please tell me what's going on?"

"I'm calling the chief," Rose said as he headed out the door.

"Can I get you a bottle of water or soda?" Dozer asked Eden.

"No, I'm fine. I just need to know what you're going to do about the abduction of my sister." Eden appraised Dozer Davis as one would scrutinize a new employee.

Dozer was easy on the eyes. At six feet six and two hundred fifty pounds, he certainly fit his name. Thick blond hair curled over his head, making him look much more angelic than he was.

"Could you go over the abduction one more time?" Dozer encouraged her, trying to kill time.

"Why don't you simply replay the recordings from the first six times I told the story?" Eden glared at him.

Dozer breathed a sigh of relief when Wayne Rose entered the bull pen. "Chief wants us to escort Miss Daye to his office." Wayne motioned for Eden to follow them.

In silence, they rode the elevator to the top floor of the Fort Worth Criminal Building that housed the Special Investigations Unit of Central, Texas. The elevator opened directly into a huge area that housed the chief and his staff.

Chief Frank Canton rose to greet Eden and the detectives. "I'm sorry we must meet again under such dire circumstances," he said as he shook hands with the woman.

"I suppose you want me to retell my story." Eden scowled.

"No, that won't be necessary," Canton said. "Detective Rose has provided me the details.

"I would appreciate it if you could describe your sister's abductor to me. Please try to recall everything you can. Even the minutest details will help us."

"It was dark." Eden closed her eyes, visualizing the event. "There was a full moon. I was watching my sister from the second-floor window as she walked in the garden. I thought I saw a movement in the shadows. Then there was nothing. I decided I had imagined it. The security around our home is state-of-the-art, impenetrable.

"Suddenly something darted from the shadows, threw Sharon over its shoulder, and jumped the garden wall. Just like that, Sharon was gone. No alarms went off, nothing."

"How tall is the garden wall?" Chief Canton frowned as he made notes.

"Eight feet," Eden answered. "Whatever took my sister was only a little shorter than the wall."

Silence fell over the room as everyone digested Eden's story. Even she was beginning to wonder if her eyes had deceived her.

"You said, 'whatever took my sister,'" Canton reiterated. "You couldn't tell if it was a man or a woman?"

"I'm not even certain it was human," Eden whispered.

Canton looked at his officers. "Detectives, you may return to your office. I've already assigned this case to Special Agent Knight."

As Rose and Dozer turned to leave, the elevator doors whooshed open.

Eden was certain a cold wind blew into the office as the woman stepped from the elevator. She was tall and incredibly beautiful. Her mane of thick dark hair billowed around her face as if battling for a place to rest on her shoulders. Piercing blue eyes and perfectly shaped red lips completed the look of beauty and power.

"Here's Agent Knight now." Canton nodded in deference to the woman who dominated the room. Without taking their eyes off the brunette, Rose and Dozer slipped into the elevator and punched the button to close the doors.

Agent Knight arched perfect brows as she scanned Eden Daye from head to foot. "He took your sister?" Knight's sultry voice hummed. "It seems he left the best one behind."

Eden couldn't break the gaze of the mesmerizing blue eyes—now they were green—that seemed to pierce her soul. Agent Knight was spellbinding. She had the face of an angel but everything about her screamed power. Her black jumpsuit hugged a perfect body. The knee boots she wore looked as if they could be lethal weapons under the right conditions. Nine-millimeter Glocks rested in the holsters strapped to her hips. Agent Knight was both breathtaking and terrifying.

Only when she stepped forward did Eden realize a huge black dog accompanied the agent. "Is he a wolf?" she asked.

A slow smile played across Knight's face, "She is. Thank you for recognizing that and not trying to pet her."

Somber, she had been beautiful, but Knight was gorgeous when she smiled. Red lips framed perfect white teeth, and dimples kissed the corners of her mouth. Her eyes sparkled. As Eden gasped for breath, she wondered how long ago she had stopped breathing.

Chief Canton broke the silence. "Agent Knight will be your constant companion until we sort this out."

"My constant companion?" Eden fought back the terror that overtook her at the idea of being in constant contact with Agent Knight.

"Constant," Knight cooed and raised a salacious eyebrow.

"I . . . I don't think that's necessary," Eden said.

"Suit yourself," Knight said in a huff as she whirled back toward the elevator.

"Agent Knight, I need you on this case," the chief said. He narrowed his eyes at Eden and got to his feet.

Knight turned around to face the two. "I'm happy to help, Sir, but I won't babysit some spoiled brat with a death wish."

Eden blushed from head to toe. No one had ever called her a spoiled brat. "Who the hell do you think you are?" she snapped at the agent.

"I'm all that stands between you and certain death," Knight said. "Do you want my help or not?"

The truth almost made Eden throw up. She knew she was in danger from something. "Yes, please," she said.

##

Chapter 2

As they rode down the elevator, Knight stood beside Eden. Eden was five-eight and the agent towered over her. *She must be six feet tall*, Eden thought. Knight shifted from one foot to the other, and a soft, pleasing fragrance filled the elevator. *She smells good too.* Eden studied the woman beside her from the corner of her eye.

As the elevator door opened, Eden realized that once again she was holding her breath in Knight's presence.

"Where's your car?" Knight asked.

"I . . . I don't have it with me. The police picked me up at my home and brought me here."

"I have mine," the brunette said. "Is that okay with you?"

Eden nodded. She was surprised Knight had asked her approval. They walked to the parking garage, where an unbelievable car backed from its parking space and pulled to a stop in front of them.

Knight approached the car, and the front doors opened automatically. The back falcon-wing doors lifted, and the wolf glided into the back seat. The car looked like a giant hawk preparing to take flight.

Eden took her seat and the seatbelt locked around her as the door closed on its own. Knight slipped into the driver's seat and all the doors closed. "Address?" she said, one brow cocked at Eden.

Eden recited her address and watched as the information appeared on the car's computer screen. Without making a sound the vehicle moved forward.

"What kind of car is this?" Eden inquired.

"Electric," Knight answered. "Tesla prototype, test vehicle."

Eden watched as the agent steered the car out of downtown Ft. Worth and onto I-30 West.

With all her wealth, Eden had never ridden in a car as smooth and luxurious. The eerie silence of the vehicle was almost unnerving.

"I'm surprised you drive an electric car," Eden said. "I expected you to be more the hopped-up speedster type. You know, like a Bugatti Veyron SS."

Knight glanced at Eden and smiled. "Tess will go from zero to sixty in 2.5 seconds and tops out at speeds over a hundred and fifty miles per hour. I figure that's all the car I need."

"You call your car Tess?"

"I name everything that is important to me, Miss Daye." Knight narrowed her eyes and looked at the blonde.

Eden glanced over her shoulder. The sleeping wolf lay on her stomach and covered the entire seat. Eden guessed her weight at over a hundred pounds.

"What's her name

"El Cazador. I call her Caz," Knight replied.

"The Hunter," Eden said.

Knight cast an approving glance at the blonde next to her and nodded.

"What about you? Do you have a name?" Eden said.

"You may call me Agent Knight." The brunette smirked. "K-n-i-g-h-t."

"I bet you're no one's white knight," Eden's caustic tone made Agent Knight look at her, again.

Agent Knight didn't respond.

##

The GPS system led them around a beautifully manicured golf course. Knight recognized it as River Crest Country Club. Her family had belonged to the elite club for more years than she could remember. Tess eased to a stop in front of an imposing set of gates. Knight waited as Eden dug thru her purse for a remote device.

"I . . . I'm sorry," Eden muttered. "The gates automatically open when they recognize my car. I've never used the remote before." She finally pulled the small box from her purse and pushed the button. The gates swung open to allow the car admittance then closed behind it.

Agent Knight surveyed the grounds as far as she could see. A winding road ducked behind tall shrubs and trees, hiding the gate and entrance road from sight. They were in their own little world.

"Follow this road to the back," Eden instructed. "You can park Tess in the garage."

Knight chuckled. "Thank you, Miss Daye."

Agent Knight pulled the Tesla into the garage and the car doors opened by some unseen command. Caz leaped from the back seat and stretched. Knight watched the wolf as the animal slinked into the woods around the Daye mansion. *Let me know if you find anything unusual.*

The wolf stopped and looked back over her shoulder as if acknowledging her master's thoughts before disappearing into the woods.

"I need to go home and get a few things," Knight said as she walked into the library of the mansion. "If I'm to stay here, I'll need clean clothes and a toothbrush." Her glorious smile captivated Eden. "I assume you'll take me out in public."

"Probably not," Eden huffed. "I don't even know your name. How can I introduce you to people? Do you want others to know you're with the police?"

"Darke," Agent Knight said.

"You'll be back before dark?" Eden snorted. "That's reassuring. What if that . . . that thing comes back for me?"

"D-a-r-k-e," Knight said. "My name is Darke Knight. I'll leave Caz to protect you. You'll be safe, and I'm not exactly with the police." Knight turned on her heel then hesitated at the door. "Don't leave the house until I return."

Eden walked to the door. Her mouth hung open as she watched the dark beauty getting into her car.

"Darke Knight?" Eden said. "Who the hell names their daughter Darke Knight?"

Eden jumped when Margaret, her estate manager, entered the room. "Miss Eden, there's a huge black dog lying on the back terrace. Should I call security?"

"No, Margaret. That's a guard . . . dog. Her name is Caz. Please inform the rest of the staff of her presence." Eden started up the stairs to dress for dinner. "Oh, and Margaret, a tall brunette will be here in an hour. Please put her in the gold room. She'll be staying with us for a while."

Eden wasn't certain how long she could stand Darke Knight. The woman made her uneasy. Knight was too smug, too self-assured. Eden had been on edge from the moment Knight stepped from the elevator.

Of course, she's confident and at ease, Eden thought. *She's been in her element. She has the police wrapped around her little finger, a wolf and a car—Tess—that do her bidding.* Eden chastised herself for using the car's name. *Only children named inanimate objects.*

A soft knock on her door drew Eden from her thoughts. "Come in."

"Miss Eden, are you attending the dinner at the country club tonight, or do you wish to dine at home?" Margaret inquired. "It's the beginning of the holiday celebrations."

"I'll dine at home. No, on second thought, I'll attend the dinner."

Eden walked to her window overlooking the mansion's courtyard. *Yes, dinner at the club will be interesting. Let's see how at ease Agent Darke Knight is in my world.*

##

Eden surveyed her image in the full-length mirror. She had selected a burgundy dress with long sleeves and a scooped neck. Pearl earrings and necklace complemented the dress. Her long blonde hair fell freely around her shoulders. She examined her reflection and wondered if Agent Knight would approve of her appearance. It troubled her when she realized what Knight thought mattered to her.

Eden located Margaret in the kitchen. "When Miss Knight arrives, please ask her to join me in the clubhouse for dinner," Eden said.

The evening was pleasant with a slight breeze whispering through the trees. Eden decided to walk to the clubhouse. It felt good to get outside and walk. She'd been cooped up in the mansion since her sister's disappearance.

##

Eden was nursing her second drink at her table in the back of the dining room when a hush fell over the merrymakers. She looked up to see what had caused the stillness. She watched as Darke Knight glided toward her table. Eden realized that every eye in the room was on the ravishing brunette.

Darke wore an amber-colored floor-length dress, plunged low in the front to reveal perfect cleavage. A floor-to-thigh slit provided a fleeting glimpse of the woman's long, toned legs.

Darke stopped at Eden's table and waited to be invited to sit with her. Her gaze locked with Eden's as she stood across from her.

Eden cleared her throat. For some reason, she couldn't make her lips move. She nodded at the chair.

Darke's lips twisted into a half smile. Eden knew the woman wasn't going to make this easy. She gulped the rest of her drink and cleared her throat again. "Please join me."

Darke nodded her head and reached for her chair. A man appeared from nowhere. "Please, allow me."

Darke smiled and thanked him as she took her seat. A waiter appeared with a bottle of wine and another glass.

The sommelier joined them and bowed as he uncorked the wine. "It is a privilege to have you with us tonight, Miss Knight." It was obvious Darke was no stranger to those who worked at the country club. He waited as Darke sipped the wine and gave her approval of the selection.

Eden was surprised to see that Darke was as at home with the country club set as she had been with the law enforcement officers.

Darke waited until the waiter took their order and left the table before she spoke to Eden. "I told you to stay in your home."

"You can't order me around," Eden muttered through clenched teeth.

"I wasn't ordering you around." Darke's voice was calm. "I was trying to save your life."

Eden watched, spellbound, as Darke moved her head from side to side and seemed to sniff the air. Her blue eyes turned darker and narrowed. Her nostrils flared. She surveyed the room and settled on the man approaching their table.

The man bent down and kissed the blonde's lips. "Hello, Eden. Have you heard any news about your sister?"

Eden shook her head and watched in silence as Carter Winthrop scrutinized her dining companion.

After what seemed like several minutes, Eden broke the silence. "Carter, this is my friend Darke Knight. Darke, this is my fiancée, Carter Winthrop."

Darke nodded but said nothing.

"She's visiting me for a while," Eden added.

"Miss Knight," Carter said with a slight dip of his head. He opened his mouth as if to say more but snapped it shut without uttering a sound. He seemed stunned by the woman's beauty. She had certainly rendered him speechless.

Eden cleared her throat. "Would you like to join us for dinner, Carter?"

"No, I'm with clients," he said, his eyes glued to Darke's. "I had hoped you would join us, but it would be rude to leave your guest."

"Yes," Darke murmured, her husky voice sending shivers through Eden. "We'll be leaving soon."

Carter turned away from Darke and addressed Eden. "Don't forget we're going horseback riding tomorrow."

"I'm not sure I can," Eden said, casting a look at Darke.

"I would love to go horseback riding," Darke looked up at Carter. "I will be staying close to Eden until the situation with her sister is resolved. Like a body guard."

Carter nodded as an unhappy look flited across his face.

##

"Where's your car?" Darke asked as they left the country club.

"I walked," Eden replied.

"In those shoes?"

Eden reached into her oversized purse and pulled out a pair of tennis shoes. "I wore these."

"You should put them on," Darke instructed.

"I won't need them in Tess," Eden said with a smirk.

"I walked," Darke's tone was flat.

"In those shoes?" Eden gasped as she stared at the six-inch stilettos worn by the agent.

"They're more comfortable than they look." Darke's blue eyes sparkled in the moonlight as if she were enjoying toying with the blonde.

Eden changed her shoes and almost ran to keep up with the other woman. "There's no fire," she grumbled. "Can't we slow down?"

Darke said nothing but shortened her stride and slowed their pace.

Eden suppressed a scream as Caz materialized in the dark and joined them. "She scared me," she explained.

Darke nodded but said nothing.

"Are you angry with me?" Eden moved closer to the taller woman. For some reason, she felt safe next to Darke.

"I don't want you to meet the same fate as your sister," Darke said. "If you want me to protect you, you must do as I say. This isn't a game. It's serious."

Eden was silent. After several minutes, she asked, "Do you know what happened to my sister?"

"Since the chief called me in for your case," Darke said, "I'm certain it can't be good."

"They don't call you in for the normal, everyday cases, do they?" Eden almost whispered.

"No, they don't."

The tone of Darke's voice left a coldness in the pit of Eden's stomach. She wondered what had taken her sister and killed her father. Even though Darke scared her, she was thankful for the agent's presence.

##

Eden was restless. Nightmares of Sharon's abduction kept screaming through her mind. She walked from her bed to the window. A full moon cast a brilliant light, filling the trees and statues with grotesque shadows.

She caught her breath as she realized two shadows were slinking across the lawn. *It looks like Caz has found a friend*. She watched as the two dark shapes loped across the grass and disappeared into the trees.

##

Darke smiled as Eden joined her in the garden the next morning. "I thought you were going to sleep all day."

"It's eight in the morning," Eden grumbled, rumpling her hair with both hands. "How long have you been awake?"

"Long enough to take Caz for her morning run and convince your housekeeper I would die without coffee."

Eden couldn't suppress her smile.

"She even gave me an extra cup in case you joined me." Darke poured coffee for Eden from a sterling silver carafe. Eden watched as steam curled upward from the hot coffee.

"When you feel like it," Darke said, "would you show me where your sister was when she was kidnapped?"

Eden suppressed a shudder as she thought about walking in the dark corner of the garden. "After breakfast I'll take you there."

"How long have you been engaged to Carter Winthrop?" Darke asked as she refilled her coffee cup.

"A month," Eden said.

Darke tilted her head to the side and watched Eden. "When is the wedding?"

"We haven't set a date."

"I'm sure you're anxious to marry him," Darke said. "He's quite handsome."

"I plan to finish college first," Eden said as she avoided commenting on Carter Winthrop.

They ate their breakfast in silence. Eden was amazed at the amount of food Darke consumed. *I wonder how she maintains her perfect figure.*

"I've finished with breakfast," Eden said, jumping to her feet. "Would you like to see the garden where Sharon was abducted?"

Darke followed the younger woman into the garden on the west side of the house. Eden keyed a passcode into the gate leading into the garden.

"Is this the only entrance to the garden?" Darke asked.

"It's the only outside entrance. We can enter from the house too." Eden swept her hand toward a beautiful patio with two spotless glass doors that opened to the house.

"Where do the doors lead?" Darke said.

"The left door is Sharon's suite." Eden bit her lip, fighting back the tears. "The right door leads into the breakfast room." She turned away and burst into tears.

"I'm sorry," Darke consoled her. "I know this is difficult for you."

Eden nodded, wiped the tears from her eyes with the heel of her thumb, and walked toward the far corner of the garden where yellow crime scene tape still billowed in the morning breeze.

Darke stepped over the tape and studied the tracks on the ground. "Your sister was wearing tennis shoes," Darke stated.

"Yes," Eden said. "She had just returned from the country club and was still wearing her tennis shorts and shoes. The police took her tennis racquet. It was twisted beyond recognition."

"Do you own a large dog?" Darke squatted down to study the huge prints beside those left by the tennis shoes. She picked up a handful of dirt and sniffed it.

Eden trembled. "No. Why do you ask?"

"There are three sets of prints," Darke said as she continued to stare at the ground. "The third set of prints are bare feet. Looks like a man's size eleven."

"I . . . I only saw two things," Eden said. "Sharon and that monster."

Both women watched as Caz slinked along the garden wall and began to dig in the far corner. She looked at Darke and whined.

"What have you found, girl?" Darke bent over and shoved dirt away from the object Caz had uncovered. "A pair of shoes?"

Darke looked up at the garden wall. It was easily eight feet tall or more. "The . . . abductor threw your sister on its shoulder and leaped over the wall?"

"Not over it," Eden said, her brow furrowed as she recalled the horrifying event. "To the top of it. A wall this tall is also wide. It's about four feet thick. It stood on top of the wall and . . . and—"

"And what?" Darke's voice was low and persuasive.

"Howled!" Eden slapped her hand over her mouth as if trying to keep the words from tumbling out. "It howled like a wolf."

"That wasn't in the police report," Darke said, her eyes locked on Eden's.

"I didn't tell anyone. I was afraid they would rush me to the tenth floor of John Peter Smith Hospital."

Darke nodded. "The psyche ward."

"Yes."

"So, the . . . thing jumped from where I'm standing to the top of that wall with your sister over its shoulder?" Darke asked.

The woman is either hard of hearing or she's trying to torture me. "Yes," Eden whispered.

##

Chapter 3

"Dozer, I understand." Darke's voice was hushed and exasperated. "When will he be back?"

"About an hour," Detective Dozer Davis answered.

"Why can't you pick them up by yourself? It's just a pair of shoes. I don't want to break the chain of evidence, so either you or someone in CSI needs to pick them up." Darke couldn't keep the annoyance from sounding in her voice.

"The shoes won't go anywhere in an hour," Dozer grumbled. "We'll get there as soon as Rose returns."

Darke inhaled and counted to ten. "Did you look at the photos I sent you? The paw prints?"

"Yeah. Where did you find a dog that size?"

"Jesus," Darke growled. "Give me the name and number of the CSI agent who worked the crime scene."

"That would be Zeller." Dozer rattled off the phone number. "She knows more about the evidence than I do. She just finished her shift."

"Loraine Zeller?"

"Yeah, Lori Zeller," Dozer said. "Do you know her?"

"I'll just talk to her," Darke grumbled. "Forget I called you."

Darke paced the floor. She hadn't spoken to Lori Zeller in over six months. Although they'd solved their last case together, Lori had refused to report the events as they'd happened. For that, Darke was thankful. She wondered if Lori would work with her again.

Darke frowned when Lori's answering machine picked up her call. She debated leaving a message and was about to hang up when a breathless Lori picked up the phone.

"Zeller," she said.

"I'm afraid to ask what you're doing," Darke said, unable to refrain from teasing the CSI.

"Chasing that damned wolf pup, you gave me," Lori said, as she caught her breath. "God Darke, he's incredibly smart and fast. I have to admit he has grown on me. I do love him."

"I knew you would fall in love with him," Darke chuckled.

"A call from you can't be good."

"It isn't," Darke said. "Did you work the crime scene at the Daye mansion?"

"Yeah. Did you read my report?"

"No, it wasn't included in the file they gave me."

"They probably threw it away," Lori grunted. "The boss didn't like my conclusions. He threatened to make me go on vacation. Said I was obviously exhausted."

"Off the record," Darke said, "what did you find?"

"Same as the murders you and I worked six months ago," Lori's voice dropped an octave lower as she gave her secretive answer, "wolves."

Made in the USA
Columbia, SC
14 November 2018